CRIME IN THE BOOK CLUB

A fiercely addictive mystery

CATHERINE MOLONEY

Detective Markham Mystery Book 10

JOFFE BOOKS

First published in Great Britain in 2020
Joffe Books, London
www.joffebooks.com

ISBN: 978-1-78931-641-4

PROLOGUE

There was nothing quite like an English spring, Sheila Birtle reflected as she made her way along Calder Vale High Street on the morning of Friday, 20 March.

Most of the terrace's little front gardens were adorned with cheery clusters of daffodils and vibrant purple crocuses. Those with paved forecourts had jardinières and ceramic planters crammed with hyacinths, primroses and primulas, creating a real feast for the eye. Even the more dilapidated properties sported window boxes with jaunty displays heralding the approach of Easter.

Sheila was headed for the little heritage railway station located at the far end of the high street. From there, aficionados could take the steam train at weekends for a winding twelve-mile trip through the hilly countryside and quaint traditional towns and villages. She had made the journey herself a few times, rattling along in an open-top carriage — at least until Rob had started grumbling about the draughts making his arthritis play up, at which point they adjourned to one of the covered compartments.

Cleaning the railway office, waiting room and café was Sheila's responsibility as lead volunteer, and she looked forward to it every week as a colourful diversion from her regular job, pulling on the marigolds as a cleaner at the council offices and a roster of private customers.

After her morning stint at the station, it would be back to Bromgrove and her clients in Grasmere Park, a leafy private enclave leading down to the river Brom and the garden festival displays along Brom Promenade.

Puffing slightly as she reached the top of the high street, Sheila — a sturdy middle-aged peroxide blonde with the compact build of a cob pony — sank onto the bench at the station entrance. Time for a quick breather and then she'd crack on.

Idly, she wondered if there was any chance of bumping into Michael Dominguez, her fellow volunteer and one of her favourite Grasmere Park regulars.

Rob was unimpressed by her susceptibility to the charms of the sixty-something retired lecturer. 'Stuck-up ponce,' was his unflattering verdict after a single unfortunate encounter in the town centre. 'Like a cross between Nicholas Parsons and that smarmy bloke who does the railway programmes.'

'Michael Portillo?' she'd ventured.

'That's right. Dead oily with his teddy-boy quiff an' all the highfalutin blather. As for the get-up: pink jackets an' green trousers . . . *I ask you*. It's a wonder the guy doesn't get lynched wearing that kind of clobber. Makes me eyes water just looking at him.'

'Mr Dominguez doesn't dress like that,' she had protested.

But Rob just shook his head darkly making it clear that he considered the man eminently punchable. 'Bound ter be a Tory an' all . . .'

Dress sense aside, she supposed the comparison wasn't all that far-fetched given Mr Dominguez's Spanish ancestry, somewhat bouffant (suspiciously tawny) coiffure and resonant baritone. Plus, he had charm you could *surf off*. When he flashed that twinkly smile of his, the corners of his eyes crinkling roguishly, she felt he could talk her into just about anything. Mind you, she didn't think women were really his thing, despite the flirtatiousness and old-world manners. Not that she'd ever seen anything to confirm it . . . it was just a *feeling* she had.

Mr Dominguez's house was also her favourite to clean. A modernist detached property, it was all open-plan and split-level, with acres of maple-stripped flooring and triple-glazed panels. Hard to see what he would want with five bedrooms, but then he'd earned it. Juggling a successful writing career with lecturing at the university all those years. She always gave the shelves in his double-aspect snug her special attention, dusting the spines of *Dominguez: The Collected Spanish Artists* with positively reverential devotion. *Velázquez, El Greco, Sorolla* . . . The names meant little to her, but they tripped off her tongue in an almost mystical incantation as she took down each gilt-edged volume and wiped it carefully before replacing the title precisely where she had found it. Mr Dominguez was fussy like that.

The day was so mild, and the spring scents so tantalizing, that Sheila allowed her mind to drift.

She thought of the rest of them in Grasmere Park. There was no one half as nice as Mr Dominguez.

Nerys Wynne, the retired civil servant who lived with her son in the rather boring red-brick dormer bungalow next door, clearly thought she was a bit familiar with him. But Mr Dominguez just chuckled. 'She's old-school is Nerys. Probably makes Simon dress for dinner.'

There was no doubting Nerys ran her household with a firm hand. Even so, Sheila had always found Simon Wynne friendly enough and not above offering to help carry her vacuum and other cleaning paraphernalia to and from the car whenever the weather was bad.

There was never any question of Nerys requiring Sheila's services — no way would she trust anyone to perform to her exactingly high standards — but the other residents of Grasmere were less chary and Sheila now had a little pool of clients there.

Mr Dominguez's house was far and away the most striking, but there were some other properties that she enjoyed visiting.

'They're all well off in there,' she told Rob proudly. 'And the Park's won all sorts of awards. For architecture and that kind of thing,' she added vaguely.

'Can't think why,' was her husband's repressive rejoinder. 'Some of them big old houses are downright gloomy.'

Admittedly, the period Georgian and Victorian properties — with their turrets and belfries — weren't to Sheila's far more conventional taste, but any criticism of Grasmere made her oddly defensive.

'It's a mix of styles,' she said with some hauteur. '"Eclectic", Mr Dominguez says. That's what makes it special.'

'Oh aye.' Rob remained resolutely unimpressed, thinking with some complacency of their own smart little semi in Medway. 'It's a bloody horror show with them space-age Tardis-looking places — all glass an' steel an' what have you — alongside the twiddly ones that can't decide whether they're meant to be castles or summat out of a fairy story.'

'Well, there's all sorts of posh folk living in there at any rate.' Knowing she had lost the argument, Sheila retreated to safer ground. 'Vicars and accountants — people like that.' She paused, ready to produce her trump card. 'The local MP and all.'

Rob's face darkened as though he hardly counted this as a recommendation.

Hastily, Sheila continued, 'I met some of them when they came round to the book club.'

'What's that when it's at home?' Despite himself, her husband was intrigued.

'Oh, it's Mr Dominguez who runs it. They meet once a month in his house. Neighbours from the Park mainly.' She met her husband's sceptical gaze bravely. 'They usually meet Saturdays, but I was there once when he had to move it back a day.'

'Passed round the drinks, did you?'

Her chin went up. 'Mr Dominguez did that himself. He asked if I'd like to join in actually. It was *Wuthering Heights* and I knew the story from when I went to see the film with our Julie.'

There was something oddly touching about her dignity.

'You're worth ten of any of 'em,' Rob said gruffly with a clumsy squeeze of the hand. 'I reckon your Mister Dodgy Dago knows it an' all.'

And so their tiff had ended in a truce.

Now Sheila stretched languorously. It was so peaceful just sitting outside the sleepy old ticket office. There was nobody about, just a fat tabby leering at her somnolently from the sidings where the Calder Vale Express (affectionately called 'Thomas the Tank Engine' by locals) gleamed in the sun.

But the station clock showed eleven a.m. Time to get a move on.

* * *

Forty minutes later, Sheila leaned back on her haunches in the little café, surveying the newly washed red- and black-tiled floor with satisfaction. Just because she was a volunteer didn't mean she was the sort to skimp on anything. Even Nerys bloody Wynne wouldn't be able to fault her work today!

She felt a childish compulsion to take a quick turn round the sidings. Have a look at the little locomotive slumbering in the sun. Ten minutes' break and then she'd be ready to do the gents, this being easily the least enjoyable part of her morning schedule.

The blue-painted carriages were as storybook charming as ever, she thought, running her fingers lightly along their sides. Out of the corner of his eye, the lazy tabby looked on.

On she wandered the length of the train, until she came to the very last compartment.

She was about to turn and walk back when a familiar smell struck her nostrils.

Spicy, citrus-flavoured with hints of gerbera.

Sheila knew that scent. Would know it anywhere.

Sweat pooling at the nape of her neck, she peered into the end coach. Despite the warmth of the day, she felt suddenly icy cold.

It was dark and shady inside, but still she saw it peeking out from beneath the velour banquette.

The red kerchief that he loved to wear when playing at station master.

She recalled him knotting the cravat at an impossibly rakish angle while flashing that endearing grin.

'C'mon, Sheila. Do I look the business or what?'

Moving awkwardly on legs that felt as though they had turned to rubber, Sheila Birtle made her way back along the platform and into the café.

She rummaged through her shoulder bag for her mobile and made the call.

999.

'It's Michael Dominguez . . . out at the heritage railway . . . I think he's dead.'

1. CLOUDS ON THE HORIZON

Like Sheila Birtle, DI Gilbert Markham always felt his spirits lift with the arrival of spring.

Saturday, 21 March found him pacing the grounds of St Chad's, the terraced graveyard round the back of Bromgrove Police Station.

'You'll end up with your own statue in there, you visit it that often,' DS George Noakes was wont to observe. And it was true: the DI invariably sought refuge here before plunging into the sordid realities of whichever homicide investigation he happened to be working.

It was a beautiful morning, white clouds scudding across a sky so intensely blue that it almost hurt to look at it. The daffodils tossed their little trumpet heads in true poetic fashion and sunshine softened the austere grey monuments and crosses which crowded the paths in serried ranks. Clusters of dog violets, windflowers and saxifrage stippled the foot of the cenotaph like exotic pincushions, while thrushes and blackbirds chirruped contentedly from somewhere in the tall elms that had protected the church since time immemorial.

It would have been perfect but for the consciousness of his profession. The canker in the bud.

Markham sat on a bench next to the cenotaph and turned his thoughts to the previous day's discovery.

There had been something truly horrifying about the spectacle of Michael Dominguez's battered corpse as the paramedics extracted it from beneath the railcar banquette. Worst of all was the contrast between the man's mashed and bloodied features, and the perky red cravat around his neck.

'It was his trademark,' Sheila Birtle sobbed. 'He liked to send himself up . . . said you couldn't be a stationmaster without a bandana.'

Arriving amid the usual vile squealing of brakes, DS Noakes lost no time in steering the hysterical woman away from the gruesome scene, keeping up a stream of soothing prattle which contrasted sharply with the bullishness he reserved for his own sex.

'You don' want to remember your friend like that, luv,' he told her with gruff solicitude, his own innards twisting at the thought of that mangled head dripping pulpy matter onto the floor of the train compartment. 'You an' him helped out here, right? Well, I reckon he'd want you to get that café open so we can have a brew all round.'

Crashingly tactless in every other context, Noakes invariably struck the right chord when dealing with the stricken and vulnerable. In no time at all, Shirley was busy making hot drinks and sorting biscuits for the ambulance crew, pathologist Doug 'Dimples' Davidson and the police. Strictly speaking the café should have been cordoned off, but Shirley swore that the door had been locked when she arrived for duty. The same was true of the waiting room and its interconnecting ticket office.

'It was deliberate, you know,' she said softly just before Markham arranged for a uniform to drive her home. 'Putting the scarf round his neck after doing . . . *that* to him.' Her voice was thick, her blue eyes brimming once more. '*Downright wicked*,' she added with vehemence.

Once she had gone, Dimples withdrew a plastic evidence bag from his pocket with gloved hands and handed it to the DI. 'I think the poor woman was right about it being a sick joke. This bookplate was in there as well, pinned to his jacket like the man was some kind of exhibit.' Bluff and ruddy-complexioned, he'd always had more of the farmer about him than the sawbones.

'What's it say?' Noakes squinted at the blood-smeared evidence bag with distaste.

'*Grasmere Park Book Club*,' Dimples replied. 'Only someone's drawn a skull and crossbones in the corner.'

The DS scowled, pudgy bulldog face full of concentrated disgust.

'Great,' he muttered. 'So we're looking for a clever-dick nutter.'

'You're looking for a psychopath,' came the blunt rejoinder. 'It's a while since I've seen a body mauled about as badly as that.'

'Time of death?'

'Now you know better than that, Markham,' the pathologist tut-tutted. Then, seeing the DI's sombre expression, he relented. 'I'd say between eight and ten on Thursday night.'

Noakes cleared his throat. 'Was he . . . well, tortured or owt?'

'Battered with, at a guess, a steel jack or wrench.' It was Dimples' turn to swallow. 'The victim put up quite a fight, but it was such a frenzied attack he stood no chance.'

'Never saw it coming, then?' Markham probed.

'Doesn't look like it.' The pathologist took a long gulp of tea as though to clear his throat. 'I recognize the name,' he said at last. 'Michael Dominguez, yes?'

'You know him, doc?' Noakes was eager.

'The wife dragged me to a couple of his talks at the art gallery . . . Spanish painters or some such malarkey.' Dimples seemed aggrieved at the memory. 'Could've been worse, I suppose. Bucketloads of ham, but the ladies lapped it up.'

'What was he then — an *art expert*?' The DS was evidently no fonder of the breed than Dimples.

Between replacing items of kit in what Noakes irreverently called his 'bag of tricks', the doctor offered up some nuggets about the dead man. 'Retired from the university . . . big cheese in academic circles, apparently . . . published a few books into the bargain . . . house in Grasmere Park.' Now the medical man looked sad. 'Actually, as I recall, there was something quite endearing about him — a sort of childlike enthusiasm. And he wasn't totally up himself like most of that lot at the university.'

Noakes nodded grimly as though to say, *I know what you mean*.

'Was he a dago then?'

Markham winced but the doctor, inured to the sergeant's contempt for anything resembling a PC lexicon, didn't turn a hair.

'Spanish ancestry. Quite swarthy looking . . . big sprawling nose that took over half his face . . . good head of hair, mind.' He winked at Noakes. 'Helped along from a bottle, I'd wager.' Another swig of tea. 'Handsome enough in a continental sort of way . . . seemed a bit too exotic for the university, though no trace of a foreign accent — pure BBC.'

'You said the ladies liked him,' Markham observed delicately.

'Not sure he liked them back, if you get me.' Dimples was thoughtful. 'I could be barking up the wrong tree, of course, and the women certainly went gaga for him . . .'

'Keeping his options open then,' Noakes grunted.

Amused, the doctor nodded. 'Quite possibly, Sergeant.' A cloud passed over his face. 'He was a bit over the top for my taste, but there was something open and trusting about him . . .'

The DI pondered. Could that same naiveté have prevented him seeing the danger rushing towards him until it was too late?

'Whoever he was, he didn't deserve to die like that.' Dimples snapped his medical bag shut with unnecessary force. 'Be sure to catch whoever did this, Markham.' He paused impressively. 'And do it fast. I'd say he could develop a taste for it.'

After Dimples was gone, Markham and Noakes watched the uniforms cordon off the railway sidings with yellow crime-scene tape.

'Looks like ole Dimples took a shine to the vic,' Noakes ruminated.

'Yes.' Markham's face was shaded with melancholy. 'Quite a character by the sound of it.'

'Grasmere Park's poshville,' the DS volunteered. Then, with a hint of pride creeping into his voice, 'One of the missus's pals from the Women's Guild lives there.'

'Indeed, Sergeant. That could be very useful.'

Noakes's pouchy features radiated gratification.

'The missus says it's all very nicey-nicey on the surface, but you wouldn't believe the bitching that goes on.'

'Oh, but I would, Noakes. A closed community is a like a petri dish for all manner of grudges and resentment . . . and when a virus breaks loose, all hell follows in its wake.'

Remembering his words a day later — here in St Chad's — it occurred to Markham that they must have sounded melodramatic. Certainly DCI Sidney (whose moniker 'Slimy Sid' was justly earned) would baulk at talk of petri dishes and viruses. 'Save the poetry and twiddles for when you write your first novel, Markham,' Sid had told his subordinate with ill-concealed jealousy.

And Markham knew that, on some level, Slimy Sid must be right. He *did* need to keep a check on the philosophical streak that formed such a strong part of his make-up.

But it was hard not to feel a sense of acute foreboding at the thought of that scrap of red cloth tied round the dead man's neck . . . the jaunty calling card, encrusted with blood and gore.

Downright wicked.

The DI got to his feet and, casting one last look at nature's outspread tapestry, headed towards the station.

* * *

The CID office was quiet as Markham passed through to his own corner sanctum. Glass-walled, it offered an unrivalled view of the station carpark. Sighing, it occurred to him that his workplace looked staler and shabbier than ever in contrast with the glowing panorama of St Chad's. But in the current economic climate, the chances of his superiors sanctioning a splurge on interior décor were vanishingly small.

He smiled at the sight of the miniature bonsai tree adorning DS Kate Burton's desk — set in a gravel tray with its own tiny bamboo rake. In the wake of her broken engagement, his earnest, capable sergeant had developed a passion for all things Zen. God help her if Noakes decided to lend a hand with the watering . . .

He shut the door of his office and sat down heavily in the 'ergonomic' chair behind his desk.

How do you solve a problem like DS George Noakes?

A grizzled veteran, Noakes had long been in DCI Sidney's cross hairs as an ideal candidate for redundancy, due to the same qualities that made him indispensable to Markham: his outspokenness (leading to politically incorrect gaffes which never failed to leave the liberals aghast); his lack of reverence for authority in general and 'the gold-braid mob' in particular; his determination to fight for the underdog at any cost.

Despite them being polar opposites, a strange affinity had existed between the DI and Noakes right from the beginning of their association, only deepening as the years went by. Noakes's truculent loyalty to his boss never faltered, rendering him impervious to the machinations of those who envied Markham's meteoric rise and would be only too happy to see him humbled.

The DS might be CID's resident dinosaur, but he was unusually sensitive to undercurrents which lay below the surface. Without the need for words, Noakes had guessed the tragedy of Markham's adolescence — the abusive stepfather who had blighted his formative years and made him bury his emotions deep inside.

Markham's girlfriend Olivia Mullen, an English teacher at Hope Academy, had clicked with Noakes from the start. Their inexplicable mutual admiration was a source of ill-disguised irritation to Mrs Muriel Noakes. 'I think she must have bewitched my husband,' she was wont to say, with a brittle laugh that deceived no one.

But when Noakes dug his heels in, that was that. There was no doubting his devotion to his snobbish, overbearing wife, whom he had met (bafflingly to those who knew them) on the ballroom-dancing circuit. Even so, he regarded his boss's willowy red-haired partner with all the reverence of a medieval squire sprung from the pages of Arthurian legend. Olivia, in turn, was teasing and playful with 'George'. Like her boyfriend, she relished his unvarnished honesty and knew he would always have Markham's back.

Somehow Kate Burton had never been admitted to this magic circle of intimacy.

Dedicated and conscientious, the psychology graduate's path into the police had not been easy. Eventually overcoming parental opposition ('no job for a woman,' her father had said), Burton had worked hard to reach her present position in CID. It took a while before she and Noakes surmounted their personality clash — his political incorrectness versus her right-on sensibilities and eager-beaver work ethic — but somehow they had reached a mutual understanding, united in their allegiance to Markham and equally tenacious in hunting down murderers. Seeing Burton blunder into danger in recent investigations had even brought out Noakes's protective streak. And so their truce looked set to hold.

Lately, Markham had noticed a curious restraint and self-consciousness in Burton's manner towards him. It bothered him. He knew she envied the closeness between himself and Noakes but somehow didn't think that was the root of the problem. The broken engagement had made her withdraw still further into her shell ('she's well rid cos the guy's a no-mark, if you ask me,' was Noakes's withering verdict on

Kate's stolid ex-fiancé) and she showed no appetite for taking her Inspector's exams.

Somehow he would have to get to the bottom of it. He couldn't allow a talented detective like Burton to drift along the way she was going.

But Noakes posed the more troubling dilemma. A cloud hung over Markham's relationship with his wingman and he didn't know how to dispel it.

Their most recent murder investigation at the Bluebell Dance Studio had seen a skeleton tumble out of the Noakes family closet. To the DS's shock, it transpired that Natalie Noakes — the apple of his eye — was most likely not his biological daughter but the result of Muriel's youthful fling with another man. The father had left her high and dry. To make matters worse, it was eminently probable that Noakes, on discovering the truth, had taken the law into his own hands.

Now an enquiry was underway, and the police watchdog involved. The DI didn't doubt that his number two would eventually be exonerated — not least since the IOPC wasn't privy to Noakes's family history — but Noakes was closer to him than just about anybody else. And it hurt to know his wingman had failed to confide in him, leaving Markham to piece the story together from other sources.

'It's chivalry,' Olivia tried to reassure him. 'George's code of honour, you see. He can't bear the thought of anyone looking down on Muriel . . . or knowing that Natalie isn't his.'

Markham did see, but these days a shadow still hung over the relationship, leaving him to wonder if things would ever return to the way they were.

Noakes had no idea that Markham knew his secret and the DI didn't know how to broach the subject.

'He'll talk when he's ready, Gil,' was Olivia's opinion.

Markham could only hope she was right. Somehow it felt contrary to the natural order of things that there should be any constraint between him and Noakes.

At least DC Doyle, the fourth member of the team, was causing the DI no anxiety. A lanky carrot-top, with an easy-going manner that belied his keen ambition, he was approaching the end of his distance-learning degree in criminal law and studying hard for his sergeant's exams. Proud to be in 'Markham's gang', he enjoyed a relaxed friendship with Noakes whose avuncular affection somehow survived their heated discussions about Bromgrove Rovers. Doyle's attitude to Kate Burton was respectful, though he and Noakes indulged in expressive eye-rolling displays whenever she 'went off on one' — as she was prone to do when it came to her beloved psychology. Indeed, the two men had bets on the *Diagnostic and Statistical Manual of Mental Disorders* being their colleague's preferred bedside reading.

All in all, the DI prized his little team highly and strongly resisted all attempts at infiltration — not that DCI Sidney hadn't tried to break them up.

Idly, Markham wondered who was behind the series of leaks that had plagued the Bluebell case and made a mental note to keep this upcoming murder investigation firmly under wraps.

Michael Dominguez sounded like he'd been someone worth knowing. According to the poet John Donne, 'any man's death diminishes me'. Yet Markham could not help feeling that Dominguez was no ordinary character and vowed with more than usual intensity that he would see the man's brutish killing duly avenged.

It occasionally happened in the team's investigations that a victim's personality coloured the case to such a degree that it seemed almost as though strings were being pulled from beyond the grave. It had been like that with the George Baranov ballet murder, and the DI had a suspicion the same thing was about to happen again.

There was the sound of voices from the outer office.

'If you overwater them, it's fatal.' Kate Burton's voice was tight.

Markham suppressed a grin. More than likely, her fellow sergeant had been interfering with that poor little bonsai. Just because he donated the odd yucca plant to CID, the DS now seemed to regard himself as being on a par with Monty Don.

Indeed, as Noakes came shambling into the DI's office, he bore more than a passing resemblance to a park groundsman or gardener, sporting a grubby Aran sweater and sludge-coloured cords. His hair was a salt-and-pepper thatch, standing wildly on end as though it had been curry-combed rather than brushed. Somewhat less chunky these days owing to what he bemoaned as a 'crappy' diet of chickpeas and couscous imposed by 'the missus', he still fell far short of a lean, mean crime-fighting machine. Even so, he had miraculously squeaked through his recent appraisal (Markham having called in various favours in the process).

Yes, Noakes would require sprucing up before they attended Grasmere Park. Perhaps Burton could see her way to dropping the necessary hint . . .

His other DS, needless to say, was smart and well-groomed even in her civvies. Despite a lack of sparkle in her demeanour, Burton looked the epitome of laid-back professionalism in straight-leg jeans, dark polo neck, ankle boots and blazer. Her trademark hairstyle — a chocolate pageboy with old-fashioned bangs — offset her intelligent brown eyes and tip-tilted nose, lending her features a certain quirky charm.

Doyle too 'looked the business' in well-pressed denim and button-down shirt. Markham would have no cause to blush for him should the DCI suddenly materialize like an evil genie.

Two out of three wasn't bad going and, with it being Saturday, he could only hope Sidney was elsewhere, safely hitting the fairway at Medway Golf Club.

His subordinates settled themselves round his desk in their usual fashion, Kate Burton with her soy latte, and the other two with cappuccinos and muffins from Dunkin'

Donuts. Markham sent up a silent prayer of gratitude that he'd been spared the usual grease-fest from McDonald's.

Burton reached into her blazer for her spectacles, which made her eyes look like enormous lollipops, before flipping open a pristine notebook and regarding Markham with the rapt attention of a religious acolyte.

This in itself wasn't enough to elicit eye-rolls from her male colleagues. But Noakes slouched back in his chair, as if in implicit rebuke to such bushy-tailed enthusiasm.

'So, what's with these poshos at Grasmere Park?' was his opening gambit. 'Cos it's got to be one of them seeing as there was that bookplate thingy pinned to him.'

'One of the reading group, you mean?' Burton asked eagerly.

'Book club,' Noakes amended sourly.

'Yes, I think we can narrow it down to members of the Grasmere Park Book Club, which I believe met at Mr Dominguez's house once a month,' Markham said.

'What about the railway volunteers?' Doyle enquired. 'Wasn't he some sort of train buff?'

'They'll have to be checked out, obviously,' came the reply. 'But that bookplate suggests to me his neighbours in the Park represent our prime suspects.'

'Could be a double bluff, of course.' Noakes's lips were pursed. 'A trainspotter trying to make us look at the neighbours when it's *ackshually* one of them Thomas the Tank weirdos.'

Burton frowned at hearing railway enthusiasts thus described, but she wisely kept her opinion to herself.

'Do we have a list of book-club members, sir?'

'It so happens I have one here, Kate.' The DI smiled at her. 'I'll make sure you each have a copy . . . It looks like quite an intimate set-up, so only a half-dozen names or so.'

Burton's fountain pen hovered over the immaculate notebook. Typically, she was keen to record her own marginalia. Noakes meanwhile tapped the side of his forehead as though to say, *It's all in here, mate*. The DC merely grinned.

Markham scanned his list. 'Fenella Staunton, retired academic . . . The university's history of art department.'

Noakes's mouth turned down at the corners. He'd had enough of bleeding art historians after that series of murders at the gallery.

'The Reverend Derek Worthington,' Markham continued smoothly, only too aware of his wingman's malevolent inner commentary. 'Vicar of Saint Barnabas's. That's the little church at the entrance to the Park. Rosemary Kernan—'

'Hey, she's the MP.' Doyle was alert and interested.

'Correct, Constable.'

'Not that ordinary folk ever see much of her,' Noakes groused. 'Too busy brown-nosing people in high places.'

'Then there's Bernard Gallagher, retired principal of Calder Vale FE College.'

'Sounds like they're all wrinklies.' Noakes scratched his chin viciously. 'Hard to see how any of 'em could've battered Dominguez to death.'

'Age-wise, they range from late forties through to early seventies,' Markham pointed out. 'All vigorous enough to have done it, particularly with the element of surprise.'

Burton cast a reproving look at her fellow sergeant. Evidently, she wanted to hear the full roll call.

'Andrew Boughton is a local amateur organist,' the DI went on. 'There's a librarian from Bromgrove Central Library — Judith Lockyer. Plus, we've got a teacher from Hope Academy—'

'*Oh, chuffing Nora, not that place again.*' Noakes sounded anguished, no doubt at the remembrance of their visits to the local secondary in various investigations and his own prickly encounters with school management.

'Afraid so, Sergeant. One Susan Caldicott from the maths department.'

'At least she's not a pigging art freak,' was the tetchy rejoinder.

'Finally, we have Timothy Appleyard, retired accountant.'

Noakes sat up straighter. 'That name rings a bell.' Another scratch of the chin. '*Yeah, I've got it.*' The DS sounded excited now. 'He's the one whose wife went missing an' they never found her. Our lot thought he was good for it but couldn't make owt stick . . .'

'Yes, Mr Appleyard is connected to one of our cold cases.' Markham's tone held a warning note. 'But let's not make any hasty assumptions.'

Despite this admonition, it was all too obvious from Noakes's baleful expression that Appleyard had shot straight to the top of his own shit list.

'Oh yes, and I nearly forgot. There's Nerys and Simon Wynne, mother and son. Live next door to Mr Dominguez. He's a surveyor with the council. I believe she's a widow.'

Markham looked at them steadily.

'So there we have it,' he concluded. 'And I propose to get started this afternoon. Noakes, you'll be with me giving Mr Dominguez's house the once-over before we have another word with Sheila Birtle. I want to hear *her* take on the residents before we move to interviews.'

Seeing that Burton looked slightly downcast, he added, 'I need you to set up the incident room with DC Doyle, Kate. Your matchless efficiency means we can hit the ground running.'

She brightened at that, though the youngster looked somewhat like he had drawn the short straw. 'Don't worry. I'll see everyone gets a slice of the action,' Markham added wryly, causing the DC to crimson to the roots of his hair.

'What about the rapes, sir?' Doyle asked tentatively. CID were currently investigating a string of sexual assaults.

'I'll speak to DCI Sidney about that,' Markham reassured him. 'I'm sure he won't mind my poaching you from DI Gregg.'

Too bloody bad if he did.

'Right, team. We need to pull out all the stops on this one. Mr Dominguez deserves nothing less.'

Burton noted the formality. Markham was never casual in the way that he referred to victims. Never disrespectful. And woe betide anyone who resorted to gallows humour in his hearing. Then their austere chilly boss could turn glacial in a heartbeat.

'There will be a pattern here,' the DI concluded as they rose to their feet. 'A criss-cross of human motives. And it's our job to make it out.'

2. PICKING UP THE VIBES

'Before we head over to Grasmere, let's check out the heritage station one more time,' Markham instructed Noakes as they settled into the latter's Fiesta. 'It was important to Mr Dominguez, so I want to get a feel for the place. Pick up the vibes.'

'Them choo-choo types jus' never grow up,' the DS declared sententiously.

'*Choo-choo types*?'

'Oh, you know what I mean, guv.' Noakes ground the gears with his usual gusto. 'On the telly those train fanatics allus come across dead creepy. All shiny-eyed an' blathering on.'

Noakes's clutch began emitting some truly horrible noises, but the DS was unfazed.

'God help their kids having embarrassing dads like that . . . That's if they ever manage to find some poor cow who'll take 'em on.'

'You make the whole thing sound positively perverted, Sergeant.' Markham's voice was dry. 'But it's just possible they admire the workmanship and creativity that goes into it all.'

'Oh, aye.' Noakes returned to the attack. 'But you wouldn't want to set your watch by one of them locomotives, would you?'

'I suppose not.' The DI was amused. 'That's not the point though, Noakesy. It's about living life at a different pace . . . savouring the beautiful countryside . . . enjoying the experience of being on a narrow-gauge railway.' He warmed to his theme. 'Then there's the moments between stations.'

'*Eh?*'

'When you get that sense of being almost outside of time. In a sort of twilight zone where you're in neither one place nor the other . . . No man's land.'

'Well, I s'pose there's always a trip to the pub at the end of it.' Noakes was prepared to be generous. 'Them outdoor seats must be bloody hard on folks' rear ends, so reckon they're ready for a pint when it's all over.'

'The point is, it's meant to be a *pleasure outing*, Sergeant. Not a cruel and unusual punishment!'

But the DI's tone was affectionate. It felt comfortable to be ribbing his DS like this. The air of constraint had lifted and he sensed they were both relieved to be back in harness, facing the challenge of a new investigation.

For his part, it was a guilty relief. At times he felt like some ghastly horseman of the apocalypse herding innocent souls into the netherworld before their time. He knew it was irrational but couldn't help confiding his superstition in Noakes.

'Yeah,' Noakes agreed straightaway. ''S like them dark rider blokes in that film, *Lord of the Rings*. The ones in black cloaks with no faces who wanna get the hobbits,' he added with some relish.

That was the thing about Noakes. He made the unbearable bearable by virtue of his blessedly *normal* take on the evil that stalked in their wake, thereby destroying its potency. Like some fairy tale where the demons crackled and withered and disappeared all at once in a puff of smoke with only a pile of incinerated rags to show they were ever there.

But the tectonic plates had shifted beneath Markham's feet during their last investigation. Now he'd had a glimpse of his wingman's own hinterland and it felt as though there was no going back for either of them.

The DI recalled Olivia's admonition: he just needed to give it time.

Yes, he would just have to be patient and hope that Noakesy would open up eventually.

If he didn't — well, dammit. Along with Olivia, the man was the nearest thing he had to family and he wasn't going to throw it all overboard . . .

Noakes too was reflecting on his boss's vagaries.

All that guff about the magic of — what was it? — being *suspended outside time* and *twilight zones*. Like a train was one of them diver's decompression thingies.

Most likely the guv'nor was thinking back to childhood outings. Times when he got a break from that bastard of a stepdad.

Still, it was good to hear the DI coming over all poetic. Meant they were settling back into their old familiar groove. Happen he'd be able to tell Markham how it really was during the Bluebell case . . . but not just yet . . .

* * *

All was quiet at the little heritage station when they arrived.

'No funny types hanging around?' Noakes enquired of the pimply uniform posted at the entrance. 'Weirdos in flasher macs?' he added by way of clarification.

'My sergeant means trainspotters,' Markham said drily.

'I meant the killer!' The DS was indignant.

'Come along, Noakesy.' This was no time to be disputing the difference between train enthusiasts and homicidal maniacs. 'Keep up the good work, Constable.'

With that, the DI moved towards the sidings. The SOCOs were nowhere to be seen, from which he deduced that their forensic sweep had been concluded.

'*Good work*,' Noakes snorted. 'The lad's bored out of his skull.' Then, with real fellow feeling, 'An' he can't even get a brew.'

'There's a perfectly adequate snack machine outside the ticket office, Sergeant. He won't perish for want of sustenance.'

Noakes's expression suggested that Snickers bars were a poor substitute for tea and a bacon butty, but he merely grunted.

They ducked under the crime-scene tape and made their way towards the covered end carriage where Michael Dominguez's body had been discovered.

Inside the carriage felt cramped and musty, but Noakes stroked the velour upholstery of the banquettes approvingly.

'Nice,' he said before plonking himself down on the right-hand bench. 'Okay,' he conceded, testing the springs. 'Mebbe it wouldn't be too bad for forty-five minutes or so. So . . . What would ole Manuel have done for this volunteering lark, then?'

'Don't let Kate hear you call him that,' Markham admonished. 'I believe Mr Dominguez was of Basque ancestry, but the family came here during the Spanish Civil War and he regarded himself as an Englishman through and through.'

'Oh aye.' Noakes was unimpressed. Then, with an air of meritorious condescension to the unfortunately born victim, he declared, 'Very public-spirited of him to, er, help out here at any rate.'

The DI suppressed a grin.

'I'm not entirely sure myself what exactly the volunteers do,' he admitted. 'Probably help out in the ticket office and café—'

'D'you think they get to drive a loco?'

'I believe they can help out the qualified crew. Apparently, there's a range of steam experience courses people can follow if they want a hands-on role.'

'Mebbe they could be guards or operate the whatchamacallit . . . signals.'

'Exactly.' Markham looked through the window of the stale little compartment. 'There'd be lots of outdoor jobs on offer as well . . . looking after the rolling stock, helping to maintain tracks . . .'

'Dressing up like the Fat Controller.'

The DI let it pass.

'As you say, Sergeant, it showed admirable community spirit.'

'How many trains have they got here, boss?'

'Just three, I believe. The others are in the engine house behind the platform across from this one. There's a little subway connecting the two.'

Noakes ruminated. 'Mister D was defo killed in this carriage, then?'

'We'll need results from the PM and forensics, but it looks that way.' There was a note of real regret in Markham's tone as he added, 'I think the drama of a cloak-and-dagger meeting on the train would have appealed to Mr Dominguez . . . easy enough to lure him out here by playing on that side of his character.'

'An' you don' see one of them other volunteers for it, guv? I mean, mebbe the vic got up someone's nose.' Noakes spoke as if he considered this all too probable.

'We'll run checks, obviously, but I think the answer lies in Grasmere Park,' Markham replied slowly. 'I reckon Sheila Birtle thinks so too.'

'We're gonna have another word, right?'

'Yes, but first I want a look at Mr Dominguez's house.'

'The missus says the places round there are like summat out of *Ideal Home.*' At Markham's quizzical expression, the DS qualified gruffly, 'Not that I read it meself.' *Perish the thought.* 'But Grasmere's dead exclusive. They use it for film shoots an' stuff like that.'

'You're quite the mine of useful information, Sergeant.' His boss smiled.

They walked slowly back towards the main entrance.

'No CCTV,' Markham noted, 'and no visible security. Presumably they have a rota for patrols and the like. That'll need looking into.'

'Well, it's jus' a little outfit, innit?' Noakes guffawed. 'An' no chance of pinching a loco, so it'd be a waste of money splashing out on high-end gadgets.'

'Indeed.' The DI took one final glance about him. 'Whereas the Grasmere Park residences will no doubt be bristling with all kinds of expensive security devices.' He nodded his head. 'Our killer chose cleverly. And he knew his man alright.'

Back in the car, Markham reflected, 'Small communities have their own kind of awareness. It's not about detection or high-powered psychology . . . more a kind of instinctive feeling for human nature, like water diviners in folklore.'

Uh-oh. Noakes sensed another poetic digression was imminent. Hastily, he revved the engine and reversed out of the forecourt in a hail of gravel.

* * *

In the event, Noakes was awed almost to mutism by the glories of Michael Dominguez's residence.

'Gotta be worth half a million easy, guv,' was all he said as they explored the architecturally bespoke property set in half an acre of beautifully landscaped grounds.

It was certainly impressive, Markham reflected as they went from the undercroft double garage to the cosy snug, perched on its own mezzanine, with square porthole windows on either side and light pouring down from a roof lantern above.

The DS was in a dream of wonder as they passed through room after room of high-spec fixtures and fittings. ''S like summat out of *Star Trek*,' he muttered, looking at the Quooker taps and endless stainless steel. 'An' all for one bloke.'

To Markham it felt like some sort of beautifully designed Scandinavian show house. Spread over two floors, the exterior was built from pale yellow brick, topped with a striking metal-faced roof. On the upper level, Markham saw a projecting zinc-panelled elevation. On the ground floor, the rooms flowed into each other around a central courtyard, with unexpected surprises in the form of split levels, alcoves and secret spaces — all of which took the visitor unawares.

Upstairs was equally impressive.

'Not short of dosh, then,' Noakes gazed wistfully down from the master bedroom's feature window to the rear garden with its decked patio, pond, feature timber bridge and exotic shrubs. Determined not to sound too impressed, as they headed back downstairs he added, 'Burton'd like the Chinky courtyard with them little rocks an' the stumpy trees.'

'I think you mean the Japanese garden, Noakes,' the DI amended mildly.

'Same difference.'

'It's certainly a most attractive feature,' Markham agreed.

The cloistered internal space at the heart of the house was the jewel in the crown as far as he was concerned — that and the delightful snug. The bookcases in this room amply attested the intellectually omnivorous mind of Michael Dominguez.

'What did he want with all them bedrooms, though?'

'Who can say, Sergeant,' the DI mused before saying briskly, 'I'll get Kate to make an appointment with Mr Dominguez's housekeeper — Sheila can give us the details. Then she and Doyle can do a top-down search.'

'D'you reckon they'll find owt useful, boss?'

'Unlikely.' Markham exhaled heavily. 'Our killer's fingerprints will be here — along with those of all the neighbours — so he knew it would be safe to come back after the murder and remove anything that might be incriminating.' Another sigh. 'You may have noticed—'

'No computer.'

'Correct, Sergeant.' Restlessly, the DI paced the maple-floored hallway. 'So, any secrets on his laptop are lost to us.'

'How'd the killer get in without waking half the Park up, boss?' Noakes gestured towards the wide in-and-out driveway. 'I mean, I know it's all leafy an' quiet an' whatnot cos that's what you're paying for. But Domingo's got neighbours an' someone must've heard something.'

'Not if the killer had keys and knew how to disable the alarm, Sergeant.'

Noakes looked startled.

'You reckon that was it, guv?'

The sunlight streaming into the hallway made it feel uncomfortably warm inside, so they headed back out into the forecourt where another dispirited uniform waited to lock up behind them.

'But won't that mean we're looking for . . . well, someone in a relationship with the vic? Cos it stands to reason, you don' jus' let any ole Tom, Dick or Harry into your gaff.'

'That's one possibility, certainly. But there are others. Maybe someone exploited a Neighbourhood Watch scenario or somehow tricked Mr Dominguez into giving them access. Perhaps a builder or tradesman was careless . . .'

'I don' see that Sheila slipping up.'

'No,' Markham agreed. 'I'd say she's highly conscientious and trustworthy.'

He smiled at the uniform who endeavoured to look super-alert before turning back to the DS.

'Let's go and catch up with Ms Birtle. I'd be interested to hear her impressions of the neighbours. She's a shrewd, sensible sort of woman, so worth seeing if she can give us the low-down on Grasmere's other residents.' Easing himself into the front seat of the Fiesta, he added grimly, 'A way to breach their defences if we're lucky.'

* * *

Sheila Birtle lived on Bromgrove Rise in a neat little terraced property. Cluttered with knick-knacks, the place nevertheless sparkled with cleanliness and the two detectives were soon comfortably ensconced in armchairs with tea and (to Noakes's delight) home-made coffee cake.

It was obvious that Sheila had been very fond of Michael Dominguez.

'He was like an overgrown schoolboy at times,' she smiled. 'Full of energy. A bit exhausting even when he got started on his latest fad or whatever it was. And always quoting stuff at me . . . went right over my head, but that never put him off.'

Sounds like him and the guv'nor could have been besties, thought Noakes munching away.

'Was he the kind of man to have made enemies?' Markham asked gently, taking in Sheila's red-rimmed eyes and doleful expression.

'I s'pose he could have done, yes. But everyone in Grasmere knew what he was like. It's hard to imagine any of the neighbours hating him enough to do . . . *that*.'

Her lower lip began to tremble.

Noakes was quick to notice.

'Hey, luv,' he rallied her. 'You're our secret weapon for catching the scumbag who did this.' Lying through his teeth, the DS added, 'Mister D was bashed so hard over the head he wouldn't have known a thing. The . . . other stuff . . . that happened after he was out sparko.'

He stared fiercely at the DI as though daring him to say it wasn't so.

Markham gave an imperceptible nod. *Simmer down, Noakesy. I've got this.*

'I gather there's no next of kin,' he continued.

'That's right,' she said shakily. 'Michael was an only child. Parents were middle-aged when he came along and they're both dead now. I think there are some cousins out in Spain but that's it really.'

'You weren't aware of any run-ins with the neighbours, anything like that?' Markham asked.

'You wouldn't believe how many folk fall out over hedges an' paths an' walls — all kinds of stuff,' the DS put in cheerfully through a mouthful of cake.

Secateurs at dawn, Markham reflected, watching Sheila's face carefully.

'Oh, I'm sure there was the odd tiff from time to time,' she replied. 'But nothing serious. Like I say, people would have said it was just Michael being Michael. He didn't have much of a filter . . . childlike . . . loved his *Thomas the Tank Engine* lunch box I gave him.'

There's a bloody surprise. But Noakes kept his expression studiedly bland and sunny. Poor bint was miserable enough as it was.

'And yet he was an academic,' the DI observed.

'Oh yes, very intellectual. Always had his nose in a book. Jane Austen was his favourite.' Sheila smiled shyly. 'I told him I liked *Pride and Prejudice* when it was on the telly and he gave it me to read.'

Christ. This is worse than bleeding Radio 4. But again, the DS kept shtum.

'Would you say Mr Dominguez might have been absent-minded when it came to security, Ms Birtle?' Markham's mind was running on that missing computer. 'Is there any chance a set of house keys might be out there? Did other people know the code for his alarm?'

'I was always nagging him about that,' she admitted ruefully. 'He *did* lose a set of keys and I told him he needed to get the locks changed. He promised he'd get round to it but somehow never did.' Her face fell. 'I should have insisted.'

'Not your fault, luv. You weren't to know he was in any danger,' Noakes told her.

'The chair of Neighbourhood Watch has a set of keys,' she continued. 'That's Mr Gallagher. And the vicar has one too.'

'Derek Worthington.' The DI recalled his roster of Grasmere residents.

'That's right. But they're both ever so reliable. I just can't see them being careless.'

From Noakes's expression, it was clear the DS wasn't about to let them off that easily.

'Old geezers, are they?' he asked bluntly before adding hastily, 'No offence, luv, but they could've, er, taken their eye off the ball . . . specially the reverend if he's got folk traipsing in an' out.'

'Mr Gallagher's in his early seventies,' she retorted smartly, 'and Mr Worthington's sixty-something. But they're not what you'd call "past it" by a long way.' She paused, struck by a sudden recollection. 'And Nerys Wynne has a set of keys as well.'

'From the dormer bungalow next door to Mr Dominguez?'

'Yes, Nerys and Simon — that's her son — looked out for him.'

'What're they like?'

Noakes eyed the last remaining slice of cake as he put this question.

Sheila's expression was indulgent. 'Go on, Sergeant,' she encouraged in a motherly tone. 'Force yourself.'

'Don' mind if I do.'

'Nerys is a bit stiff and starchy — *genteel*. You'd want to mind your Ps and Qs. But good-hearted enough underneath it all. Simon's not really into all that railway stuff, but he pretended to be interested out of politeness.' She smiled. 'Nerys brought him up well.'

'What about the other residents?' Markham enquired, seeing that Noakes was intent on polishing off every last crumb.

'Well, let me see . . . There's Mrs Staunton. That's Fenella Staunton. She—' Sheila's face suddenly assumed the expression of one who has caught herself on the verge of committing an indiscretion.

'Go on, luv. You can trust us,' the DS urged, with a crafty leer. 'Sweet on him, was she?'

'As a matter of fact, I think she might have been a bit keen—'

''Cept he batted for the other side, yeah?'

'Well, I wouldn't want to speak out of turn,' Sheila said turning red.

'Don' you worry 'bout that,' Noakes reassured her.

'I never saw anything . . . but I did wonder . . .' The woman fiddled with the tea things. 'Fenella was very possessive and clingy, but he just didn't seem that interested. I think she might have been a bit jealous too cos he was so charming he had everyone eating out of his hand. And she liked to be queen bee, if you know what I mean.'

'There were three other ladies in the book club, I believe,' Markham resumed. 'Mrs Rosemary Kernan MP . . . Then there was Ms Lockyer and Mrs Caldicott. Have I got that right?'

'Susan Caldicott . . . yes, she's a nice woman. Teaches at Hope. Husband's something in finance' — Sheila bit her lip — 'bit of a bully between you and me.'

'Don't worry.' The DI flashed her a charming smile. 'We won't tell if you don't.'

She smiled back at him. A tall, dark figure, he'd seemed a bit intimidating at first, but he had such a kind way about him.

'Their place isn't as smart as the other houses,' she continued. 'But with four children it's not surprising.'

'And Ms Lockyer?'

'That's Judith. She works in the library, but Mr Dominguez told me she's a writer on the side . . . had a few books published.' Sheila looked embarrassed. 'I don't think they're any great shakes cos he was laughing when he told me.'

'How about Mrs Kernan?' Noakes was curious.

'She never had a word for the likes of me.' There was an edge to Sheila Birtle's voice. 'Mr Dominguez didn't like it. He wasn't at all snobbish.' Again, that nervous lip chewing. 'She wasn't happy when he asked me to join them at book club one day. I just happened to be there, you see, but it put Mrs Kernan in a bad mood. They had an argument afterwards, only I don't think it was about me . . . something to do with one of his students from when he worked at the university.'

It was obvious she was uncomfortable at the appearance of eavesdropping, but Markham spoke warmly.

'You're being a tremendous help to us, Ms Birtle — or perhaps I can call you Sheila?'

Oh pur-lease. Noakes jiggled in his seat but the DI sailed smoothly on.

'Then there's Andrew Boughton.'

She pulled a face.

'I take it you're not a fan,' Markham said.

'Thinks he's the Great I Am, that one.' This was uttered with surprising asperity. 'Ego the size of . . . a cathedral!'

It sounded to the DI as if there were quite a few egos among the residents of Grasmere Park.

'Musicians can be a bit like that,' he agreed.

'I don't know how Mr Worthington puts up with him. But then that man's halfway to being a saint.'

'What about Timothy Appleyard?' Noakes's expression was intent.

Sheila became suddenly wary.

'I know about his wife going missing, if that's what you mean. But it happened years ago, before I started coming to Grasmere.' She shifted uneasily on the little two-seater sofa facing them. 'He's a quiet man, very shy.'

With bloody good reason, thought Noakes sourly.

'But he's always been okay with me. "Live and let live" is my motto.'

'And a very good one,' the DI was quick to point out.

'How many of 'em do you clean for?' the DS asked. Always useful to have a spy in the camp.

'I used to clean for Mrs Caldicott, but she had to let me go. Time to tighten their belts, was what she told me. No one else from the book club, but there's a few others I do in the Park . . .'

'I believe there's around thirty households in all.'

'That's right, Inspector.' A touching note of pride. 'It's very exclusive, see.'

Nothing exclusive about murder, luv, Noakes said to himself.

* * *

Afterwards, the DI said, 'Obviously all the other residents in Grasmere have to be checked out.'

'But you don' think it's any of that lot, do you, guv?'

'No, Noakes, I don't.'

Sheila Birtle had confirmed that Michael Dominguez's main associates within Grasmere Park were the members of the reading group. Given the discovery of the bookplate and the fact that the book club was 'his baby', the DI was more convinced than ever that their killer was somewhere on that list.

One of them was possessed by a devil which had gone undercover, deep down, concealed by a veneer of suburban respectability.

It was his job to lure that devil out into the open.

3. A SPANNER IN THE WORKS

Sunday morning broke bright and clear over Bromgrove, finding Markham and Olivia at home in their apartment at The Sweepstakes, an upmarket complex off Bromgrove Avenue.

Over a leisurely brunch of bagels, scrambled eggs and fearsomely strong coffee, Markham described the events of the previous day.

'You should have seen Noakesy's face. He was bowled over by that house in Grasmere Park. Goggling at the fixtures and fittings . . . you'd have thought he was memorizing it all for an exam or something.'

'Well, I suppose in a manner of speaking he was,' Olivia said wryly. 'She Who Must Be Obeyed is bound to have given him the third degree when he got home. You know what Muriel's like when it comes to property envy!'

Markham chuckled. 'It was impressive alright. And there's something delightful about being so close to the river. The air *tastes* different somehow.'

'Did you never think of Grasmere for yourself, Gil?' Olivia asked curiously before breaking into a laugh. 'But, of course, it doesn't have a view of the cemetery, does it?'

Markham grinned. His predilection for graveyards was a standing joke, the flat's panoramic view of Bromgrove North

Municipal Cemetery having reeled him in off-plan before the building was even finished.

Olivia understood his affinity with the place. Understood that the proximity of the cemetery and its tussocky mounds acted like some revivifying elixir when the demands of his job were dragging him down, reminding him what he owed to those lost souls who were powerless to obtain vengeance for themselves. It was almost as if there was a shadowy host, invisible to others, following closely at Markham's heels; a ghostly tag team that he'd never been able to shake off — didn't *want* to shake off. It was part of why she loved him. Markham was a sensitive man whose austere, even forbidding, exterior concealed a heart which never ceased to ache for the dead.

A lapsed Catholic, he nonetheless had a vivid awareness of the next world, to the extent that she sometimes felt he *vibrated* with supernatural impressions and fears.

Now Michael Dominguez had joined the cavalcade of spectres clamouring in Markham's ears to say that he was their last hope of justice. That unearthly message would hold him spellbound and possess him wholly, like a man in a hypnotic trance, until he unmasked the killer.

Lightly, she asked, 'How about the residents, then? Have you started interviewing them?'

Markham looked lovingly at her across the kitchen table.

Clad only in a dressing gown and bare of make-up, her long red hair tumbling about her shoulders in a heavy mass, there was a translucent, ethereal beauty about her this morning. She seemed to have sprung straight from a painting by Rossetti or Millais. Small wonder that Mrs Noakes suspected her of sorcery.

'We've scheduled formal interviews for Tuesday,' he told her. 'Derek Worthington, the local vicar, said we can use St Barnabas's church hall.'

'What's he like, the vicar?'

'Faded, timid, tired eyes. There was something defeated about him.' Markham scooped up the last of his scrambled egg and washed it down with a scalding mouthful of coffee. 'God, that was good, Liv. He looked as though he was going to pass out when Noakes and I appeared on his doorstep, but I gather he's got heart problems, which would explain it.'

'That and the fact of his neighbour being bludgeoned to death.'

'Well, we're keeping the details under wraps for now,' he frowned, 'but the local tom-toms will likely be busy.'

'Did you get round the rest of them in this book club or whatever it was?'

'They were all at home when we did the circuit.'

'And George behaved himself?' Olivia quirked an eyebrow. 'Didn't go all Citizen Smith at the sight of so many manicured lawns?'

'Well, as far as he's concerned, we already have our man and it merely remains to deliver him into custody.'

She leaned forward, intrigued.

'And who might that be?'

'A retired accountant in his sixties. Name of Timothy Appleyard.' Markham reached across and squeezed her hand apologetically. 'I'm afraid I have to go out to Calder Vale this afternoon with Kate Burton so we can speak to Jim McLeod about him.'

The former DCI now worked with Bromgrove CID as a cold-case consultant, Markham holding his old boss in high regard.

Olivia looked at him expectantly.

'Appleyard's wife is one of our unsolveds . . . went missing in 2009. But there was no trace of a body' — he shrugged — 'and they couldn't get a result, though God knows they tried.'

'Presumably George was ready to arrest him on the spot.'

'Oh yes, chafing at the bit. Luckily, he and Muriel are tripping the light fantastic at some dance shindig today, which should keep him out of mischief.'

'I imagine Slimy Sid won't want you "polluting the shades" of Grasmere Park by dredging up another murder.'

From the hardening of her delicate features, it might be deduced that Olivia was no great admirer of Markham's boss.

Markham pulled a face.

'I've got to brief Sidney this evening.'

'Aren't his weekends sacrosanct, Gil?' she said sarcastically. 'I can't imagine him thanking you for dragging him off the links.'

'He's prepared to make an exception for this case. And Noakes said he'll be back for it, so at least I'll have some moral support.'

Olivia cut to the chase. 'D'you think there's a connection between the missing wife and what happened to Mr Dominguez?'

Her boyfriend sighed.

'Not got the foggiest, sweetheart. I'm hoping Jim can shed some light.'

'What's Appleyard like?'

'Stocky, silver-haired, craggy features, drinker's complexion, cultured accent.'

'Did he look like a wife-killer to you?'

'No, but who knows what goes on behind closed doors.'

She nibbled thoughtfully on her bagel.

'From what you said, Mr Dominguez sounded larger than life . . .'

'That's right, Liv. "Flamboyant" is the word we keep hearing.'

'People like that often stir up strong emotions.'

'Well, it sounds like Fenella Staunton fancied her chances with him.'

'I've seen that woman around the university, Gil.' Olivia taught adult education classes in creative writing. 'Quite a presence but very overbearing from the looks of it. Affected, too. At one time she made a habit of waltzing about the place sporting a pince-nez, would you believe.'

'Yes, Grasmere Park's answer to Germaine Greer. Let's just say she and Noakesy didn't exactly hit it off.'

‘I can imagine.’ Olivia rocked with mirth. ‘Did he insist on calling her “luv”?’

‘Despite my best efforts to shut him down, unfortunately yes.’

‘Did Mr Dominguez fancy her back?’

‘It would appear not. I have a suspicion she was quite disgruntled about it. And, as you say, a domineering personality into the bargain . . . It was obvious she resented the way everyone fell down like ninepins before him.’

Olivia smiled. ‘He sounds quite a smoothie. But’ — her face clouded over — ‘d’you think it was a crime of passion, Gil? I know what they say about a lover scorned and all that, but could a woman really have bashed him over the head?’

‘Dimples says yes if his guard was down.’

Markham had kept the full details of Michael Dominguez’s horribly bloodied corpse to himself. Observing Olivia’s distress, he knew it was the right decision.

‘What about the other women in the Park?’ she asked. ‘Were they smitten too?’

‘Rosemary Kernan certainly wasn’t,’ he said drily. ‘A big bosomy dame with horsey features and a voice like a megaphone.’ Markham gulped down more coffee as though desperate to kick-start his synapses. ‘She didn’t give an inch. The cleaning lady told us there’d been a falling-out between Mrs Kernan and Dominguez, but Kernan was having none of it . . . insisted everything between them was sweetness and light.’ He toyed with a bagel. ‘However, I’m inclined to believe there *was* a contretemps of some sort which led to a souring of relations.’

Olivia grimaced. ‘Not a groupie then?’

‘God, no.’ Markham poured himself another cup. ‘And Judith Lockyer was clearly a bit uptight about him.’ He cast his mind back to their talk with the librarian. ‘She looked like one of those Wiccan types. Long grey hair and what Noakes would call hippie attire . . . put me in mind of that historian, Mary Beard.’

'Oh right. Didn't some pig-ignorant critic say she was too ugly for television?'

'I wouldn't be surprised,' Markham replied. 'Anyway, Ms Lockyer churns out bodice-rippers as a sideline. She didn't say anything explicit, but I got the feeling Michael Dominguez might've poked fun. Just something about her defensiveness.'

'He wound folk up, then,' Olivia observed.

'Well, Susan Caldicott seemed to like him—'

'*Caldicott*.' Olivia sat up. 'She's from our maths department.'

'Sorry, dearest. I should have mentioned it before. Lives in one of those stucco-covered villas that's seen better days . . . middle-aged, washed-out . . . something a bit down at heel about her.'

'Yep, that's her.'

'You don't sound particularly enamoured.' Markham picked up on a certain reserve in her tone.

'Oh, she's just a bit . . . well, *dreary* . . .' Olivia hesitated, evidently torn between a desire to be charitable and the impulse to be indiscreet. The struggle was brief. 'There's something a bit sneaky about her. Strikes me as the sort who listens at doors, spies on colleagues and runs to management at the drop of a hat.'

'But didn't you tell me your place is pretty much "Stasiland" — riddled with informers?'

'True . . . and I don't think her home life's a bundle of laughs, so maybe it's her only outlet.'

'The husband's a bully apparently.'

'That would fit.' Olivia nodded slowly. 'There are four kids — two of them in Hope — so she's got her hands full.'

'Sheila Birtle — that's the cleaning lady who found Mr Dominguez — said Mrs Caldicott was nice but had to let her go because money was tight.'

'I only know Susan from school, Gil. Could be she's a different person away from the swamp of fear and loathing.'

'What you say about her being the type who listens at doors is interesting, though,' Markham observed, his brow corrugated. 'I'd almost forgotten about that . . .'

Olivia regarded him interrogatively.

'Well, Mrs Caldicott mentioned overhearing a snatch of conversation between Timothy Appleyard and Dominguez which she said struck her as odd. She put up some pretence of being reluctant to bad-mouth a neighbour.' Markham's lips were tightly compressed, a sure sign of distaste. 'But it was clear she wanted to mark our card.'

'What was it she heard?'

'Appleyard said something like, "You've enjoyed turning the screw all these years, haven't you?" Then Dominguez replied, "I put my neck on the line for you and you know it" — or words to that effect. She didn't hear the rest, but she said when Appleyard came out, he looked like someone on the rack.'

'Very poetic,' was Olivia's acid rejoinder. 'I didn't think our mathematician could wax so lyrical.'

'If she's right about that exchange, it suggests Michael Dominguez may have covered for Appleyard somehow.'

'As in *murder*?'

'I'm keeping an open mind, but you can see why Noakes wanted to whip out the handcuffs.'

'Sounds fishy, certainly . . . assuming she didn't make it up for effect.'

Or to send us up a blind alley.

'Well, that's all the women.' Markham swallowed a yawn. 'Oh, and there's the next-door neighbour . . . Nerys Wynne.'

'*Nerys*. Is that a Welsh name?'

'Hmm, sounds Celtic, doesn't it? But there wasn't a trace of any accent . . . Stumpy little sore-eyed woman. In her sixties like Dominguez but looks decades older. Walks with a limp and none too steady on her pins. Seems to have been genuinely fond of him. I got the feeling she was used to looking the other way when it came to his, er, eccentricities.'

Olivia grinned. 'You mean his colourful private life?'

'Something like that. Mrs Wynne is very correct — what you'd call a stickler for doing the right thing — but kind-hearted once you've got past the prim-and-proper bit.'

'What's *her* place like?'

'Oh, nothing special. At least, not in the same league as Dominguez's house. That's the thing about Grasmere. Architecturally it's a lunatic hotchpotch — the odd red-brick Lego monstrosity mixed in with Victorian Gothic follies and quaint Georgian villas.'

Olivia raised her eyebrows. 'Must have given Nerys an inferiority complex living next door to a modernist palace like Dominguez's.'

'I doubt it,' her boyfriend replied. 'She and Simon — that's the son — sounded faintly pitying when they talked about his pad —. as though it was somehow a breach of good taste. I'd say they're both very traditional.'

'What did you make of the son?'

'Middle-aged before his time, sandy-haired . . . a bit lumpy . . . works for the council . . . easy-going in a jogtrot kind of way.'

'None of them sound like a killer,' she pointed out.

'*You're telling me*,' Markham groaned.

'Was that the lot, then?'

'There's a retired principal from Calder Vale FE College: Bernard Gallagher. A dry old stick but sharp as a tack. He spoke affectionately about Dominguez, but I sense a little intellectual jealousy below the surface. I wouldn't be surprised if Dominguez needled him . . . got under his skin somehow.'

'Sounds like he's a bit behind Mr Dominguez in the charisma stakes.'

'Oh, undoubtedly.' Markham stretched luxuriously, enjoying these precious minutes with Olivia before murder claimed him again. 'Dominguez wore his learning lightly. He was an academic but *fun* with it, whereas Gallagher . . . let's just say he doesn't come across as red-blooded.'

'So, if you put a drop under a magnifying glass it would be all semicolons and parentheses!'

Markham smiled, recognizing a literary allusion.

'Well, if Gallagher was lacking, Andrew Boughton certainly didn't regard himself as being deficient in the manliness department.'

'Where does *he* fit in then?'

'Organist at St Barnabas's and no doubt a heavy cross for the poor vicar.'

'You didn't like him, Gil?'

'He's one of those flashy overbearing types . . . made sure we knew he came from money and didn't have to work for a living.'

'I'm sure that went down well with George.'

'Like a lead balloon.' Markham gave a reluctant chuckle. 'It was like watching two silverbacks square up to each other.'

'How did this Boughton bloke get on with Mr Dominguez?'

'Hard to tell . . . though he was careful to rattle off the appropriate platitudes.'

'Was he jealous of him like some of the others?'

'I wouldn't be surprised,' Markham said evenly. 'There was a flicker when I touched on Dominguez's eminence in the academic world, but it was gone so quickly I wondered afterwards if I hadn't imagined it.'

'I went to a lecture by Michael Dominguez,' Olivia said thoughtfully. 'He had flair, no doubt about it.'

'Dimples went along a couple of times when Dominguez was doing talks at the art gallery.' Markham pulled a comical face. 'He said it was really hammy and over-the-top.'

'Oh, I know what Doug means. Dominguez was terribly over-exuberant and unselfconscious . . . cracked some awful jokes too. It was obvious he didn't care two hoots what anyone thought of him.' She smiled reminiscently. 'But there was something so infectious about his enthusiasm and excitement that you couldn't help liking him. I remember thinking he'd make a good TV presenter because he just drew you in.'

'Interesting you should say that, Liv.' Markham knew it was time to be off, but somehow he couldn't bear to break up their cosy tête-à-tête. 'Someone in the Park said something about Dominguez setting his sights on a media career . . . Now who was it? Oh yes, that's right. Nerys Wynne said the BBC had approached him about doing a series.'

Hearing the regret in his voice, Olivia said gently, 'What a waste of all that energy and talent.'

Markham dug deep. 'At least Michael Dominguez enjoyed the time allotted to him, Liv. At least when he came to the end of the line, it couldn't be said of him that he had not lived.'

'True, dearest.' Her voice was very tender. 'If ever a man "sucked out all the marrow of life", it was him.' Her voice rang with conviction. 'And I know you'll see he gets justice in the end.'

* * *

Oddly enough, Kate Burton used practically the same words later that day. She and Markham were driving back to the station after calling on retired DCI Jim McLeod at his quaint terraced cottage in Calder Vale.

'DS Noakes will be well browned off to have missed Mrs McLeod's home cooking,' she said, a smile playing about her lips. Then, more seriously, 'Mr McLeod knows you'll nail this killer, sir. It's just a matter of time.'

He was touched by the sincerity in her voice.

'Noakes thinks Appleyard's our man. And Mr McLeod certainly found plenty of circumstantial evidence to say he could've murdered his wife.'

'Yes.' Despite the intriguing subject under discussion, Burton drove as carefully as ever, pulling wide to avoid a cyclist. There was something restful about it after Noakes's Formula-One-style manoeuvres.

'An unhappy marriage,' the DS continued after negotiating the obstacle, 'plus a failing business and an autistic daughter in care . . . He was under a lot of stress. Wouldn't surprise me if he'd snapped.'

'Why would Mr Dominguez cover for him, though?'

'Perhaps he sympathized with Appleyard, sir. The wife sounded a right harridan.' She blushed at her own vehemence. 'Or Dominguez could've enjoyed holding something over him.'

'You mean blackmail?'

'Not necessarily the financial kind, boss.' Burton puzzled over the conundrum. 'From the sound of it, Michael Dominguez was the kind of man who liked to be liked.'

'Hmmm. You mean he needed a coterie?'

'Something like that . . . with himself as top dog.'

'So, Appleyard was a sort of faithful retainer,' Markham mused. 'And then the worm turned.'

Dogs and worms, he thought. The natural order.

Burton pursued her theory. 'Say Dominguez kept him on a tight leash. We could be looking at years of resentment bubbling away under the surface and then finally — *whoosh*!'

'If that's the game Mr Dominguez was playing, it was a risky one.'

'Maybe things just crept up on them, sir. There was this connection between them and it became toxic over the years.'

The DI suppressed a smile, knowing his colleague was itching to look up *Dysfunctional co-dependency* in the index of her trusty *Diagnostic and Statistical Manual of Mental Disorders*.

'Perhaps they kept each other's secrets,' he said. 'Perhaps Mr Dominguez enjoyed flirting with danger and paid the ultimate price.'

'Mind you, Appleyard hardly looks like he's got the strength for an attack like that.'

'Dimples says Dominguez was battered with a double-ended spanner, and I had a call earlier to say the SOCOs found one a couple of hundred yards further up the track covered in blood. It's the murder weapon alright.'

'So if the killer distracted Dominguez and got him looking the other way—'

'Easy enough to smash his skull like an egg,' Markham finished grimly. 'And, by the by, there's no question of you attending the PM on this one, Kate.'

Too bad if this raised Burton's feminist hackles. The thought of her watching while Doug Davidson sloshed around inside what was left of Dominguez's cranium made him feel sick.

Unusually, she looked relieved.

'What kind of secrets d'you reckon Appleyard and Dominguez might have shared, boss?'

'Could've been sexual if Mr McLeod's right about Appleyard having gay friendships.'

Burton pursed her lips. 'Never turned anything up though, did they, sir?'

'True. If that's why Appleyard's marriage was on the rocks, they never found hide nor hair of a boyfriend.' The DI looked sightlessly out of the passenger window. 'Appleyard was so far in the closet that he'd thrown away the key . . .'

Unless Michael Dominguez had it.

'Perhaps we're overcomplicating things, sir, and it was something like a tax fiddle or a property scam.'

'Hmmm. From the look of that house, Mr Dominguez had a taste for the finer things in life. But then, he had the income to match.

They drove on for a time in silence, leaving behind the foxgloves and lush green foliage of Calder Vale as they drew closer to Bromgrove.

'What's the plan now, boss?'

'Well, I've got to brief the DCI,' Markham said neutrally. 'Your fellow sergeant can share the honours on that one. I calculate that Sidney is bound to be distracted by Noakes's sartorial deficiencies and therefore less likely to turn his firepower on me.'

He was pleased to see Burton allow herself a tiny smile.

'The DCI won't like it if rumours start up about Grasmere Park,' she said. 'Doesn't the ACC's sister live there?'

Markham stifled a groan. *Please no!*

'He'll want this squared away as soon as possible — a freak incident down to some climate-change protesters or student anarchists,' she went on remorselessly. 'The *Gazette*'s doing wall-to-wall coverage on the rapes, so that's the PR-friendly case as far as Sidney's concerned.'

'Kate, you're turning very cynical in your old age!'

'I've been around DS Noakes too long,' came the stoic reply.

As they turned into the station car park, the DI asked casually, 'How are things with you these days, Kate? In general, I mean.'

He saw her decide to grasp the nettle.

'It was difficult when I broke up with Colin, sir. But' — a twitch of the narrow shoulders — 'probably for the best. Mum and Dad were very keen on him and, well, I think I got carried away.'

The notion of his earnest, sensible sergeant getting 'carried away' strained credulity but Markham nodded gravely, considerately looking anywhere but at her face.

'What about those inspector's exams of yours?' he enquired gently after a pause. 'You should be heading up your own team by now.'

With false brightness she replied, 'I know and I'm on it, sir. Sent off for the registration forms last week.'

'Excellent.'

Time to leave it for now. But he wished he knew what was troubling her. Noakes had dropped sly hints about 'a bad case of hero worship', but it was inconceivable to Markham that an officer of Burton's calibre and temperament should sacrifice her career to sentiment. Olivia had gone further and suggested the DS viewed him in a romantic light . . . a theory which, on looking at his colleague's stolidly phlegmatic profile, he rejected as being equally improbable.

One way or another he'd have it out with her.

In the meantime, he was ready to tackle the DCI.

* * *

'Well, that weren't too bad,' Noakes ventured later that day after their interview with the DCI.

Sidney's marsupial secretary Miss Peabody had greeted them at the entrance to his office sanctum and then bustled off to inform the DCI of his underlings' arrival.

'Can't think why Sidney don' have a dolly-bird PA like Superintendent Bretherton,' Noakes muttered as soon as she left them. 'Peabody's a nice ole trout but, well, there ain't much kudos in having a blue-rinser 'stead of a bit of skirt.'

'That's a remarkably ageist observation, Sergeant. And, anyway, you forget that *Mrs Sidney* might not want "a bit of skirt" sashaying round the DCI.'

'Right you are, guv, I'm with you.' Noakes tapped the side of his nose with an air of ineffable sagacity. 'No danger of any hanky-panky with Peabody.'

Minutes later, they were admitted into the holy of holies. Valkyrie-like, Mrs Sidney herself now stared imperiously out at them from various silver-framed portraits ranged along the rosewood sideboard, as though to attest to her part in the recruitment process. On the wall above, a photo montage — irreverently dubbed 'the Hall of Fame' by station wags — showed her husband rubbing shoulders with assorted luminaries of the North West as well as minor royals and C-listers. All in all, it ensured there was no mistaking Sidney's priorities.

Tugging distractedly at his goatee — fondly cultivated by Sidney as a way to counterbalance his lack of hair on top (he'd finally ditched what Noakes called his 'Bruce Willis buzz cut') — the DCI was clearly preoccupied with the rape investigation to the exclusion of all else.

'You could practically see him planning his next photo-spread in the *Gazette*,' grumped Noakes afterwards. '"Tough on crime, tough on the causes of crime" an' all that bollocks. C'n you imagine it? Sidney asking that little scrote Gavin Conors which is his best side.' There was no love lost between Noakes and the *Gazette*'s star reporter, their animosity having exploded into fisticuffs on various occasions. Many of which had passed into station lore.

As predicted, the DCI had been decidedly unenthusiastic at the prospect of raking up the Timothy Appleyard case.

‘Just covering all the bases, sir . . .’ Markham operated on autopilot on such occasions, parroting meaningless but soothing phrases designed to reassure the DCI that there was no question of his ‘going over the side’.

The DI even managed to listen to Sidney’s admonishments against relying on his ‘famous flair’ with every appearance of servile acquiescence.

‘Distrust it, Markham,’ the DCI honked in his unpleasantly nasal tones. ‘Solid down-to-earth legwork, that’s what’s required here. No flights of fancy.’

‘He don’ mind taking the credit for your clear-up rate though, guv,’ Noakes exclaimed wrathfully afterwards. ‘*That’s* all fine an’ dandy. No grumbling ’bout you having too much imagination when it means *he* can hog the headlines . . . *oh no*!’

‘So long as we get our man, Noakesy. That’s all that matters.’

The DCI had agreed to them bringing in Appleyard for questioning on Monday morning provided they were *discreet.*

‘No theatrics, though, Markham. I don’t want to be fielding complaints from respected local figures.’

As Burton had foreseen, Sidney plumped for his favoured ‘random nutter’ theory.

‘Obviously we’ll be checking local troublemakers and student activists, sir,’ the DI reassured him. ‘In addition to mental-health outpatients.’

He could count on DI Chris Carstairs in Vice for help in blindsiding Sidney with spreadsheets and data, in return for the occasional loan of DC Doyle and sundry other favours.

All in all, as Noakes said, they’d got off lightly.

Like the skins of an onion, they were gradually peeling back the layers of Michael Dominguez’s complex personality. Perhaps tomorrow they would uncover the secrets of his killer.

4. INTO REVERSE

The following morning, the team sat huddled in Markham's office.

'So the DCI's given us the green light to bring Appleyard in?' DC Doyle was clearly excited at the prospect.

'I wouldn't go getting your hopes up,' Noakes said. 'We ain't got nowhere near enough to charge him — jus' the tail end of a conversation some dopey bird was earwigging in on.' He rumpled his hair so vigorously that it gave him the appearance of having been electrocuted. 'Coulda meant anything . . .'

'Those phrases about Dominguez "turning the screw" and "putting his neck on the line" have the ring of authenticity,' Markham said. 'I'm willing to bet Mrs Caldicott's recollection is accurate.'

'Don' mean they were talking about Appleyard topping his missus,' the DS insisted stubbornly.

'*You've* changed your tune,' the DI said to his wingman. 'I thought you couldn't wait to see Mr Appleyard in the slammer.'

'Playing devil's wotsit, weren't I?' Noakes huffed in reply.

'Well, if you're playing devil's advocate, what else do you figure they might have been talking about?' the DI enquired drily.

'Happen Appleyard cooked the books for someone an' Dominguez knew about it. Or p'raps it was summat to do with sex.' Noakes had his witchfinder general's face on. 'Summat pervy . . . cos both of 'em were that way inclined.'

Burton's expression turned stony. It was obvious she objected to this swingeing designation, but she swallowed the acerbic reproof she was clearly yearning to deliver.

'The fact that they were gay doesn't mean anything of the sort, Sergeant,' the DI pointed out.

Noakes's underlip shot out mutinously, giving him the air of a choleric mastiff.

'Yeah, but there could've been' — he groped for a non-pejorative adjective — '*romantic* secrets an' things.' He was in deep now. 'They were both leading a double life, if you like, so things coulda got awkward.'

'What did Dominguez tell the police when Appleyard's wife went missing?' Doyle asked suddenly. 'Could he have provided a false alibi or something like that?'

'Good thinking, Constable.' Markham smiled approvingly at the youngster, who squirmed with gratification in a manner that made Noakes look at him sardonically.

'Actually, they were never able to pinpoint when precisely his wife disappeared,' the DI continued. 'He didn't report her missing for some time after she supposedly "walked out on him" and accounts varied as to when she was last seen. So the question of an alibi was a moot point . . . But Dominguez still came out strongly for Appleyard. Said he couldn't possibly have done it and that the Appleyards were happy together — not a sign of trouble between them.'

The DC was puzzled. 'Didn't Mr McLeod say Appleyard's wife was a bit of a bitch though, boss?'

'Yes, which means Dominguez's version of events never rang true. But they couldn't budge him . . . and there was no evidence to suggest a conspiracy.'

'But you think Dominguez knew the truth — about what happened to her?' Doyle asked eagerly.

'I think maybe he did, yes.'

'*Strewth!*' The DC boggled. 'As in *helped* Appleyard get rid of the body?'

'Possibly,' Markham said levelly. 'Or maybe he figured it out for himself. Maybe he saw something that put him on to Appleyard.'

'And then kept quiet about what he knew?'

'Precisely, Constable.'

Like Burton earlier, Doyle sought to apply logic. 'Having something on Appleyard might've been useful if he wanted the bloke at his beck and call, I s'pose.'

'It may not have been as cold-blooded a decision as that to start with,' Markham said. 'From what we've heard so far, Mr Dominguez was impulsive, quixotic . . . but not fundamentally evil.'

'But over time the relationship became toxic because he had Appleyard in a chokehold,' put in Burton quietly. 'Then something happened, and Appleyard snapped.' She looked wistfully over at her own desk, with its shelf of psychology reference books — all neatly arranged by height. 'If Appleyard had dependent personality disorder then, according to Professor Cermak, that would impact his functioning.'

Noakes looked meaningfully at Doyle.

Oh, God. This is all we need. Next thing she'll be yakking on about that Freud bloke and how it all goes back to potty training or Appleyard's parents not giving him enough hugs or him having a small willy . . .

Markham knew exactly what the two men were thinking.

'Let me have what you've got on that, Kate,' he said warmly. 'By way of building a psychological profile.'

Colour flooded her cheeks. 'Will do, guv,' she said earnestly. 'I'll do a chart of comorbid risk factors as well.'

Just so long as we don't have to listen to you go through them, luv.

Time for a pre-emptive strike, Noakes decided. Before his colleague got her second wind.

'Are we gonna arrest Appleyard, guv?' he asked. 'Seeing as no one else looks good for it?'

'That hardly sounds like a ringing endorsement, Sergeant,' Markham said wryly.

'Jus' telling it like it is.'

'Hmm . . . Well, my plan is that we ask Mr Appleyard to help us with our enquiries — attend the station voluntarily in the first instance?'

'What if he tells us to bog off?'

'We'll cross that bridge when we come to it, Noakes.'

'He might be afraid we'll try to fit him up for Dominguez cos of his wife—' Doyle blenched in the face of the implacable granite expression Markham turned on him.

But all the DI said was, 'It will be our responsibility to convince him we're not in the business of stitching people up.'

There was a knock at the office door and a rabbity secretary appeared. To Burton, she looked frightened — perhaps owing to the wolfish grin bestowed on her by Noakes.

'I know you've had your calls diverted, sir. But there's an urgent message from the Central Library.'

'*Central Library*? C'mon, luv. Don' tell us he's in trouble for all them unpaid fines.'

'Button it, Noakesy.' The DI too had noticed the woman's strained expression. 'That's perfectly alright — Brenda, isn't it?' She was agitatedly folding and unfolding a slip of paper. 'Is that for me?' he added kindly.

Dropping the note on his desk as though it burned her fingers, she ducked out of the room.

'What's up, sir?' Burton half-rose in alarm observing Markham's swift intake of breath and the tightening of his jaw muscles.

Outside the day was bright, but in Markham's office if felt as though a shadow had fallen across the room.

'They've found Timothy Appleyard's body.' The DI's voice was very low.

'*What . . . He topped hisself? In the bleeding library?*' Noakes was defeated at the news. Clearly it was the choice of location that had him flummoxed. 'I mean, he must've guessed we were on to him. But why do it *there*?'

'This wasn't suicide, Sergeant.' The DI's expression was so taut that it seemed almost as though his high cheekbones must pierce his skin. 'The man was murdered.'

* * *

There was something decidedly morgue-like about the Central Library's basement, with all that gunmetal steel and the tall locker-type shelves anchored to tracks on the floor.

Perhaps that was why Dimples Davidson looked so relaxed, thought Noakes, eyeing the pathologist sourly. *Like bleeding home from home.*

'How does this set-up work, then?' he grunted.

Despite the horror of the situation, Kate Burton wasn't going to miss a pedagogic opportunity.

'They're called "rolling stacks", sarge,' she said. 'It's all about saving space.'

Noakes's expression suggested he preferred a more traditional arrangement.

'How do folk get at the books, then?' he enquired with a look of dark mistrust.

'You turn the wheel on the side of the shelf to get to a particular section,' she explained.

'Freaking scary to be trapped an' squished cos someone else is moving 'em,' Noakes commented.

'They're pretty much foolproof these days — fitted with sensors to detect blockages,' Doyle chipped in with all the confidence of a man close to completing his degree in criminal law.

'Oh aye. Then how come that poor sod got no warning?'

Markham left Dimples and came over to join their little huddle.

'The head librarian says they've had engineers in over the last two weeks,' he told them. 'Problems with motor currents and floor plates apparently.'

Noakes flashed Doyle a triumphant look.

'So not safe then, guv?'

'Safe enough for maintenance staff to work on but potentially lethal to the general public,' the DI replied.

Burton felt shuddering relief that the remains had been sheeted and stretchered out to a waiting ambulance before they arrived.

'Not pretty,' was all the pathologist had told them of Appleyard's condition. 'We're talking massive trauma from crush injuries. Best if you don't take a look.'

No one felt inclined to argue with that decision.

Now Noakes ran gloved hands over the wheel that, when spun, had revealed Timothy Appleyard's mangled corpse lying in the aisle between two rows of shelving.

'How do we know it's murder an' not some kind of prank gone wrong?'

Markham gestured to a paper-suited technician who was busily taking photographs on the far side of the room next to a row of study cubicles. 'Brian says there's blood over by the carrels . . . signs of a struggle.'

'Could Mr Appleyard have been unconscious before he was . . . put in between the shelves?' Burton asked hopefully, her brown eyes huge in her wan face.

For all his earlier irritation with her — he hated when Burton brandished her university 'educayshun' — Noakes felt a sharp pang of compunction at her woebegone expression.

'Had to have been out of it,' he said, shooting a look at the other two men which dared them to contradict him. 'A whack on the bonce an' then *finito* . . . jus' never woke up.'

The others were happy to go along with it. Unbearable to imagine Appleyard's final moments as bones shattered, blood vessels ruptured and organs exploded in a delirium of red-hot agony.

'Appleyard didn't murder Dominguez then,' Noakes mused. 'But he must've known who the killer was.'

'Or it could be he saw or heard something but didn't realize what it meant,' Burton said. 'And then he let it slip—'

'So the killer decided it was too dangerous to let him live,' Doyle concluded.

'Exactly.' The DI approved of their reasoning.

'But Appleyard was the ideal decoy for him to finger,' Noakes burst out. 'I mean, let's face it, he was allus gonna be our number-one suspect cos of what happened to his missus. All sonny boy had to do was sit tight an' wait for us to—'

'Fit him up?' Markham enquired with a dangerous expression.

'Find some 'criminating evidence,' the DS replied with an expression of injured merit. 'An' mebbe he'd have planted a few clues to help us out.'

'You're correct that it was hardly in the killer's interest to eliminate Mr Appleyard,' the DI conceded. 'Which means that whatever Appleyard uncovered posed a real threat.'

'Why did Appleyard agree to meet him?' Doyle was bemused. 'And why *here*?'

'He didn't realize what he was dealing with,' Burton answered. 'Didn't think the killer had anything to do with what happened to Mr Dominguez.' She looked round the air-conditioned basement and shivered. 'Maybe he thought it was just a case of "tea and sympathy".'

'Yeah, but why come to the library?' Doyle persisted. 'Why didn't the killer finish Appleyard off back at the Park?' He cast an eye over the rows of steel and metal. 'That had to be more convenient than schlepping down here.'

'Mebbe it was the thought of all them twitching net curtains. Got the wind up him.' Noakes ran a finger around the inside of his grimy shirt collar as though struggling to breathe in the atmosphere of the basement.

'They're not exactly overlooked in Grasmere, though — are they, sarge?' Doyle countered. 'I mean, what with all those trees and massive gardens . . . it's not like living on a council estate.'

'Who knows what was going through his mind,' the DI observed quietly. 'Even somewhere that exclusive, he could have felt it was potentially a "neighbourhood of voluntary spies".'

Noakes knew the guv'nor was quoting out of some book, because this was a phrase he'd heard before. Nonetheless, he was pleased to have his theory corroborated.

'Yeah,' he nodded approvingly. 'You allus get nosy parkers an' snoopers in places like that. My missus says poshos are the worst.'

It takes one to know one, Markham thought grimly then reproached himself for being uncharitable.

'And don't forget,' Burton pointed out, 'they're all professionals and academic types in Grasmere — probably in and out of this place by the minute — so meeting up in the library wouldn't necessarily have struck Mr Appleyard as odd. Maybe with a killer on the loose, he'd have *liked* the idea of a public place — other people around, all nice and safe.' She glanced about her as though trying to envisage a procession of visitors and researchers. 'The library's open at weekends till six p.m., so it's handy too.'

'What about this engineering malarkey?' Noakes demanded. 'Won't they have turfed everyone out early? I mean, it's not like the killer could've got stuck into Appleyard while folk were sitting around reading, is it?' Heavily sarcastic, 'They might've noticed someone getting clobbered over the head an' flattened between them bookshelves.'

Burton winced perceptibly.

'Sorry, luv,' he said, eliciting a weak smile.

Ever focused on the job in hand, Burton soon rallied.

'He must have had special access,' she said slowly. 'A pass key or fob or some such that meant he was able to come and go freely outside the usual opening hours.'

Markham was thoughtful. 'The head librarian said they were overhauling the alarm systems and cameras . . . using a private security patrol while maintenance was ongoing.'

'There you go then.' Noakes was exultant. 'All he had to do was wait till everyone else had cleared out an' then time to party!'

'Who'd be entitled to a pass key?' Doyle asked. 'University types? Important people from the community? *Christ*, that's just about all of them in Grasmere.'

'You're forgetting, it might not even have been the killer's own pass key . . . perhaps he was just borrowing it. Or got hold of it somehow without the owner knowing. It'd be easy enough to con Appleyard into thinking he had special privileges.' The DI digested the implications of this while his team regarded him in dismay.

'Chuffing Nora,' Noakes groaned. 'That means checking *all* the passes an' what have you.'

'Yes,' Markham agreed, 'and even then I don't think it'll lead to our murderer.'

'Not if he nicked a lanyard thingy,' Noakes lamented. 'That means it could be pigging *anyone*.'

'We know that Appleyard *trusted* him,' Burton said. 'Whatever Appleyard knew or thought he knew, he was happy to come out here for a chat.'

'Must've scared him shitless when me laddo suddenly turned on him.' Noakes cast a furtive glance at the carrels. 'But he weren't quite as weedy as the reverend an' the retired headmaster fella. Seemed like he'd not be the sort to go without a fight.'

'I'm not so sure about that, Sergeant.' Markham watched the SOCOs intent on their fingertip search of the basement. 'As with Mr Dominguez, we have to factor in the element of surprise.'

'So a woman could've done it,' the DS opined gloomily.

'Dimples thinks it can't be ruled out.'

'What did they bash Appleyard with? One of them encyclopaedia things?' Noakes guffawed slightly and then checked himself with the air of a guilty schoolboy who's been discovered laughing in church.

'As it happens, yes,' Markham replied gravely. 'A heavy volume of community records. It's likely the force of the initial impact broke Appleyard's nose, hence the blood.'

The DS looked sickened. 'Poor bastard.' Sensing there was more to come, he added, 'They used summat else on him, right?'

'Some sort of workman's tool — a tack hammer or mallet, something like that.'

'*The railway again*,' breathed Doyle. 'God, you don't think it could be a nutter who works there do you, sir? Some psycho with a thing for shiny gadgets?'

'That's probably the DCI's preferred scenario,' the DI observed with massive understatement. 'And no doubt the killer would be happy if we wasted time and energy on the railway angle—'

'But you ain't gonna do that.'

'Correct, Noakes.'

When the DI took that tone, Burton reflected, it would be a brave officer who attempted to deflect him.

'I think the answer lies in Grasmere Park and the members of that reading group,' Markham continued. 'There are secrets hidden out of sight behind those net curtains DS Noakes was talking about. It's our job to drag them out into the light. *Every last one*.'

'Yeah, guv, but you'll see — the residents will all close ranks now.' Expressively, Noakes drew a hand across his lips. '*Zipped . . . Shtum*.'

'We'll see about that.'

The tone of his reply sent chills up Burton's spine.

'What now, sir?' she asked.

'I want to have a word with the head librarian,' the DI said. There was sly malice in his tone as he added, 'I believe that's your old friend Miss Todd, Noakesy. So I'd like you to attend.'

The DS appeared resigned to his fate.

'I remember her from the art-gallery case,' he said, shooting a baleful glance at Burton. 'This one tole her I was mad about them pervy Victorian painters who had a thing for big lasses getting their kit off.'

Such was Noakes's summing up of the Pre-Raphaelite movement.

'Not to worry, Sergeant,' came the DI's bracing response. 'The lady's got more on her mind at the moment than your cultural preferences.'

'Was she the one who found Appleyard then?'

'Unfortunately, yes.'

'Poor old bat. Prob'ly put her off coming down here for life.'

'Well, she's made of stern stuff but even so . . .'

'Mebbe we should interview her in that Costa place,' Noakes said craftily, having found the library's café a handy refuge on previous visits. 'Change of scene an' all that.'

'How very caring, Sergeant,' the DI replied deadpan. 'You must have read my mind.'

He turned to Kate Burton. 'I'd like you and DC Doyle back at base checking details for all the contractors doing work here.'

It was just the kind of tedious grunt work at which she excelled.

'You'll also need to look into the situation regarding lanyards and arrangements for special access to the library outside normal hours,' he continued. 'The facilities manager Mr Harrison can help you with that.'

Seeing DC Doyle's glum expression, Markham added, 'Not the kind of task to set pulses racing. But we need to narrow down the field and — who knows? — it's possible a workman or visitor may have noticed something out of place. Something a hair's breadth off.'

The young DC was shamefaced. 'It's just that, whoever we're looking for, he doesn't seem the type to make a mistake, sir.'

'Maybe not, but I want a watertight case for when we finally nail him . . . or her.'

'Like the advert says, *Every little helps*,' Noakes observed with a wink.

'Kate, I also want you to liaise with Mr Worthington—'

'The sky pilot?' Noakes didn't relish the involvement of local clergy.

'The vicar of St Barnabas's.' Markham's flinty expression discouraged his wingman from further embellishment. 'We need to interview everyone on our initial list first thing tomorrow. After that, we can widen it to include other residents.'

'Do we tell the vicar about Mr Appleyard, sir?'

'You can say there's been a tragic incident at the library. Mr Appleyard has been found dead and we're treating the circumstances as suspicious.'

'It'll leak anyway,' Noakes said. 'Bound to once the library bods start blabbing. An' then that sleazeball Gavin Conors'll be all over us.' His brawny fists flexed instinctively at the mention of the journalist's name.

'Maybe he'll be too busy with the rapes,' Doyle said, without any real conviction.

The young DC absorbed their startled expressions. 'There was another one last night, you know.'

'Where?' Burton enquired alertly.

'Bromgrove Rise . . . where the woods start.'

'What is it with those freaking woods?' Noakes muttered as though anyone needed reminding of the gruesome discovery that had triggered the Newman Hospital murder investigation — which had nearly ended in the loss of Burton's life.

There was something unsettling in the thought of two predators bent on parallel paths. Like twin halves of an evil whole.

Markham shook off his malaise.

'As you say, Constable, Gavin Conors currently has other fish to fry.' He met the eyes of each of them in turn. 'Which gives us a little breathing space . . . So let's make it count.'

* * *

With her brutalist crop and beige two-piece, Miss Todd undoubtedly resembled what Noakes called 'one of them warders from *Prisoner Cell Block H*'. But today, her gimlet eyes were unfocused with shock. Even a triple shot macchiato and jumbo chocolate muffin failed to restore their customary sharpness.

Seeing her reject such choice victuals caused Noakes no small amount of consternation. Under normal circumstances, it might have been comical.

'C'mon, luv,' he murmured. 'Gotta keep your strength up. Look, I'll go halves on the muffin.'

'You're very kind, Sergeant, but . . . it was such a shock. I'll never forget the sight of that poor man.'

'He won't have known owt about it, luv.' Only the jiggling of Noakes's feet under the table gave the lie to this assertion. 'The doc said he was sparko as soon as he hit the deck.'

'You're bound to be affected by something so awful, Miss Todd,' the DI said very gently. 'You're likely suffering from post-traumatic stress. Can we contact your GP . . . arrange for someone to be with you?'

The Old Soldier, as Noakes subsequently dubbed her, sat up straighter, a faint flush colouring her sallow cheeks.

'I'll be fine, Inspector. I just need time to process things.' She squared her shoulders. 'Now, how can I help you?'

'I take it you were on duty over the weekend, Miss Todd?'

'That's correct, Inspector. And everything was in order both nights. I only realized something was wrong this morning after I saw the blood. And then, when I went to check the shelves . . . I found him.' She shuddered. 'Laid out like a carcass at the butcher's.'

'Would you happen to remember who visited the basement on each of those evenings, Miss Todd?'

Crestfallen, she shook her head. 'I was just doing my rounds, Inspector. And there was no one at the service desk. The first warning bell had gone to let readers know the library would be closing, so it was just a few people in the carrels getting ready to pack up.'

'What's down there then?' Noakes asked.

'The contents of what used to be the Medway Family History Library, before it was relocated to the basement here.'

'An' it's open to anyone, yeah?'

‘Oh, absolutely.’ The woman looked slightly less haunted. ‘It’s very popular and there’s study booths as well as the reading tables.’

‘Your usual security systems have been deactivated on account of the renovations, yes?’

‘That’s right, Inspector. Instead, we’ve been using OneGuard. They have contracts with the diocese and education authority as well as the university. I think they’ve taken over the art gallery too. Mr Harrison could tell you more. He organizes facilities and procurement.’

‘Don’t worry, Miss Todd. We’ll follow up with him.’ The DI could see she was flagging. ‘A last question for you . . . Do OneGuard carry out checks of the whole building throughout the night or was this a standing patrol?’

‘I think they just man the main entrance. Once the warning bells go off, the building should be secure. Only authorized personnel are allowed after that.’

‘And that would include folk with one of them special pass jobbies, would it?’

‘That’s right, Sergeant. But they’d have to exit through the main entrance. Everyone signs out for security.’

‘Only it wasn’t secure, was it?’ Noakes said afterwards once they had arranged a lift home for the librarian.

‘Well, the killer and Mr Appleyard didn’t leave with the rest,’ Markham replied. ‘And I have a feeling we’ll find no one signed out later via the OneGuard system.’

‘So there must be another exit.’

‘Correct. We’ll need a floor plan of the place.’

‘Burton c’n do that. She gets off on charts an’ drawings an’ all that jazz.’

They reached Noakes’s car.

‘What a bleeding mess!’ Noakes exclaimed, kicking a tyre tetchily. ‘Feels like we’re going into reverse. An’ as for that library . . . talk about making it up as you go along!’

‘Amateurish, certainly,’ the DI observed. ‘And our killer exploited it. Chose his moment well.’

'Hey' — Noakes had thought of something — 'don' that Lockyer woman work here? The one who writes mucky books?'

'Yes, she's a librarian.'

'Reckon she goes to the top of the list then,' the DS said more cheerfully.

'Right, Noakesy, back to the station,' his boss chivvied. 'Best foot forward. Let's have no more talk of that reverse gear!'

5. AN OPEN FIELD

Tuesday, 24 March was one of those mild days which hold the promise of a languorous summer to come.

It also appeared to herald the start of hay-fever season given the way Kate Burton was sneezing and snuffling at her desk.

'It's one reason I like bonsais, sir. No pollen,' she told the DI between sniffs. 'But round our way they're all mowing their lawns and what have you, so that sets it off.'

Noakes's eyes fastened on his colleague's miniature garden. It was obvious he wanted one for his own desk but feared this might dent his macho credentials.

'Come into my office for a minute,' the DI invited. 'We need to divvy up our interviewees.'

Observing a greasy paper bag in Noakes's hand, he added resignedly, 'You can bring your breakfast.'

Cranking open his window the measly few inches it permitted, Markham mitigated the worst effects of Noakes's Big Mac. Even so, Burton's bleak expression suggested she could hardly wait to escape to the sanitized interior of her immaculate Corsa.

'Bags I the woman from Hope an' that headteacher fella,' Noakes mumbled through a mouthful of mayo. 'The rest of 'em are godawful.'

'You're with me, Sergeant,' the DI stated. 'We'll be taking Mrs Kernan, Ms Lockyer, Mrs Staunton and Mr Worthington.'

The DS pulled a face. 'Kernan's a juggernaut — total motormouth jus' like all them politicos.'

Burton flipped open her trusty notebook. 'The *Gazette* ran a piece on her husband a while back. He was a trustee of Everglades Children's Home—'

Noakes's head came up. 'That's the place they shut down for kiddie fiddling.'

'Yes. Well, he died just after they announced there was going to be an official enquiry—'

'Off the hook then.' Her fellow DS sounded disgusted.

'I remember it,' Markham said slowly. 'Joe Kernan . . . The investigation didn't come up with anything concrete against him.'

'That's right, sir. But the *Gazette* insisted there'd been a cover-up. Said his wife pulled strings so his name was kept out of it and got her "friends in the police" to bury the mess six feet under. There were hints about calling in favours from high-ranking officers but then the paper backed off.'

'I imagine the prospect of legal action was a powerful deterrent.'

'Looks that way, sir.' She hesitated.

'What is it, Kate?'

'I'm just wondering if that's what Mrs Kernan and Mr Dominguez were arguing about,' she replied. 'Though it's difficult to see how he could've been connected with what went on at Everglades.'

'Hmm . . . Do some digging, Kate. See what else you can turn up. I believe DI Carstairs had some input into the Everglades enquiry, so he may be able to help you join up the dots.'

'Will do, boss.'

Noakes groused, 'Burton'd be better with the Lockyer woman, guv'nor. They c'n talk books an' literature an' all that cobblers.'

'Cheers, sarge.'

Damned with faint praise, thought the DI suppressing a grin.

'I want us to throw Ms Lockyer off balance, Sergeant.'

And you're the man for that.

'I s'pose Lockyer'll know summat about who gets to have them pass thingies.'

'I checked with Mr Harrison,' Burton said brightly. 'People with special access have swipe-card lanyards.'

'That means access all areas, yeah?'

'Pretty much, sarge,' she confirmed with a determinedly positive air. 'It's mostly university staff and academics. You can get passes for a week, three months and six months. After that you have to apply to get the card renewed.'

The DI contemplated his own computer. 'Presumably there's a centralized database with details of who's applied.'

She grimaced. 'In some cases, it's the university faculty or a particular department that requests a job lot of temporary passes. Whether or not library staff input details for every individual user depends—'

'On whether they can be arsed,' Noakes finished for her.

'They're tightening things up. Passes kept getting lost or going missing, so the library decided to charge for them.'

'*Jesus wept.*' Noakes's face was a picture of concentrated derision. 'Sounds like that lot couldn't organize their way out of a paper bag.'

'What's the betting our killer has a generic departmental ID card?' The DI sighed. 'He could have got his hands on one that went missing. That way, there's no risk of it leading back to him.'

Noakes ruminated, scratching his bristly and inexpertly shaven chin. 'Wouldn't someone report a lost card? So they could get another one.'

'Mr Harrison said lots of users never got round to it — couldn't be bothered.' Burton clearly deplored this kind of inefficiency. 'I get the impression there might be quite a few lost passes knocking about. It would be easy enough to pick one up.'

'Needle in a bleeding haystack,' groaned Noakes.

'It's not all bad news.' Burton was resolutely upbeat.

'How d'you make that out then?' her grouchy colleague demanded.

'Mr Harrison told me there are two doors located at the back of the repository — that's where they keep historical manuscripts and the most valuable books — plus another door behind the Oak Room, which houses all the natural-history exhibits.'

'Don' tell me,' Noakes groaned. 'They use the same swipe cards for them special doors.'

Burton's smile faltered slightly.

'*Ye-es*,' she said slowly. 'It didn't seem worth having separate cards because those doors weren't in everyday use.' The DS got her game face back on, chin lifting slightly as though to issue a challenge. 'But at least we know how he got out of the building without the security guards clocking him.'

'Were these doors for the special collections common knowledge, Kate?'

'That's another thing, sir. Mr Harrison says not. He was quite adamant only senior personnel knew about them. That's why they didn't bother to create different swipe cards.'

That didn't exactly narrow things down, Markham thought wearily. As Burton herself had pointed out, pretty much all their suspects moved in the kind of circles which revolved around the Central Library and Bromgrove's other cultural institutions.

'It helps to give us a picture of what happened,' he said with an encouraging smile at Burton. 'And explains why Mr Appleyard was lulled into a false sense of security.'

'Everything was at sixes and sevens in the library,' Burton said eagerly. 'The usual pack drill meant that all visitors should have been gone by ten p.m. — even the ones with special passes who got to stay on. After that, the alarms were set and they had CCTV monitoring the building. This weekend was different because of all the maintenance work.'

'Them managers took their eye off the pigging ball,' Noakes muttered.

'Yes they did,' she agreed. 'And that's when he struck. Mr Appleyard died because the killer got lucky.' Another tilt of the chin. 'Look, we only have to be lucky *once*. He has to be lucky *all the time* . . . That's why we'll get him in the end.'

'You're right, Kate.' Markham spoke with grave deliberation. 'Just a sliver of an opportunity and he was in there—'

'Like a rat up a drain,' Noakes put in.

'Like someone who kept a cool head, Noakes, and knew how to disarm his prey. Calculating and clever.'

'You call that *cool*, guv? Battering Appleyard with some book an' then splatting him between them shelves so even his own mum wouldn't recognize him!'

'That was gratuitous cruelty,' the DI retorted. 'The sadism of someone who, once started, rapidly loses control. A red mist descends, if you like.'

'So we're looking for a cross between a droid an' Hannibal Lecter. *Jesus*.'

Markham famously loathed profanity and would normally cut an offender off at the knees. But, Burton noted with a sharp niggle of resentment, he was uncharacteristically indulgent with his wingman. *As ever*.

'We have to wait for him to screw up, Noakesy.'

'You mean wait for some other poor sod to die.'

The DI didn't contradict him.

'In the meantime,' Markham continued after a pause, 'I want Kate and DC Doyle to interview Mr Boughton, Mr Gallagher and Mrs Caldicott.'

He really *couldn't* risk letting Noakes loose on a self-opinionated pseud like Andrew Boughton, since the most likely outcome would be a slew of complaints to Sidney.

Such men were Noakes's bêtes noires. From the truculent expression on his face, it was clear he fancied a crack at Boughton. All the more reason to keep the two men apart.

'Mrs Caldicott won't be available till the end of the school day and Mr Gallagher is attending an event at the university,' the DI told Burton. 'You'll have to fit around them.'

'Hmph.' As far as Noakes was concerned, waiting on suspects was contrary to the natural order of things.

'We'll meet to compare notes later on this afternoon,' the DI continued. 'Then Kate and Doyle will check in with the library staff — see if anyone noticed anything unusual over the weekend — while we tie up any loose ends at Grasmere.'

'Don' know why we're even bothering with alibis.' Noakes scrunched up his McDonald's bag and lobbed it at Markham's wastepaper bin, missing by several inches as usual. 'They'll all say they were tucked up in bed both nights or home alone crying into their Horlicks or summat like that. We won' get diddly squat.'

'We'll be able to observe their reactions, Sergeant. And, as Kate said, we only have to be lucky *once*.'

Maybe this would prove to be the day that luck was on their side.

* * *

'Blimey, that were a bit of a turn-up for the books, guv.'

Markham and Noakes were sitting in a pew at the back of St Barnabas's church, having decided to adjourn from the parish hall where they were conducting their interviews.

The church was located at the entrance to Grasmere Park. Beneath the overlay of modern cleanliness — odours of Dettol and Pledge — the smell of the ugly little mid-Victorian church asserted itself in a mildewed commingling of old mortar, damp courses, decaying woodwork and ancient floorboards. Somehow the chill stone subdued even the warmth of the mild spring day, making Noakes shift rheumatically on the oak bench. But Markham felt mysteriously at ease. It was always this way with him in churches — a sense of 'time no longer' — and he was rather taken with the squat sandstone building. He didn't even dislike the funny octagonal turrets at either end of the gabled facade — the desperate flourish of an architect resolved on subverting his brief.

Noakes darted a furtive glance up at a large painting of the Crucifixion, as though he feared its saintly figures weren't above a spot of eavesdropping. 'Who'd have thought it?' he declared at last.

'I gather you've decided Mrs Caldicott must give way to the Reverend Worthington as our prime suspect, Sergeant.'

'Flippin' heck *yeah*.' Noakes was flushed with the excitement of discovery. 'The man's got form, guv!'

'Mr Worthington's case never came to trial, Sergeant. And' — Markham's face softened with compassion — 'I'm not convinced a prosecution should ever have been contemplated in the first place.'

'Yeah, but we're talking *sexual assault*, guv. Perviness 'gainst minors.'

Another shifty look at the holy painting followed by an awkward little duck of the head as though to ward off divine thunderbolts.

'The man's superiors supported him, Noakes. And he's been a dedicated parish priest for many years since then.'

'But he admitted Dominguez *knew* about his background, boss.' Noakes pressed home his advantage.

'Because Worthington confided in him. They were fellow railway buffs. He found Mr Dominguez sympathetic . . . a kindred spirit.'

'But who's to say Dominguez didn't put the squeeze on him later?'

Now Noakes was squinting into the shadows at a reproduction of *The Ship of Fools* which, by a bizarre association of ideas, hung to the left of them above a shallow recess containing the church's Book of Remembrance. Suddenly, the DS withdrew his gaze. It appeared the depiction of lost souls drifting towards their 'fool's paradise' was even less to his taste than the Crucifixion. At least that was based on historical fact.

'You think Mr Dominguez was blackmailing the vicar, Sergeant?'

'Look, guv.' Noakes shuffled out of his oatmeal tweed jacket, which was hopelessly unsuitable for a warm spring day, disclosing soup plates of sweat under each armpit, 'We're talking birds of a feather an' all that. Who c'n say what Dominguez might've needed from him?'

'There's no evidence to say Mr Worthington is homosexual, Noakes.'

'Oh *c'mon*, boss. You gotta see he's light in them loafers.'

'Unlike you, Noakesy, I don't have such highly tuned gaydar antennae.'

Or what Burton would call rank bigotry.

'But you gotta admit it means he's in the frame.'

'Yes,' Markham conceded reluctantly, for he had liked the vicar with his shy diffidence and sad eyes. 'Actually, Noakes, I got the feeling he was worried about something.'

'Us finding out about his rap sheet, you mean?'

'How many times do I have to tell you, he doesn't *have* a "rap sheet"!' Markham glanced around the shadowy little church. In that moment, the statues seemed to be leaning in confidentially, anxious to hear their clergyman exonerated.

'No, it wasn't that.' The DI breathed in deeply, filling his lungs with the motes of ancient wisdom dancing in the air of St Barnabas's church. 'There was something else that was bothering him. I had the feeling he was weighing up whether or not to share it with us.'

'Well, you *tole* him, guv.' Noakes wrenched savagely at his horrible crimplene tie. 'You *said* if there was anything on his mind, now was the time to get it off his chest.' With the DS, mixed metaphors were a sure sign his passions were running high.

'There was *something* alright, Noakesy. But I'm not sure I got through to him.'

The DS sighed virtuously as though to say, *None so blind as those who will not see.*

Abruptly, he changed tack.

'That Penelope Pitstop woman. *Jeez*, what a bitch.'

Another bob of the head as though to request absolution for his language.

'Fenella Staunton,' Markham amended. 'Yes, a very tricky customer.'

'You could tell she fancied Dominguez something rotten.'

'But he didn't fancy her back,' Markham said. 'The chemistry just wasn't there.'

'No bloody wonder.' Noakes shuddered. 'That freaking monocle thing or whatever it was she was wearing. An' that bird's nest of a hairdo. I mean, for fuck's sake . . . Who'd fancy *that*?'

'You'd be surprised, Sergeant.' Markham's tone held a wealth of meaning, but he didn't expand. 'There was something she wasn't telling us . . .'

'D'you mean a pity-bonk?'

'Where *do* you get these dreadful terms, Sergeant?'

'Our Nat, boss. She keeps me in the loop.'

The DI regarded his wingman from beneath hooded lids.

Noakes's mentions of Natalie were becoming ever rarer, now that Markham knew the truth about her parentage.

How far did you go for her sake, Noakesy?

The question hung in the air between them along with the centuries-old dust.

He'll tell you when he's ready, Gil.

Like Olivia said, he needed to keep the faith and trust that one day the barriers would come down and Noakes would finally open up about the Bluebell case. In the meantime, keep things normal, low-key.

'I'm not sure the tension between Mrs Staunton and Mr Dominguez was wholly sexual,' he said.

'Yeah, there were that plaguey wotsit.'

'Plagiarism, yes.' Markham smiled. 'She owned up to being unhappy about Dominguez "borrowing" her ideas.'

'Enough to make her . . . *do that*?'

'Sexual and intellectual jealousy — it's a potent combination, Sergeant.'

'That Lockyer bird . . . *she* were jealous too.'

Noakes wrinkled his nose.

'Her hair was even worse than Pitstop's,' he observed. 'Like she were auditioning to be a druid or summat.'

Markham grinned. 'Mrs Staunton's was expensively dishevelled, Sergeant, while Ms Lockyer's was just—'

'Freaking awful.' The DS frowned. 'Must scare the living daylights out of kids in the library. Like she's the Wicked Witch of the West . . . An' did you clock that whopping great wart on her nose?'

'She wasn't particularly prepossessing, I grant you. But it doesn't make her a murderer.'

Noakes shrugged, ready to return to his main point.

'Didn't like the way Domingo talked about her writing, though, did she? Tried to laugh it off, but you could tell she'd had it up to *here* with his "jokes" about heaving bazookas an' the rest of it.'

'Yes, I think she resented Mr Dominguez's raillery — however innocently it was meant.'

'He made her feel like she were second best, guv . . . not the genuine article . . . Dreary Ville.'

The DI cast his mind back to their interview with Judith Lockyer. Her sharp darting glances at her interlocutors, like a blackbird hunting for earthworms.

'Mr Dominguez's sneers flicked her on the raw . . .'

'And the Pitstop creature made sure she heard about 'em.'

'Well, it probably made Mrs Staunton feel better — knowing that she wasn't the only woman to be knocked back by him.'

'Safety in numbers,' grunted Noakes.

'Something like that.'

'Lockyer had the run of the library an' a staff pass,' the DS went on. 'What's to say she didn't sweet-talk Appleyard into a meeting in the basement?'

'Nothing. Except her own statement that she was at home glued to an episode of *Vera*.'

Noakes kicked the kneeler viciously by way of relieving his frustration before changing the subject again.

'Kernan came over as dead shifty, boss.'

'To be fair to her, the Everglades investigation is probably an episode she doesn't care to revisit.'

'What d'you reckon she meant by saying we didn't ought to bite the hand that feeds us?' The DS ran a beefy paw through his salt-and-pepper mop, which could have benefited from a more professional 'do' than that provided by Mario's Salon on Marsh Lane ('unless I get change from a tenner, it's a con' being Noakesy's guiding rule).

'D'you think Superintendent Bretherton's the one she's got in her pocket?' In Noakes's book, 'Blethering' Bretherton was capable of just about anything. 'Or did she mean Sidney?'

'There've always been close ties between the authorities and CID, Sergeant.'

'Too bloody close if you ask me.'

'It's possible she was simply warning us to let sleeping dogs lie lest we cause embarrassment to our lords and masters.'

'What if Domingo was on to summat about the Everglades story an' wouldn't let it go?'

'Such as?'

'Oh, I dunno. Mebbe he knew someone who'd been there . . . someone Joe Kernan molested . . . or someone who never got justice.'

Noakes felt uncomfortable with the whole subject given what he had intuited about Markham's own experience of childhood abuse. But, like a dog with a bone, he couldn't let it go.

The DI's dark gaze was unfathomable, but his voice was perfectly calm.

'It's possible, Sergeant,' he said. 'We know that there was an argument between Mr Dominguez and Rosemary Kernan—'

'An' it weren't nothing to do with whether they liked Charlotte Bronte or ruddy Jane Austen best.'

'No,' Markham smiled thinly. 'I imagine the quarrel had somewhat more substance than that.'

He rested a hand on the slim granite pillar which divided their pew from the neighbouring bench, almost as though invoking the deity of the church.

'I don't see Mr Dominguez as the type of man to be intimidated by Rosemary Kernan,' he said finally. 'Nor is he likely to have been blackmailing her.'

'But if he planned to drag up the past, boss . . .'

'It would have made him a threat, yes,' Markham said quietly. 'A threat to that hard-won political career she's fought tooth and nail to keep alive despite all the scandal.'

'An' she'd have been furious with him an' all.' The DS swatted an errant bluebottle with a hymn book. 'Got a bit of a temper on her, y'know. There was that bloke who accused her of kicking him in the goolies.'

'It's quite a step from precision taekwondo aimed at a lecherous civil servant to the kind of punishment dealt out to Dominguez and Appleyard . . .'

But the DI remembered the smouldering anger at the back of the woman's flat, pebble-grey eyes and the involuntary flexing of brawny hands whose bright-red nail varnish seemed like a shocking anachronism.

Could she have acted in tandem with someone?

A door creaked in the porch and their two colleagues joined them, slipping into the pew in front. Markham was amused to note that Burton attempted a sort of genuflexion along the way.

Noakes went straight on the attack. 'How was Bromgrove's answer to Gareth Malone then?'

'Giving it large,' Doyle groaned. 'You'd think the parish couldn't run without him — ego the size of a cathedral.'

'Thought so,' the DS retorted with considerable satisfaction.

‘Would you say he and Dominguez clashed?’ the DI enquired. ‘With both of them having outsized personalities, I’d presume there was some locking of horns from time to time.’

Doyle grimaced. ‘Well, when we got hold of Susan Caldicott, she let it slip that Boughton wanted a character reference from Dominguez when he applied to be a magistrate, but it was no dice.’

‘“Let it slip”, did she?’ Noakes rumbled. ‘As in accidentally on purpose.’

The DI recalled Olivia telling him that Mrs Caldicott was the snitchy type.

‘Did you tackle Boughton about this, Kate?’

‘He brushed it off as nothing, sir. Said it was easy to provoke envy with him being an artist and prominent in cultural circles.’

‘Pass the sick bag.’ Noakes’s eyes narrowed. ‘Betcha he didn’t get to be a JP neither.’

The DS looked thoughtfully up at the stained glass in the louvred lancet above the main altar. Depicting St Michael the Archangel, something about its martial splendour triggered domestic associations in his mind. ‘If they didn’t take my Muriel, they sure wouldn’t have a jumped-up ponce like Boughton.’

‘I didn’t know Mrs Noakes had applied for the bench, Sergeant.’ Markham tried to keep the incredulity out of his tone.

‘Oh yeah, after she did them evening classes on local government.’ Noakes puffed out his chest. ‘But the committee thingy thought she had enough on her plate already, what with doing the Women’s Guild an’ Friends of the Cathedral an’ all her other stuff.’

‘I’m sure it was their loss,’ the DI murmured politely not daring to meet Kate Burton’s eye.

‘Oh aye.’

Noakes’s eyes were drawn upwards again to the curly-haired messenger, whose locks, now Markham came to think of it, had something eerily in common with Noakes's lady wife's lacquered bouffant.

'She's a slave to duty,' the DS pronounced, no doubt echoing the received wisdom, 'but a body c'n only do so much after all.'

'Indeed.'

The DI allowed a respectful pause to elapse before continuing.

'What about Mr Gallagher? How did he come across?'

'Seriously boring.' Doyle suppressed a yawn. 'Made me feel sorry for those students of his.'

'Ex-students,' Burton corrected primly. 'He retired from Calder Vale FE.'

'Whatever.' The DC was unabashed. 'His voice made me want to go to sleep.'

'There's no flies on Mr Gallagher,' Burton put in tartly. 'That absent-minded professor thing's a bit of an act. Underneath it all, he's a shrewd cookie.'

'D'you reckon he had one of them special library passes?' Noakes grunted.

'All of them have done at some time or another,' Burton sighed. 'But Gallagher and Boughton said theirs had lapsed. I think it happened like the guv'nor said. The killer pinched one he saw lying around. That way, there was no risk of anything being traced back to him . . . no chance of the system throwing up his name.'

'They don't even *have* a bleeding system,' her fellow DS snarled. 'Totally random if you ask me.'

'Anything come up to indicate ill-feeling between Gallagher and Mr Dominguez, Kate?'

'Nothing you could really put your finger on, boss. Gallagher was a few years ahead of Dominguez at Oxford, but they moved in different circles.' She smoothed down an errant wing of hair as though wishing their suspects could be so easily marshalled into order. 'There was probably the usual rivalry, but other than that . . .'

'The way Gallagher told it, Dominguez muscled in on his publishing contacts. Stole his thunder big style.' Doyle swallowed another gargantuan yawn.

'They're both art historians, is that right?' asked the DI.

'Yeah, boss.' Now Doyle shrugged off his Hugo Boss blazer, folding it neatly beside him on the bench with a faintly scandalized glance at the crumpled ball of Noakes's jacket. 'But Dominguez was media-friendly whereas Gallagher—'

'Don' speak human.'

'Something like that,' Doyle agreed, flashing a grin at his politically incorrect mentor.

'D'you think Gallagher's a ponce an' all?'

Kate Burton closed her eyes briefly as though in prayer.

The DC's grin broadened.

'If you mean is he gay, sarge, yeah, I wouldn't be surprised. But he an' Dominguez were chalk and cheese. I can't see them being part of a love triangle or anything like that.'

'What about Mrs Caldicott?' Markham deemed it best to move on from Bernard Gallagher's sexual preferences. 'Anything useful there, Kate?'

'She came across like your typical harassed mum, boss.'

'Yeah,' Doyle concurred. 'Didn't seem like she'd have any energy left over for worrying 'bout Dominguez. Mind you . . .'

'What, Constable?'

'Well, she said something a bit snappy along the lines of "he wasn't the one to be dishing out relationship advice".'

'Oh, yes.' Burton nodded vigorously. 'That was a bit odd. But if the cleaning lady's right about Caldicott's husband being a bully, maybe Dominguez stuck his oar in where it wasn't wanted . . . interfered and made himself unpopular.'

'You didn't take to her, though,' Markham pointed out.

'No, boss.' Burton didn't usually allow personal reactions to cloud her professional judgement, but there was no hiding her dislike. 'There was something snippy and grudging in the way she spoke about Dominguez — class envy or jealousy — and she never said a word of regret.'

Maybe she was just more honest that the rest of them, the DI thought.

'What about their reactions to the news about Appleyard?' he asked.

'Just shock and bewilderment. Pretty much like you'd expect,' Burton said.

At that moment the church door creaked open.

Markham turned around swiftly.

There was just time to register the sight of a young woman with long blonde hair. Then she disappeared as quickly as she had appeared.

'Kate,' he said urgently. 'See who that is, will you?'

The DS complied with alacrity only to return a few seconds later.

'Sorry, boss. Whoever she was, she moved like the clappers — gone by the time I got there.'

'No matter.' Yet somewhere at the back of his mind, a voice told him it *did* matter and they had missed something significant.

The door creaked again to admit two new arrivals.

Nerys Wynne trailed by her apologetic-looking son.

'We were going to call on you later this afternoon, Mrs Wynne,' Markham lied smoothly, though in truth he had completely forgotten about Michael Dominguez's next-door neighbours.

'That's alright, Inspector,' came the brisk response. With a certain twinkle, she added, 'We can wait our turn.'

Markham found himself warming to the little woman, whose reddened eyelids appeared to betoken a bad case of the same hay fever that afflicted Kate Burton.

'Did you happen to pass a young woman on your way in?' he asked. 'Tall and slim with blonde hair.'

'No, Inspector. Was she a parishioner?' Nerys eased herself onto the pew behind them with an audible sigh of relief which suggested sciatica as well as rhinitis. Simon Wynne hovered uncertainly at the end of the bench, clearly concerned about his mother.

'That must be it,' the DI said easily. 'Anyway, thank you for making the time to see us.'

'Is it true that Mr Appleyard was . . . *murdered*?'

The woman's face was clayey white.

Easy, Markham told himself. *This one can't take too much strain.*

'We're treating his death as suspicious,' he said gently. 'You'll appreciate we can't say more than that right now.'

'Of course, Inspector.'

Simon Wynne too looked shaken. 'He and Mr Dominguez were good neighbours.' Then his plain, squarish face relaxed into an unexpectedly puckish smile. 'Well, Michael could be maddening sometimes,' he admitted. 'No common sense and, as for DIY well, forget it . . . Just as well Mum's got her head screwed on, otherwise he'd have flooded that utility room of his more times than I've had hot dinners.'

Nerys's colour was returning. 'Sheila Birtle and I somehow managed him between us,' she chuckled.

Afterwards, Noakes pondered, 'D'you reckon Dominguez got on their wick, guv? It sounded a bit like they were at his beck an' call.'

'They seemed happy enough to keep an eye out,' Doyle said. 'Though she clammed up when you asked about his private life.'

'With them types, it's allus a case of *see no evil, hear no evil*,' Noakes put in sagaciously. 'No imagination when all's said an' done.'

'What's next, boss?' Burton had the air of a beagle keen to pick up the scent.

'I'd like you and Doyle to catch up with staff at the library, Kate.' The small of Markham's back was beginning to ache, as though centuries of damp were leaching into his very bones. 'I don't hold out any great hope that they'll provide a eureka moment, but let's see if anyone remembers who was hanging around that basement over the weekend.'

‘It’s a pigging open field, ain’t it, guv?’ Noakes grumbled at his colleagues’ retreating backs. ‘Any of ’em could’ve done it. *Any of ’em.*’

‘Come on, Noakesy. Show me some of your vaunted Dunkirk spirit,’ the DI admonished him gently. ‘We’ve been here before, remember? This is just another investigation like all the others.’

But the memory of that long, blonde hair, whisking round the corner of the church door, niggled at the edge of his consciousness even as he uttered the words.

He had an uneasy feeling that this particular investigation might be their most challenging to date.

6. LULL BEFORE THE STORM

Markham chose the café on the first floor of Waterstones for his breakfast meeting with Kate Burton on the morning of Wednesday, 25 March. He hadn't wanted to press Miss Todd too hard in the aftermath of her appalling discovery, but he felt he couldn't rest until he got his mind around the Central Library set-up and Kate Burton was certainly the woman to illuminate its mysteries. There was also the matter of Rosemary Kernan and the Everglades enquiry, which had shown the MP's husband in a decidedly murky light.

Judging from the way Burton was looking round happily at their surroundings, it was obvious his DS approved the choice of venue. Her soy caramel macchiato and gluten-free blueberry muffin also appeared to hit the spot, though Noakes would doubtless have decried the notion of gluten-free cake as something dangerously akin to blasphemy.

Markham too savoured the peace and quiet, sipping his excellent cappuccino with evident appreciation.

Whenever he came into this bookshop, he thought of his friend Ned Chester, the arts correspondent from the *Gazette*, whose brutal murder during the art-gallery investigation had left a gaping hole in his life.

What would that rumpled, lanky journalist, with his droll manner, have made of their suspects, he wondered. No doubt he and Noakes — who pronounced Chester a 'gent' despite the handicap of his cultural interests — would be on the same page when it came to the likes of Andrew Boughton.

Burton watched her boss surreptitiously from beneath demurely lowered eyelids, wishing she could bottle the moment.

She knew Markham felt nothing for her beyond platonic kindness and professional regard. And that he and Olivia Mullen were a perfect match — physically, intellectually, every which way . . . Sometimes it felt degrading to hanker after a closer relationship with her boss — like she was some pitiful, grovelling monomaniac sighing for the moon — but it was a habit she seemed unable to break.

It hadn't been the reason for her break-up with Colin. At least she could acquit herself of *that*. With hindsight, she could see she had rushed into the engagement to please her parents, kidding herself that an easy-going friendship could one day ripen into love. Gallingly, when she suggested to Colin that they call time on the relationship, she had the sense her fiancé was actually *relieved*.

Was she always going to measure every man she encountered by the lodestar of her boss? If so, she risked becoming Bromgrove CID's answer to Bridget Jones, living a life where her major relationships were with a bottle of Chardonnay and a succession of cats.

The DI smiled at her quizzically and she felt hot colour rise in her cheeks.

Cop on, Kate! At such moments, she clung to her mother's Celtic common sense like a drowning woman to a lifebuoy. Carefully, she set down her macchiato and, unobserved by the DI, dug her fingernails into her palms until the stinging pain recalled her to herself.

'You alright, Kate? Thought for a moment there I'd lost you.'

'Fine and dandy, sir.'

Fine and dandy! Now she sounded like some Edwardian stereotype. God, what must he be thinking!

But Markham merely regarded her with his usual kindness.

'I'm just like you, Kate. Always zone out when I'm in here. Something to do with the red-leather moon chairs and the hiss of the coffee maker . . . Feels like I'm on holiday.' He smiled ruefully. 'Or at least a million miles away from CID.'

Burton smiled shyly.

'Yeah, I like coming in here to get away from it all,' she admitted. 'I dragged Noakes and Doyle along once, but they just thought I wanted to show off.'

'Oh, I think Noakesy has considerable respect for your "book learning", Kate. You can take all the muttering as a backhanded compliment.'

Carefully, the DI added, 'Has he said anything to you about the Bluebell enquiry?'

'Nothing, boss. But it looks like everything's squared away. They won't be taking it any further.'

Burton's eyes met his steadily.

We'll never know the whole truth, boss. Whatever went down, Noakes isn't telling.

'I think he's worried about Natalie, sir,' she ventured.

'Completely understandable when you think about what she went through.'

'Not the Bluebell . . . something else . . . Can't put my finger on it, but there's definitely *something*.'

'She's having CBT for the trauma, yes?'

'That's right. When I mentioned it a while back, sarge said the therapy was going fine. But then last week when I asked after her, he shut me down. Began sounding off about it being all emperor's new clothes and he didn't know why they bothered.'

The DI felt uneasy. This was a red flag, but he didn't know what to do about it.

'Just continue to lend an ear when he needs it, Kate. Time's a great healer.'

He hoped he sounded like he believed it.

Now to grasp the nettle.

'What have you got on the Everglades case?' he asked.

Burton looked troubled, carefully dabbing some stray foam from her upper lip before she answered.

'DCI Sidney was the SIO on that one, sir. And there *was* some talk . . .'

'You can speak freely in here, Kate, never fear.'

She glanced wistfully across at a couple of teenagers two tables away, their eyes locked on one another as though no one else in the world existed, before dragging herself back to the matter in hand.

'DCI Sidney took personal responsibility for checking out Joe Kernan, sir.' She fiddled awkwardly with her paper napkin. 'But later he told DI Carstairs — Chris was a DS back then — to drop it . . . case closed, *wham*, just like that.'

Markham chose his words with care. 'Did DCI Sidney give the team any reason for his decision?'

'Just said there were no credible witnesses and nothing to support a prosecution.'

'Did anyone challenge him?'

She shrugged helplessly.

'Well, the DCI's position was he and Mr Bretherton had been into it very thoroughly. And he didn't want to say too much for reasons of confidentiality — with Mrs Kernan being a public figure.'

Been into it very thoroughly my backside, thought Markham, his face darkening. *In other words, something was rotten, but no way were they going to dig up the stinking mess.*

'The Kernans were big supporters of Mrs Sidney's literacy foundation, sir. They got Princess Alexandra on board too.'

She looked more uncomfortable than ever.

'There *was* gossip on account of them all being so cosy, but DI Carstairs said the paperwork was legit. It was two teenagers who made the allegations about Mr Kernan, but later they backed down and changed their story — said it was all attention-seeking and a wind-up, and they never meant it to go that far.'

'Have *you* seen the file, Kate?'

'Yes boss. All looked pretty kosher plus a psychologist from the adolescent mental-health unit signed off on it . . . not in the kids' best interests to drag them into court, blah blah.'

A tame quack. He might have known.

'What happened to these youngsters afterwards?'

'One went off the rails and committed suicide.'

Markham clenched his jaws until they ached.

I won't think of it now, he told himself as the face of his younger brother — lost long ago to drink and drugs — swam momentarily before his eyes.

Burton recognized the expression, though the casual observer would have noticed nothing more than a tightening of the handsome features.

Noakes would know how to reach their boss, she thought miserably as the silence lengthened . . . know how to bring him back from that place he kept inviolate deep inside.

And then Markham was with her once more, his gaze clear again.

'What about the second teenager?'

'Went to art college in London, guv. Saint Martin's — did textile design or something like that.'

'Contactable?'

Her eyes slid away from his.

'DI Carstairs thinks there's a page missing from the file. Looks like it was torn out . . . most likely an accident . . .'

Bloody Sidney. You scratch my back, I'll scratch yours.

But he wasn't about to vent to a junior officer. Human beings were complex, and he knew the DCI was a fundamentally good man — albeit one with an overdeveloped reverence for money and celebrity. However often Noakes derided their superior as an 'arse-wipe', Markham knew it was often a fine line between arrangements of mutual convenience and police corruption. The Newman Hospital murder investigation had taught him that.

'D'you think Mr Dominguez had some connection with those kids, boss? Or somehow found out about Joe Kernan and threatened to rake it all up again. Maybe he even threatened to go to the press if she didn't resign.'

'I'll speak to Sidney,' Markham said as a spasm of distaste rippled across his face. 'See how ugly it was.'

Something inside him whispered that it was *very ugly*.

'If Rosemary Kernan's the one who did for Dominguez and Appleyard, what's to stop her killing again?' Like Markham, the DS had difficulty getting those twitching hands and the blood-red fingernails out of her head.

'I believe she's got her constituency surgery today and most of tomorrow,' the DI replied. 'I've had a discreet word with the office staff asking them to keep close tabs on her appointments and the rest of it.'

'Won't they say something to her, sir?'

'I fed them some guff about reviewing security arrangements for anyone high-profile.' He smiled grimly. 'Don't worry, her PA fell for the whole VIP safety spiel. She'll be checking in with you at regular intervals — no doubt thoroughly enjoying the whole cloak-and-dagger subterfuge.'

Surveillance dressed up as police protection. But hopefully it meant they could monitor the MP's movements without giving the game away.

Markham drained the last of his cappuccino. 'Any luck with the library staff?' he enquired with a discreet look at his watch. 'I suppose it's too much to hope anyone stood out as hanging round the place over the weekend.'

'Sorry, guv.' Burton shook her head regretfully. 'None of them even remembered Mr Appleyard.'

'Well, libraries can be like that. Visitors sink into anonymity, swallowed up by the silence and concentration.'

She smiled. 'I guess that's why sarge calls it a giant aquarium.'

Only something deadly and venomous had slipped in there without anyone noticing. Like a basking shark.

'And nothing from the library passes?'

Another slow shake of the head.

'All our suspects had swipe cards. Everyone except for Mr Worthington, the Wynnes and Mrs Caldicott.'

'Did Mr Appleyard have one?'

'No, boss. The university issued job lots via different faculties. Department heads were technically supposed to supply details of cardholders to the central services manager . . . but the whole databank was due to be redigitized and library staff were playing catch-up.' Burton's conker-brown pageboy swung with the force of her disapproval. 'Miss Todd talked me through it, but it was obvious even *she* didn't have a handle on the situation.'

Markham rather suspected his DS and Miss Todd were sisters under the skin and that any species of administrative inefficiency could be a cause of almost physical discomfort to both of them.

'So, what was the drill when someone rolled up with their freshly minted special-access visitor's card? How did it work?'

'Well, basically that's when the cardholder's details would be registered and go onto the system — the first time they came in.' She frowned. 'At least that's how it was *supposed* to work.'

'I have a feeling I'm not going to like this.'

'The library's due for a major overhaul, sir. All kinds of reconstruction and refurbishment projects are in the works: a fancy business centre plus new conservation studios, a computer-games sound-box and interactive kiosks . . . all very high-spec.'

'Makes one nostalgic for the days when libraries were places you went to *read books*,' the DI observed drily.

Burton grinned. 'I know what you mean, boss, but they've got to do something with all that lovely lottery money.' The moment of levity over, she resumed her explanation. 'The renovations are happening in stages and there's going to be a whole new registration system for readers and visitors. So they were pretty much winding down the existing set-up and basically just activated someone's card the first time they came in. If you were on a faculty list or what have you, then you just got waved through.' Another frown. 'Like I say, that's not what was *supposed* to be happening, but it looks like they were cutting corners. So the way things are, it's hit and miss as to whether or not you get a name or any personal details logged with a visitor's card.'

Burton's tone left no doubt that, had *she* been the one in charge, matters would have been organized very differently.

'Now I see how it is,' Markham said slowly, smothering a smile. 'Supposing our killer owns one of these special swipe cards, there's a fifty-fifty chance we'll find their details on the system.'

'That's exactly right, sir. Except I doubt they'd be prepared to chance using their own card.'

'So, at some point, they likely helped themselves to another card and waved it in front of Mr Appleyard, then used it to exit the building after the murder.'

'Correct.'

'Presumably there's a record of such a card being used?' In the circumstances, this felt somewhat like the triumph of hope over experience, but Burton nodded earnestly.

'Someone swiped out at five past nine on Sunday evening via the Oak Room exit.'

'Any personal data from the swipe?'

Punctiliously, the DS smoothed the cuffs of her neat taupe Nehru jacket. 'It was issued via the university's music and performing arts faculty last month but didn't throw up a match to any particular user on the library listings.'

'A dead end in other words,' the DI sighed.

'Look like it, boss,' she agreed. 'No chance of our killer being caught out by the system.' Sounding almost like Noakes, she added acidly, 'It was so inefficient, the likelihood of that happening was sweet FA.'

Burton reached for her smart executive briefcase, an item that attracted many a sarcastic sally from her colleagues. 'I suppose the killer could've borrowed the card from someone,' she said. 'But that carried the risk of the actual owner remembering and putting two and two together when the details of Mr Appleyard's murder came out.' Carefully, she stowed her notebook away and snapped the case shut, flicking a microscopic speck from the rear leather pocket. 'More likely he came in on his own library ticket, planning to nick someone's special-access card and use it the same evening before it was reported missing.'

'A cool customer,' the DI observed.

'Very,' she agreed. 'It was the weekend, so even if someone found their pass had gone walkabout, they'd be keen to get off home and less inclined to make a fuss.' She hitched her sensible shoulder bag firmly over her shoulder and patted the executive briefcase. 'Mr Harrison said the front desk *did* have a few reports of missing cards, but no one was planning on doing anything about those until Monday at the earliest.'

If at all.

'Shouldn't Mr Appleyard have needed his own swipe card? He knew he'd be in the building after hours.'

'Technically, yes. But, in the event, it was enough that one of them had special access.' Burton grimaced. 'It'll all be different under the new system.'

'Let's hope murder serves to concentrate a few minds,' the DI said, his voice equally grim.

A thought occurred to him.

'If the killer entered on a regular library card, won't their details be logged on the system?'

'The electronic card readers at the front desk weren't working, boss — something to do with the engineering work — so staff just let everyone through.' She pulled a face. 'Apparently things were pretty relaxed in there over the weekend.'

'Our murderer couldn't have timed it better,' Markham breathed.

The aquarium drew Appleyard into its depths, never to leave alive. And the basking shark glided invisibly away.

The café was starting to fill up.

'Right, Kate. You get back to base and centralize all the info we've got so far.'

‘Will do, sir.’ There was nothing Burton liked better than a stint with her beloved spreadsheets.

‘I need you and Doyle to go door-to-door on the other Grasmere residents — the ones who weren’t in the book club. If I know human nature, there’ll be a certain amount of resentment around the Dominguez clique, in which case, I want you to capitalize on it.’

Markham ran a hand through his thick, dark hair, which curled an inch below his collar in defiance of CID norms. ‘I’m going off to do a spot of lateral thinking.’ His face twisted. ‘Not that you need to share my whereabouts with the DCI. If he asks, just say I’m following up on a lead.’

‘Lateral thinking. Following up a lead . . . Got it, sir.’

And, with that, the two detectives headed for the escalator which led to the high street below.

* * *

With Markham, ‘lateral thinking’ meant a trip to ‘Doggie’ Dickerson’s boxing club in Marsh Lane. Or Bromgrove Police Boxing Club to use its full title.

Usually, it was the first place he headed after a set-to with the DCI. Once in the ring, he could superimpose Sidney’s face onto that of his opponent and then beat the proverbial seven bells out of his sparring partner. Today, he felt badly in need of the club’s cathartic properties prior to returning to the station.

His attendance at Doggie’s was a definite black mark in the eyes of the powers that be. ‘Dreadful old villain’, ‘a dead ringer for Reggie Kray’ and ‘Bromgrove’s Mr Big’ were just some of the epithets bandied around in connection with Doggie’s name, but Markham took not a blind bit of notice. Doggie and his rather dingy premises suited him perfectly and that was that.

The man in question looked like a cross between Long John Silver and a veteran of the Napoleonic Wars, with his eyepatch, wonky jaw and unnaturally large yellow teeth. To complete the look, he wore an extraordinary bell-bottomed horsehair wig, which might have passed for that of a high-court judge — from the back at least. A whiff of Jack Daniel's always drifted in his wake, though one could never positively say that he was drunk. Such was his rheumy-eyed geniality, he remained unruffled by even the most difficult customers.

And as for his clients . . . Hugely popular with police and criminals alike, it was commonplace to see officers and city lowlifes pounding away side by side. Doggie's was a place of amicable amnesty between the two sides, even if it lasted only as long as a few sweat-soaked bouts in the ring.

The council and police authority had tried every trick in the book to get Doggie's closed down, but he had somehow outwitted them all. His grotty little outfit — boasting showers in need of regrouting, smelly locker rooms and a 'sauna' which constituted a breach of the Trade Descriptions Act — stayed open and the proprietor continued to preside over his dodgy empire with aplomb. Markham secretly admired him for it.

Noakes had been along a few times with a view to improving his overall fitness after a recent health scare. Given his ferocious resistance to 'them places where everyone ponces around in Lycra an' it's all nancy boys admiring thesselves in the mirror', Bodyworks and Accelerate in the town centre were never really an option. But, after an initially wary start, Noakes and Doggie had rather taken to each other, swapping betting tips and other worldly lore interspersed with wildly un-PC denigration of everything from local politicians to the BBC. Of course, Muriel Noakes would most likely faint clean away were she ever to get wind of the true nature of her husband's 'fitness regime', but so far they had got away with it.

Noakes had strongly disapproved of Doggie's recent flirtation with New Age astrology and cabbalism — courtesy of Marlene, his buxom squeeze from the bingo hall — which, for a while, had resulted in him floating about in a cloak of which Gandalf might have been proud. But his lady love had betaken herself to pastures new, so normal service was resumed with Doggie reverting to his usual dishabille of dressing gown-cum-overcoat.

Hearing that his 'fav'rite 'spector' was towelling off in the so-called locker room, the proprietor sloped in to pay his respects.

'Hear you gave Mr Carstairs a pasting today, Mr Markham,' he wheezed.

'Ah well, Doggie.' Markham endeavoured to look modest. 'I must have had a spurt of energy.'

Dickerson cocked an appraising eye (the one that functioned) at the tall policeman.

'You're in good shape, Mr Markham, while Mr Carstairs' young lady' — he gave a lopsided leer — 'is giving him too many puds for his tea. An' he's not burning it off later if you know what I mean.'

Wink, wink. Nudge, nudge.

Markham did his best to adopt a man-of-the-world demeanour.

'Yeah, Mr Markham,' the other continued, taking this for assent. 'He'll get soft an' flabby like all them young ones if he don' keep a sharp lookout.'

Markham swallowed his mirth at this assimilation into Doggie's fraternity of world-weary veterans (even as an internal voice protested, *I'm only thirty-four*).

'D'you do much reading these days, Dogs?' he asked inconsequentially, his mind ever running on what he now thought of as the *book-club case*.

Doggie was never fazed by such random questions.

'I rate *Bravo Two Zero*,' he declared. 'Nowt soppy about *that* lad.' Doge-like, he clasped his hands across the front of his grubby overcoat. 'Shoot first an' ask questions later, that's the way to play it.'

Markham had always wondered about Doggie's career in the army. He suspected a dishonourable discharge might well have come into it somewhere . . .

''Lo, Dogs. How's tricks?'

Breathing hard, DI Chris Carstairs plonked himself down on the bench next to Markham.

'I were jus' telling Mr Markham I like the SAS bloke who writes them thrillers.'

'Andy McNab? Me too.' Carstairs shot him a quizzical look. 'What got you on to that?'

'Fav'rite authors,' was the startling response.

Doggie drew himself up, conscious that the obligations of hospitality required him to be seen by all his people.

'Well, I better be moving along,' he said, tapping the side of his nose in a manner that recalled George Noakes. 'You'll be wanting to talk copper stuff.'

With an indulgent beam and a swish that released an overpowering scent of whisky, he left his two patrons to it.

'Don't tell me you and Doggie are swapping books now, Gil!'

Markham chuckled. 'Not exactly. My head's full of this book-club murder. I was going through all the library protocols with Kate Burton this morning — round and round in circles till it felt like I was going to explode.'

'God . . . I bet she couldn't get enough of it, though.' Carstairs grinned. 'Noakes tells me I should see her when she's got a stack of timesheets and printouts — like she's in heaven.'

'Well, the *Diagnostic and Statistical Manual of Mental Disorders* comes a close second,' Markham laughed, feeling somewhat disloyal. 'But she's the soul of thoroughness.'

'Anything for you, Gil!' his colleague laughed.

Markham didn't particularly care for the sly twinkle in Carstairs' eye.

'I was hoping there might be a lead at the library,' he said curtly, 'but nothing doing.'

'My last but one bird had a Saturday job there. Said it was a bit of a doss — dead relaxed.'

Relaxed was the word, Markham thought grimly.

'Your vic was crushed, yeah?' Carstairs now looked sober. '*Nasty* way to go.'

‘Very. And it looks as though there may be a link with the Everglades case.’

‘Yes, Burton told me about that.’ Carstairs leaned in and lowered his voice, even though it was just the two of them in the room. ‘A word to the wise, Gil. Joe Kernan might have been a slimy piece of work, but he had powerful friends. We called him Teflon Man cos nothing would stick.’

‘And Sidney?’

‘Between you and me, yeah, the DCI helped make it go away. Kernan was a sick man and the wife had a lot of sway. One way and another, those kids were never going to have their day in court.’ Carstairs towelled the back of his neck with unnecessary vigour. ‘And maybe it was for the best. They’d been through enough already. I wouldn’t have wanted them worked over by some clever-dick QC.’

‘I hear you, Chris.’ Markham stretched, his muscles aching pleasurably from their match.

Time to head for a shower.

‘Ever had any dealings with Michael Dominguez and that crowd in Grasmere Park?’ he asked Carstairs.

‘Not personally, but one of the lads went to hear Dominguez give a talk at the art gallery. Said he was like Michael Portillo: really cheesy, but you couldn’t help liking him.’

‘Yes, Dimples told me he was quite a charmer.’

‘Made it fun. Lots of stories about painters’ naughty private lives . . . It wasn’t what Giggsy was expecting at all.’

Markham felt a renewed pang at the realization that Dominguez would never again be able to share all that joy and passion with an audience.

‘Did Giggs have him down as a ladies’ man, Chris?’

‘*Nah*.’ Chris didn’t hesitate. ‘I mean, apparently he had them eating out of the palm of his hand — especially the older ones. But, by the sound of it, he didn’t swing that way.’

‘Hmm. Thanks, Chris, it helps to have a feel for who he was.’

‘Must’ve made an enemy somewhere along the line,’ Carstairs said thoughtfully. ‘Reckon you were wondering if it was something to do with that accountant guy and the wife who went missing. He and Dominguez were quite matey, weren't they? And then, of course, the accountant copped it.'

'Well, yes. Noakes did seem to think Timothy Appleyard was our man.'

Carstairs chuckled. 'How is the old monster? I heard him mouthing off in the canteen the other day. Back to his old self now he's shot of that Bluebell bollocks. I mean, he was protecting his *daughter* for Chrissake!'

Markham wished he could be sure that was *all* his wingman had been doing.

'Yes, Noakesy's back to antagonizing everyone in sight,' he said with an attempt at nonchalance. 'Go on, Chris. You'll be needing that shower after what I put you through back there.'

'You wait till the rematch, Gil, and *then* I'll show you!'

* * *

Back at the station, there was an unwelcome summons from DCI Sidney waiting for Markham.

Forewarned by Burton and Carstairs, however, he decided there was nothing to be gained by revisiting Everglades and lifting stones to see what crawled out. Refreshed by his visit to Doggie's, he managed the usual two-step with an adroitness and sangfroid that surprised even himself.

No, of course. There was absolutely no question of causing Mrs Kernan or any other Grasmere resident further unnecessary distress. It was more a case of ruling out mentally disturbed individuals — the sort who bore a grudge against prominent members of the community, yada, yada, *yada.*

'An occupational hazard for those in public service,' Sidney concurred, stroking his goatee in an ecstasy of self-regard. 'A burden to be shouldered bravely. "From those to whom much has been given, much will be expected."'

The DI was only thankful Noakes wasn't present to hear Sidney's definition of noblesse oblige.

Pass the sick bag.

If there *was* a connection between these murders and Everglades, he would have to come at it another way. The team couldn't afford to have Sidney ring-fence the Grasmere residents. Not based on a false claim of police harassment.

At least he'd have an insight into Rosemary Kernan's whereabouts for the next forty-eight hours. Something about the woman repelled him, but as yet he had nothing tangible to warrant an open move against her.

Just as he was wondering where Noakes had got to, his office door banged open.

'You look pretty good considering you've jus' been in with Sidney,' Noakes observed suspiciously.

'Needed to clear my head after going round the mulberry bush with Kate, trying to thrash out the workings of that infernal library . . .'

'Oh, I get it.' A sly wink. 'Bit of the old left hook, was it?' The DS mimed throwing a punch.

'Correct, Sergeant.'

'Don' blame you. Once Burton gets started on statistics . . . makes me feel like I want to top meself.'

'I take it she briefed you and Doyle?'

'Yeah.' Noakes rolled his eyes. 'Me laddo nicked someone's swipe card was about the size of it.'

'Essentially, yes,' Markham admitted, opting for simplicity. 'Where are the other two now?'

'Over at Grasmere poking their noses into folks' business. Not the ones in the book club — the rest of 'em.'

The DI felt a sudden overwhelming urge to get away from his stuffy office.

'Right, Noakes, let's get down there ourselves and shake a few trees.'

That tallowy frightened face glimpsed so fleetingly at the back of St Barnabas's church rose before his eyes. *Like a spirit from another world.*

He only hoped it wasn't a premonition.

7. FLASHPOINT

'You certainly have the weirdest dreams, Gil.'

'Well, this one tops the lot. You know that Disney film of *Alice in Wonderland* with the dancing playing cards? The ones with human heads, arms and legs—'

'Yes, I remember. They wear masks shaped like card symbols and chase after Alice waving cute little spears.'

'There was nothing cute about *these* characters. From a distance, they looked like cartoon playing cards. But when I got up close, I saw they were blow-up ID badges with barcodes on them and squiggly writing I couldn't read . . .'

'It's because you can't stop thinking about that damned library and poor Mr Appleyard, Gil.'

Markham and Olivia sat on the balcony of their apartment at The Sweepstakes sipping scalding-hot black coffee and watching as shafts of Jaffa-coloured sunshine gilded pale clumps of celandine and narcissi in the landscaped gardens below. Beyond the gardens, the cemetery bore such a tranquil aspect that it was impossible to imagine unquiet slumbers for anyone in its peaceful earth.

'Yes, I got myself into a regular tailspin,' he admitted. 'I was so convinced the library data would give us a lead.'

Olivia's lips twitched. 'Then Kate blinded you with science — or statistics at any rate — and it knocked you out.' She laughed the full-throated joyous peal that was the first thing to have drawn Markham's attention to her. 'You've got a bad case of overtaxed cerebral processes, sweetheart. And so would anyone after one of Kate's brainstorming sessions.'

Markham grinned. 'It *was* a bit full on. But at least by the end of it we established the library is a dead end.'

'And no doubt the visit to Doggie's helped clear your head,' she added with an indulgent smile.

'Well, it helped me get through the meeting with Sidney without punching his lights out, if that's what you mean.'

'That man! *Honestly*!'

Olivia loathed Sidney. And he, in turn, never lost an opportunity of implying to Markham that Olivia's' 'flakiness' and peripheral involvement in previous investigations made her a less than ideal 'lady friend' for CID's rising star.

'Don't tell me. He wants this pinned on one of Bromgrove's mentally afflicted as opposed to anyone with a Mercedes, swimming pool and room for a pony.'

'Something like that,' her boyfriend chuckled. 'You know what he's like.'

'Oh yes, Gil. I know all too well. He's so bloody *predictable*!'

Something in Markham's downcast face prevented her from launching into a full-on denunciation of the man she called 'first cousin to Judas Iscariot'. He always insisted his boss was an honourable man at bottom, and there was something touching about his stubborn faith in the inherent goodness of human nature (in the teeth of all evidence to the contrary).

'I take it you didn't get anything useful from Grasmere's other residents yesterday?' she said gently.

'I was hoping the folk who weren't in that book club might open up . . .'

'Dish the dirt you mean.'

'Essentially, yes.'

'But no dibs?'

'Nothing,' he sighed. 'They were all shut tighter than a clam.'

With a wicked gleam in her eye, Olivia enquired, 'Did you unleash George?'

'Oh, you could see he wanted to Exocet them. But no point alienating the entire estate.' Lips tightly compressed, he added, 'There was lots of name-dropping — "my husband's friend, the chief constable," and so forth. So it was easy to see which way the wind blew.'

'What's the plan for today?'

'I want to have another crack at the vicar,' Markham said. 'He was out visiting a sick parishioner when we called yesterday . . .'

'And you think he might know something?'

'He struck me as a decent sort—'

'It's pretty much in the job description, isn't it?'

'Well, there's that, of course. But I got the feeling he was holding something back.'

Markham hesitated, but it was always such an exquisite relief to thrash things out with Olivia.

'Worthington had accusations made against him,' he said, 'but the case never came to trial.'

'Was there anything in it, Gil?'

'Who can say?' He tried to empty his mind of his own adolescent memories, to think only of Derek Worthington. 'Child-abuse investigations have become the equivalent of Salem these days.' He hesitated. 'I'd be inclined to give him the benefit of the doubt.'

'I suppose George doesn't see it that way.'

'Not exactly, no. It was a toss-up whether he fancied Appleyard or Worthington most for Dominguez's murder.'

'And now Appleyard's out of the picture . . .'

'He's foaming at the mouth over the "pervy vicar".' Markham grimaced. 'Like the DCI, Noakesy's nothing if not predictable.'

'Did Dominguez know about Mr Worthington's . . . problems?'

'Yes. They volunteered together at the heritage railway and I think they were in each other's confidence.'

'Blackmail?'

Such an ugly word, thought Markham sadly. But he needed to face up to the possibility.

'I don't know,' he said slowly. 'If they moved in similar circles, shared certain interests . . . then there could have been all kinds of undercurrents swirling under the surface.'

'You don't sound convinced, Gil.'

'There is something gentle and haunted about the man . . . something *resigned* too. Not the murdering type—'

'Though you'd be the first to say there's no such thing as a *type*.'

'True,' he admitted ruefully. 'As you're always quoting, "There's no art to find the mind's construction in the face."'

'You like Mr Worthington.'

'Yes, I do . . . and so does Sheila Birtle. According to her, he is halfway to being a saint. And I can believe it. He'd need the patience of one to deal with that awful Andrew Boughton.'

'The organist, right?'

'Organist and all-round pain in the backside. Let's just say he and Noakesy didn't hit it off.'

Olivia's lips twitched.

'Oh dear.'

'Boughton wanted a reference from Dominguez, saw himself as JP material. But Dominguez sent him packing.'

'Not squeaky clean then?'

Markham groaned. 'I'm beginning to think none of them are.' Then his eyes flared with amusement. 'It turns out Muriel wanted a shot at the bench as well.'

She snorted in disbelief. 'God . . . Bromgrove's very own Judge Jeffreys!'

'It would appear the town's had a reprieve. As Noakes told it, the vetting panel decided she's — *ahem* — overcommitted elsewhere.'

'In other words, she's too much of a fascist even for *them*.'

'Well, Noakesy believes they've lost a shining star.'

'*Bless*.' Then with a wicked look, 'And to think of the fascinating chats you and she would have had about our criminal-justice system.'

'Oh yes. A beautiful partnership tragically nipped in the bud,' he deadpanned.

Reluctantly, he got to his feet.

'Right, I'd better go and hook up with Noakes and see if we can get any further with the vicar.'

'Won't Sidney go ape if he hears a *clergyman* is in the frame?' Olivia looked up at him quizzically. 'If the *Gazette* gets wind of it, there'll be hell to pay. Grasmere Park's well-heeled brigade won't like being splashed all over the News of the Screws.'

'I'm hoping to rule Derek Worthington *out*, Liv.' Markham looked unusually determined. 'At the moment, something's holding him back. He may not want to tell us something he's learned in confidence . . . Or perhaps he has scruples about breaching confidentiality.' A shadow crossed Markham's face at the thought of the young woman who'd disappeared from the back of the church before they had a chance to speak to her. 'Priests are like the Eyes of God, aren't they?'

'I remember that from the St Cecilia's case,' Olivia said slowly. 'That's why there's a single eye in a triangle hidden somewhere in every stained-glass window. It means the Eye of God is upon the place.' She gave a little shudder. 'Won't your vicar be at risk if the murderer thinks he knows something that could lead back to them?'

'Worthington may be saintly but he's no fool,' Markham said, though his expression was uneasy. 'Even if he's not ready to share his secret with me yet, he knows he's playing a dangerous game. And I only hope he's being careful.'

'He could still drop his guard without realizing.'

Like I did at St Cecilia's, her tone seemed to say.

'True, Liv.' He raked a hand through his dark hair. 'That's why I'm going to lay down the law today — threaten him with the bishop if that's what it takes, though God knows I don't want to go that far . . . The poor man's had enough ecclesiastical officialdom to last him a lifetime.'

'Mightn't George be able to get through to him?'

'Undoubtedly.' Markham gave a short bark. 'None better than Noakes when it comes to wheeling out the rack and thumbscrews!'

'Will Kate be present at this tête-à-tête?'

'God, no. Consenting adults only.' He grinned. 'It'd only spoil her day.'

'So where are you shunting her off to?'

'"Shunting her off"? How very cynical of you, sweetheart. Actually, she and Doyle will be down your neck of the woods having a discreet word with Susan Caldicott.'

'They may get lucky. Susan's an inveterate earwigger. But savvy enough to keep herself safe, I'd say.'

Unlike Derek Worthington . . .

Markham felt anxiety coil around his innards.

'Have to love you and leave you, sweetheart.' He endeavoured to speak lightly. 'We've got suspects to intimidate!'

Olivia smiled.

'*We're the Sweeney and we haven't had any dinner.*' It was a roguish impersonation. 'Off you go, then, guv'nor.'

Her laughter followed him to the door.

* * *

'Not the smartest gaff in the place, is it?' Noakes sniffed as they stood outside Derek Worthington's detached stone villa. Clearly the awe and wonder that Grasmere Park had initially inspired in him was starting to fade —much to the DI's amusement.

'Owned by the diocese, Noakes.'

'Fair enough. Padres shouldn't be flash.'

Remembering Worthington's well-worn suit and threadbare clerical stock, to say nothing of his ancient Morris

Minor, the DI observed mildly, '"Flash" is hardly the word I'd use to describe Mr Worthington.'

'Yeah, well, stands to reason he wouldn't want to attract attention to hisself.'

With a sigh, Markham gave it up as a bad job.

The white stucco-fronted house was probably a listed building, he reflected. Georgian, he shouldn't wonder. But peeling paint, damaged masonry and trailing remnants of wisteria gave the vicarage an air of neglect, while the wrap-around lawn was in dire need of mowing.

'Nobody in,' the DS grunted after a few goes at the antique door pull. 'Happen he's in the church doing a service or summat.'

'During the week there's just the midday Mass, so we won't be interrupting anything.'

They left Markham's car in front of the vicarage and walked around to the church at the entrance to the Park.

'It's kinda special being so close to the river,' the DS remarked somewhat wistfully. 'Even if you do end up paying an arm and a leg,' he added beadily, lest Markham should infer any dissatisfaction with the amenities Chez Noakes.

'It's a peaceful little backwater,' the DI observed neutrally. 'I like to imagine how it must have been here in the old days — with uniformed gatekeepers and gardeners dusting soot from the leaves of the trees.'

His sergeant regarded him warily. It always set his internal alarm bells ringing when the guv'nor waxed poetical like this. Him and Olivia were a right pair when it came to that.

'It must have been quite something . . . hardly any cars . . . just boys on their tandems . . . and horse-drawn carriages taking top-hatted businessmen to the city.'

Noakes cleared his throat, uncomfortable with such flights of fancy.

The DI regarded him with amusement. 'Relax, Sergeant. I'm not going all *Time Team* on you. But, as you say, there's something special about a place with its own riverside promenade.'

'Not that the Rev gets to see much of the river,' Noakes pointed out, 'what with being in that side road an' them dirty great trees in the way.'

'Well, it's the houses and apartments closest to the waterfront that are the most exclusive. Mr Worthington's residence is what you might call "second division".'

'You could see the river from Dominguez's bedroom,' the DS mused. 'No chance of *him* not getting a room with a view.'

They arrived at St Barnabas's, whose sandstone exterior sparkled in the morning sunshine. The monuments and stone lozenges in the pocket-handkerchief-sized graveyard bore their usual aspect of dignified repose, making it an attractively quaint prospect all in all.

Before the DI could fall into further raptures, however, Noakes clumped decisively up the gravel path to the porch and pushed open the heavy oak door.

'Nowt doing.' He sniffed the cobwebby air with a distinct lack of enthusiasm.

'Hold on a minute, Sergeant.'

The urgency in Markham's voice brought his subordinate up short.

There was another scent mingling with the dust and mould of ages.

A scent he knew.

Metallic. Coppery. Sickeningly sweet.

The DI's gaze was drawn to one of the icons, a bearded man whose plaque identified him as St Barnabas. On their previous visit, he hadn't taken much notice of the rigidly sombre apostle, but now it seemed to him that the uplifted hand held some dreadful import.

You are in the presence of death.

The icon's eyes held his own and would not let go.

'We need to check the sacristy.' Markham's voice was hoarse.

'Oh yeah, the poky room round the back . . . where they dress up,' the DS echoed uncertainly before leading the way.

'Empty!' he declared when they reached the bare white-washed room. Nothing here but a simple prie-dieu and kneeler in front of a plain stone altar. A missal and some liturgical books rested on the altar.

But the smell was stronger now and Noakes looked round in bewilderment, searching for the source.

There was a door on the left which he pulled open to reveal a tall cupboard on a revolving base. Heavy vestments stiff with rich embroidery hung in plastic garment bags above various smaller compartments containing what looked like church plate and metalwork.

Acting on instinct, Markham bent down and pushed the rotating platform.

At first it would not turn, but then Noakes bent to the task and finally the cupboard swung round.

Later, the DI suffered recurring flashbacks to the moment when Derek Worthington's half-open filmy eyes met his through the opaque plastic. Their expression was not exactly accusing but milkily reproachful, as if his costuming in the ornamental vestments was merely the final trick played on him by a heartless deity.

Despite the shock, Markham had the presence of mind to leave the robed corpse where it was, suspended from the heavy steel hanger like some ghastly reliquary exhibited for veneration by the faithful.

'Sergeant,' he said through stiff lips, 'you know what to do.'

* * *

'Here, Markham, have a swig.'

Dimples Davidson whipped out a hip flask and thrust it at the DI.

'And don't give me any of that twaddle about drinking on duty,' the pathologist scowled. 'You're the colour of putty, and I can do without you keeling over on me, thanks very much.'

For the first and only time in his police career, Markham succumbed and felt all the better for it.

Seeing Noakes's hopeful look, he then passed the flask to his DS.

'Don' mind if I do.'

'Good man,' Dimples said approvingly. 'Sometimes the old remedies are the best.'

Noakes promptly hiccoughed whereupon the medic winked at him. 'Never fear, my lips are sealed.'

'Can we get him taken down now?' Markham took one last look at the cling-film-wrapped body in its plastic shroud.

'Yeah,' Noakes urged. 'It ain't fitting to leave him swinging . . . like one of them carcasses down the abattoir.'

Dimples disappeared momentarily, returning with two paper-suited paramedics. Between them, they manoeuvred a wheeled stretcher.

'We can leave them to it.' He ushered Markham and Noakes back into the church. 'Why not take a load off?'

By common consent, they moved to a pew at the back of the church, as far away from the sacristy as possible.

For some minutes they sat in silence.

Light-headed, Markham gazed across at *The Ship of Fools* in its shadowy alcove.

What was he to do now a crewman had murdered the ship's captain?

Could he steer the ship to port without it being wrecked?

Then came the squeak of rubber wheels, loud as an obscenity in the silence, and the paramedics appeared in the far side-aisle with their sheeted trolley.

The three men stood and bowed their heads until the little procession had gone.

'How'd he die, doc?' Noakes whispered as though there might be something sacrilegious in the enquiry, bobbing his head apologetically in the direction of assorted statues.

'Throttled with a linen belt or stole or whatever they call it. He was dead before the killer hooked him up on the clothes rail in that damned cupboard.'

Markham tried to feel thankful for this small mercy. But he could not.

'He could have been preparing to hear confession or whatnot,' the pathologist said gruffly. 'Anglicans don't bother with the Tardis set-up, do they?'

''S right. They don' do the spooky stuff.' Noakes spoke with the authority of a fully paid-up member of the Church of England. 'Not like the other lot.'

The DI gestured towards the sacristy. 'How much strength would . . . *that* . . . have taken?'

'Well, your man weighed almost nothing. Light as air.' Davidson's brows knitted in thought. 'I met him a year ago at some shindig or other, but he's dwindled to nothing since then. Wouldn't be surprised if I find something wrong once we have him on the slab.'

Noakes screwed up his face in perplexity. 'But to get him up there . . . with all that clobber on him . . . they'd have to be pretty strong, yeah?'

'If you're asking could a woman have done it, Noakes, then I'd say yes. Standing on the base would have given the killer enough purchase. It'd just be a question of dragging the body up getting the hook of the wardrobe hanger over the clothes rail. The whole arrangement's pretty sturdy, but then I guess it'd need to be with the weight of those vestments.'

The DI's gaze was remote, speculative. 'I remember when we were on the ballet murders looking at that picture gallery they had in the theatre. There was an astonishing shot of some ballerina or other. I think it was Margot Fonteyn or one of the greats . . . Well, she was just a slip of a thing, but in this particular ballet she was actually carrying a grown man.'

'*Thassright!*' The DS was excited now. 'Burton tole me about it afterwards. The guy only weighed about ten and a half stone or summat like that. So even though she were a scrawny bird, she could carry him. All about balance an' distribution of weight, see.'

'Well, well.' The doctor grinned. 'George Noakes a balletomane. Who'd have thought it?'

The DS looked both embarrassed and proud, shuffling his feet like a bashful schoolboy. 'You learn all sorts on the job,' he muttered.

'Another possibility is that your killer throttled him with someone else's help and then the two of them added those theatrical touches,' Davidson continued grimly.

'What, you mean *a team*?' Noakes gulped audibly.

'You can't rule out two people working together,' the pathologist said. 'Or one killer doing the deed and some other sicko coming across the vicar's body—'

'An' playing dress-up?' Noakes was outraged.

'Well, let's face it, we've come across some fairly depraved individuals in our time.'

Davidson looked wistfully at his 'bag of tricks', as though he could do with a medicinal stiffener. Then he seemed to think better of it.

'Time of death, doc?'

'*Tut-tut*, Sergeant.' But then the sawbones relented. 'Not that long ago. Some time early this morning. Rigor hadn't set in.'

'So the body would have been pliable,' murmured Markham. 'Another reason why it wouldn't have needed phenomenal strength to hoist it onto the rail like that.'

'Precisely, Inspector.'

The pathologist heaved himself up.

'There's damp in this place,' he grunted. 'And it's making my arthritis play up.'

The church door creaked and the next minute Kate Burton and Doyle were beside them.

Davidson gave the courtly bow which he invariably bestowed on women, no matter how pronounced their feminist credentials.

'No doubt I'll be seeing you at the PM, m'dear,' he said, 'knowing you're a glutton for punishment.'

Markham felt with this death he could risk it. At least Worthington's face hadn't been desecrated and his body was intact.

'How goes it with the studies, Constable?'

'I get my degree this year, doc.' Doyle's voice was proud.

'Excellent, excellent.' There was almost paternal approval in the pathologist's tone, belying his somewhat fearsome reputation.

Once the door had closed behind the doctor, Markham briefed his subordinates as succinctly as he could.

'*Jesus*,' said Doyle at the conclusion of the DI's recital. Then, remembering where he was, he blushed at his outburst.

'It's alright, Constable.' Markham's voice was surprisingly mild. 'It was a shock to us as well.'

Almost unbearable to think that, while he had been watching the sunrise, the sands of Derek Worthington's life had run out.

'Susan Caldicott told us she was sure the vicar was upset about something,' Burton said.

'Yeah.' Doyle was not to be left out. 'And she was pretty certain she saw some woman slip into the church on Monday evening.'

'Would she know this woman again?' the DI asked quickly.

'She *thinks* it might have been a parishioner but couldn't say for certain, not being a regular churchgoer herself. Young and blonde was the best she could do.'

The mysterious blonde again. But who was she? And what had she confided to the vicar? Something to do with the deaths of Michael Dominguez and Timothy Appleyard? Or another matter entirely?

'D'you reckon Worthington copped it cos he knew something about the murders?'

Wincing at the infelicitous phraseology, Markham replied, 'I'm inclined to believe so, Constable.'

'What if it had something to do with the vicar's . . . *personal life*?' Doyle had seen the boss flinch and sensed this death had cut him deep.

'It's something we're going to have to consider.'

And now the note of regret in the DI's voice was clear.

Like Davidson earlier, Noakes was in some discomfort. His behind was growing numb.

'We can't do owt here,' he said. 'Let's get back to base, yeah?'

Via Greggs no doubt.

'Oh, by the way, boss.' Burton had further news to impart. 'Michael Dominguez's requiem is tomorrow at Our Lady of the Angels.'

'How'd he manage that?' her fellow DS growled, not being keen on queue-jumping even in death. 'The bloke only snuffed it five minutes ago.'

'The DCI sent a briefing note,' she said, eyes sliding away from her wrathful colleague.

I'll bet he has. A wave of weariness threatened to engulf Markham.

Burton felt a sudden desperate urge to console him.

'The station had a call from some guy claiming to be Mr Dominguez's ex-boyfriend,' she continued. 'Wouldn't give his name over the phone but he's coming in later this afternoon.'

She was rewarded by a spark of renewed animation in the dark eyes.

'Now that *is* interesting, Kate. Who knows, this might be the break we're looking for.'

Please, God, let it be so. Before anyone else has to die.

8. BOLT FROM THE BLUE

'It was him and yet not him, Liv.'

Olivia waited patiently.

'Worthington's face was . . . Oh, I don't know how to describe it. Kind of a mask — owl-like and human all at the same time.'

Markham shuddered convulsively.

'And that slippery cellophane stuff swaddling the body. Like some horrible ectoplasm . . . the creepiest thing I've ever seen.'

It was the morning of Michael Dominguez's requiem.

'Try not to think about it, sweetheart.' Olivia poured him another cup of black coffee.

She had been late home after parents' evening at Hope, so breakfast was their time to catch up.

'You should really have some toast with that, Gil.'

'Oh, black coffee's fine thanks.'

'It's getting to the point where you might as well just take that stuff intravenously,' she said sarcastically. 'You'll be bouncing off the walls before the day is out.'

'I'll risk it.'

'How come the early funeral for Mr Dominguez?' She sighed, smoothing down her black peplum jacket. 'It's less than a week since you found him.'

‘He was a major benefactor of the Catholic Church. Presumably Bishop McGettrick pushed for this to happen.’

‘Oh right. Monseigneur Slimy rides again.’

Olivia’s shrug spoke volumes. No need for her to remind him of the unctuous cleric’s involvement in the St Cecilia investigation.

‘How’d it go with your mystery interviewee yesterday afternoon?’ she asked, trying to twist her tumbling red hair into a sober chignon.

‘He claimed to be an old boyfriend of Michael Dominguez. Name of Chris Mayne.’

‘What was he like?’

‘Very suave. Retired businessman . . . what you might call a silver fox.’

‘Not what you were expecting then?’

‘Not at all. Here, sweetheart. Let me.’ With deft fingers, he scooped up her heavy tresses and secured them with a barrette. ‘There you go, job done.’

‘Better than Toni & Guy.’ Olivia appraised her new style in the mirror that hung above their wood burner. ‘So, go on. What did this Chris Mayne have to say for himself?’

‘I think it was a pre-emptive strike, in case he was outed,’ Markham replied. ‘He didn’t come in with a solicitor, but I got the feeling there might be one hovering in the wings.’

‘Was there any risk of someone blabbing?’

‘I wouldn’t have thought so, but he wasn’t taking any chances. Maybe he was afraid of reporters sniffing around.’

‘But these days no one gives a stuff about boy-on-boy action.’

‘Oh, in certain circles it can still count against you, Liv,’ Markham said thoughtfully. ‘Plus, it’s not easy to go back into the closet once tongues start wagging.’

‘Is that where Mayne wants to be, then — in the closet?’

‘I’d say so, yes. And, let’s face it, Dominguez was somewhat economical with the *verité* himself.’

‘Did this bloke whip out a prepared statement?’

'Well, he'd done a typed account of his association with Dominguez. No alibi for either of the murders, but that wasn't the interesting part . . .'

Attention arrested in the middle of her make-up routine, Olivia stowed her compact and lipstick in her clutch bag and looked at him expectantly.

'There was a jealous ex on the scene,' Markham said. 'Dominguez made a joke of it — called him "Queen of the Night" — but underneath it all, Mayne got the impression he was genuinely scared.'

'So Mayne and Dominguez were still on good terms?'

'It would appear so. They'd both moved on to other people, but there were no hard feelings. At any rate, they were friendly enough for Dominguez to mention the ex who wouldn't let go.'

'And you don't think Mayne told you as a sort of lightning conductor? So you won't be looking too closely at whatever went on between himself and Dominguez?'

Markham watched affectionately as she carefully brushed his pinstriped jacket.

'Can't have you letting the side down,' she muttered. 'Bad enough that George'll probably turn up looking like Beetlejuice.'

'Oh, I think he'll make an effort,' he chuckled. 'With it being a pukka funeral, Muriel's decided to grace us with her presence.'

Olivia gave vent to her feelings in a loud groan.

'To answer your question,' he said, moving on smartly from the subject of Muriel Noakes, 'I don't think this story of the jealous ex was a smokescreen. Mayne struck me as truthful.'

'So you think Dominguez was being harassed — he had a stalker?'

'I think it's a distinct possibility.' Markham slipped on the jacket over his broad shoulders. 'I ran the idea past Sheila Birtle yesterday. Apparently, there was one day when she caught him in a thunderous mood. He was ripping a letter to shreds. It stuck in her mind because he was generally very relaxed — "so laid-back he was almost horizontal," was how she put it — and she hardly ever saw him out of temper.'

'A threatening letter . . . ?'

'Could be,' he agreed.

Olivia produced a comb and reached up to complete her beau's toilette. Markham submitted to her ministrations with an amused tolerance which would have flabbergasted the junior ranks of CID, accustomed as they were to treading warily around the formidable DI.

'So you let Mayne go then?'

'Had to, Liv. There was no reason to keep him.' Markham grinned. 'Despite Noakesy's conviction that we should "put the squeeze on him".'

'No leads on this Queen of the Night character, then?'

'Nada. Mind you, when I ran our suspects' names past him, Mayne admitted to *knowing* both Andrew Boughton and Bernard Gallagher.'

Olivia was intrigued. 'As in the biblical sense?'

'He certainly wasn't telling.'

'Don't tell me George didn't ask!'

'I could see he was going to, so—'

'You gave him the death stare.'

'Correct.' Markham sighed. 'Mayne would have pulled up the drawbridge once Noakesy started on the innuendo.'

'*Insinuendo*, you mean.'

A wry chuckle. 'I took the line that they all mixed in the same . . . artistic circles. It seemed a safe enough bet.'

'How did he react to that?'

'Oh, practically sagged with relief.'

Olivia gazed at him thoughtfully. 'So, either Boughton or Gallagher could be the stalker then?'

'Mayne claimed not to know the identity of the person bothering Dominguez. Only that nickname: Queen of the Night.'

'From what you said about the organist bloke, he sounds the more likely candidate.'

'Hmm. Boughton came across as thinking he was God's gift to women, but it may not be the full picture. That business about the reference showed Dominguez was wary of him.' Markham frowned. 'On the other hand, he's not particularly subtle — more in-your-face obnoxious than the stalker type . . .'

'But isn't Gallagher too respectable for that sort of caper?' Olivia ruminated. 'An ex-principal harassing his former lover . . . ?'

'Oh, I get the impression he can be viperish behind the rectitude,' Markham said. 'And he was definitely conflicted about Dominguez.'

'No chance this Queen of the Night could be a woman?'

'Mayne said Dominguez was talking about a male lover, Liv.'

'He might have felt embarrassed about admitting to Mayne that he was scared of a woman,' she countered. 'And let's face it, Fenella Staunton and the MP woman are pretty scary. Plus' — she was clearly warming to her theory — 'Staunton had hopes of him. And then there's the librarian—'

'Judith Lockyer.'

'Right. Well, she had hang-ups about him too, didn't she?'

'God. At this rate you'll be saying Dominguez was swinging from the chandelier with Nerys from next door!'

She bit her lip.

'I'm getting carried away, aren't I?' Her voice was small now, crestfallen.

'Just a tad.' But his smile was tender. 'Old Mother Wynne would be scandalized to hear you. But I think the son has a sense of humour. Bet he never imagined he was living alongside so many *femmes fatales*.'

'Hey, what about him — the son?' Olivia was staging a recovery.

'Sheila Birtle said there's a girlfriend on the scene,' he replied with a grin. 'She used to think he might be a bit AC/DC, but then she ran into the two of them in town . . .'

'Bit late flying the nest, isn't he?'

'Oh, I think when the lovebirds settle down it'll be a case of "And Mother Makes Three".'

Olivia laughed. 'D'you want another coffee?'

'Why not? We've got time.'

When they were settled with refills, she returned to the fray.

'Who gets to inherit Mr Dominguez's property, Gil? I mean, he was very well off, wasn't he?'

'His will specifies an arts foundation in Málaga.'

'Ah, the land of Picasso.' Olivia was approving.

'Turns out its director Antonio Escobar embarked on a relationship with Dominguez last summer . . . despite being married.'

'Blimey.' She choked and spluttered. 'Sorry, coffee went down the wrong way.' A grimace. 'Or maybe I'm not quite so liberal as I imagined. Can't get my head around someone running two relationships in tandem like that.'

'Well, Senor Escobar was devastated when we broke the news of Dominguez's death. It sounded like the two of them really had something special.'

'Will he be at the funeral?'

'He's coordinating a spring festival or some such. It's a big deal and there's no one to deputize. And *no*' — Markham registered the kindling of interest in his girlfriend's eyes — 'he was nowhere near Bromgrove when Dominguez and Appleyard died. So he's out of the running as a suspect.'

Olivia tossed her head as though to say, *I'm not beaten yet*.

'Did Chris Mayne say anything about Escobar?' she asked.

'No, it seems like the relationship was firmly *sub rosa*.'

'What about Mr Appleyard? Didn't Jim McLeod think he might have been active on the gay scene?'

'Jim has no proof of that, and Mayne didn't react when I mentioned Appleyard's name.'

A companionable silence fell as they enjoyed their coffee. But Olivia was clearly still turning things over.

'What about the MP?' she said. 'Wasn't she at loggerheads with Dominguez?'

'I've had Rosemary Kernan under discreet surveillance, Liv.' He hesitated then plunged in. 'There was a child-abuse investigation which risked coming too close to home. Her husband was involved . . . and Dominguez may have known something about it.'

Her gaze was infinitely compassionate. Other than Noakes, she was the only person in the world who had any idea of his sad history.

Matter-of-factly, she said, 'What about the vicar — could Kernan have done for him?'

Her pragmatic tone reassured him.

'Worthington was murdered some time this morning. I couldn't risk parking anyone outside Kernan's house in Grasmere—'

'Cos of Judas Iscariot?'

'Liv.'

'Sorry, Gil.' She didn't sound particularly contrite.

'Mrs Kernan's PA rang Kate on Wednesday evening to say she was back home. Apparently, her first meeting on Thursday was at midday. And I understand she kept that appointment.'

'Could've snuck out and rendezvoused with the vicar first, though.'

'There was a window of opportunity, yes.'

He looked so troubled that Olivia's heart went out to him.

'Take no notice of me, dearest.' She reached for his hand. 'I'm The Sweepstakes' answer to Miss Marple — your typical civilian busybody, always on the case.' A gentle squeeze. 'Anyway, surely it's not likely a woman could have . . . well . . . left Mr Worthington like that.'

Her voice held a plea.

'Dimples isn't ruling it out, Liv.'

'My God.'

'Actually, we even found a winch contraption in the same cupboard as Worthington's body.'

She looked at him wordlessly.

'The forensics report sets it all out with photographs. At first we thought the killer would have had to haul the body up and then hook it over the clothes rail.'

'And a woman couldn't do that . . .'

'Well, it's possible,' he said. 'Worthington weighed less than nothing — Dimples reckons we're talking the Big C — so a stronger woman could've managed it.'

'But what about this contraption thingy?'

'We didn't notice it when we were in there, but the SOCOs explained later. There's a sort of motorized lift device. You hook the hanger on there and it lifts the clothes up to the rail.'

'An automated wardrobe lift. Ingenious.'

'Very.'

She flashed him a mischievous look. 'I could do with one of those.'

But Markham wasn't smiling. 'We missed it, Liv,' he said soberly. 'Didn't imagine St Barnabas running to high-spec push-button technology like that.'

'Does it change things so much then?'

'Well, it opens the field up. Actually, Dimples says we could be looking at a pair of killers.'

'*Bloody hell.*' Olivia had good reason to remember the horrors of what criminologists would call *folie* à *deux*. Her mind wandered back to the Newman Hospital case and other investigations.

'Or it might be the work of a single murderer, with the post-mortem tableau staged by some random sicko who turned up afterwards but had nothing to do with the, er . . . main event.'

Olivia looked queasy.

‘Speaking of post-mortems,’ she said, ‘don’t tell me poor Kate has to do this one.’

‘Oh, she’s up for it, Liv.’

Markham’s face was anguished, and she knew that, for all his ‘new man’ credentials, he hated the idea of a female detective watching while Worthington’s viscera were scooped out and weighed on the pathologist’s scales.

‘At least it’s not like Dominguez. At least he’s not been splattered all over the place like some Jackson Pollock canvas . . . or squelched out of recognition like Timothy Appleyard.’

She flinched, knowing all too well that these were two of the more mangled ghosts in the procession who haunted her lover’s waking and sleeping hours.

‘Darling Gil,’ she whispered, smiling up at him. ‘“These things must not be thought after these ways. So, it will make us mad.”’

Markham blinked as though to clear his vision.

‘All gone, my Liv.’ His gaze was meltingly soft. ‘“And being gone, I am a man again.”’

Playfully, she punched his arm.

‘Right, what time’s curtain up?’

‘Half eleven.’ He strove to match her casual tone. ‘Very good of you to swell the CID turnout, Liv. How did you square it with Hope?’

‘I told Matthew it was family, Gil,’ she said firmly.

Matthew Sullivan, deputy head of Hope Academy and a friend who had found himself embroiled in various previous investigations, was firmly on their side.

And it was true, Olivia reflected, as they washed up together and prepared to leave for Michael Dominguez’s requiem.

Markham was her family. As were all those for whom he sought justice.

Family.

* * *

'I remember this place from Ashley Dean's funeral,' Olivia whispered, referring to what had become known as the Hope Academy murders.

Then, incongruously, she giggled, '*Look at George* . . . That suit's like a straitjacket! And he's gelled his hair — Rufty Tufty meets Boyzone!'

Markham bit his lip hard, trying not to laugh.

Noakes certainly looked acutely uncomfortable, though for once he didn't stand out as looking nothing like a mourner. Bizarrely, the DI caught him ducking his head to statues in the Calvary which stood to one side of the little gothic church, as if to say, *We've been here before*.

'And what in God's name is Muriel wearing?'

'Her go-to outfit for meeting a bishop, Liv.'

'*Christ*.' Then Olivia checked herself. 'Sorry, Gil.'

''S alright, sweetheart. I agree it's a bit much.'

It certainly was. Her veiled peekaboo hat and monstrous befrilled two-piece wouldn't have looked out of place in a BBC costume drama, while the blonde bouffant, lacquered into immobility, and spiky high heels carried unfortunate overtones of a dominatrix.

And yet Muriel Noakes's eyes looked somehow sadder, warier and less confident than of yore.

Had there ever been a clearing of the air between husband and wife? Had she insisted on knowing the truth — what really happened at the climax of the Bluebell investigation? Had she ever taxed Noakes with doing the unimaginable out of love for her and the daughter who was not biologically his?

Markham bowed gravely to Mrs Noakes with the old-world charm which was second nature to him. Flushing with pleasure, she fluttered her fingers at him like a coquettish teenager before sending her husband on his way with a little push.

Olivia sent up a silent prayer of gratitude that Muriel didn't see fit to accost them the way she usually did. *Gilbert*! The shrill greeting always affected Olivia like fingernails scratching a chalkboard.

As his wife bustled into the church, Noakes lurched over to join them.

'Looks like Dominguez'll get a decent send-off, guv,' he grunted. 'Sidney and Bretherton have turned up an' there's *three* sky pilots on parade.'

'Such a comfort, Sergeant.'

Noakes clocked the guv'nor's sarky tone. Couldn't blame him really. That bishop from the St Cecilia's case was a right creep — Sidney in a frock. The two of them would likely be slobbering over each other enough to make decent folk puke.

The DS caught Olivia's eye and blushed. There was something witchy about her, like she knew just what he was thinking.

She winked at him and he turned even redder, his complexion the colour of uncooked salami.

Whenever Noakes beheld his boss's partner, he felt pole-axed as if she had cast a spell on him. Not beautiful by the standards of the day ('Anorexic Annie,' was Mrs Noakes's snappish verdict), but looking at her was like stepping into a crystal-clear pool. *Streams of living water* . . . It took him back to his Sunday School days and all those exotic women. Zipporah, Sarah, Ruth—

'Shall we?'

The DI's voice recalled him to reality.

Olivia rested a hand on Noakes's arm.

'I'll go in now, boys. You'll want to wait for the others.'

A smile played about her lips. 'I've got to get back to school afterwards, so I'll have to miss the eats . . .'

'Nerys Wynne's doing the honours.' Markham sounded resigned. 'So Noakesy's counting on lots of barmbrack and bara brith. Ain't that so, Sergeant?'

'Reckon Nerys'll do a decent spread,' he said stoutly.

'Here's Kate and DC Doyle.' Olivia's gentle smile lit a fire somewhere deep inside Noakes. Like a love-struck schoolboy, he watched her vanish into the depths of the shadowy church.

* * *

It was always the same with requiems. Everyone merged into an amorphous mass, personal identity submerged in a sea of black.

Afterwards, Markham was hard-pushed to say if any of the mourners at Michael Dominguez's obsequies had stood out from the crowd.

Fenella Staunton with those hard, glittering eyes and her stagey reading from Lamentations. Judith Lockyer doing the prophet Daniel and those 'sleeping in the dust'. He'd seen her gaze flit like moth's wings round the church, brushing the stained-glass saints in their ruby and turquoise robes.

Bernard Gallagher, infrangibly dignified, as though ready to burst into a chorus of 'There'll Always Be an England'. Markham wondered how he could ever have imagined such an upright old relict being caught up in Michael Dominguez's tangled personal life.

Rosemary Kernan MP bellowed the responses like an angry bullfrog, all jutting jaw and flinty-eyed belligerence. How far would she have gone to keep her husband's involvement in the Everglades saga under wraps?

Andrew Boughton thundered overhead in the choir loft, determined to stamp his mark on the proceedings and totally obliterating the soloist, who made a brave stab at Fauré's 'Pie Jesu'. As ever, it was all about Broughton, Markham reflected grimly.

Nerys and Simon Wynne did the offertory procession, Nerys tacking uncertainly from left to right but somehow managing to get through it.

Bishop Thomas Percy McGettrick was just as Markham remembered him. Candyfloss-white hair, purplish complexion, clearly well marinated in the sauces of clerical privilege.

The eulogy was a triumph of art over substance, well-oiled phrases pouring out of McGettrick like a spigot.

Markham smiled inwardly, reflecting that Michael Dominguez would doubtless have enjoyed all the sanctuary choreography and ecclesial platitudes, gauging them at their true worth. High above in the church rafters, the gargoyles looked down on the proceedings as though to agree with this estimate, their little faces alight with wickedness.

Are you here?

In vain, the DI waited for that pricking between the shoulder blades that told him the murderer was present in the congregation, watching as the victim's remains were hefted from the trestle and carried away to their final bourn.

Chris Mayne's eyes met his as the coffin left the church before discreetly sliding away to fasten on his hymnal.

In no time at all, it was over and, after the cortège's departure for the private interment, clusters of mourners in their Sunday best lingered awkwardly outside prior to adjourning to Grasmere Park.

'We are going to the eats — right, guv?' Noakes was anxious to be clear on this point.

'Certainly, Sergeant, but ideally without hoovering up every last crumb.'

Or treating it like an all-you-can-eat buffet.

Kate Burton, spick and span in a well-cut black trouser suit, clearly thought there was precious little chance of her colleague holding back.

DC Doyle, dapper in Lacoste, looked equally sceptical.

'We'll meet you there,' Markham told Kate and Doyle, ushering Noakes to his car.

'The missus'll give your Olivia a lift back to school,' the DS assured him.

That'll make her day.

DCI Sidney and Superintendent Bretherton stood together, the former favouring them with a frigid nod while the latter managed not to see them at all.

'At least we don' have to put up with the slimy bish,' Noakes muttered. 'S'pose he's spouting off at the cemetery or wherever they've taken Dominguez.'

'His Lordship has a packed itinerary.' Markham's voice was expressionless. 'He can't attend the wake, but I gather he'll be doing the memorial service in the summer.'

'Thank fuck for that.'

Noakes looked over to the Calvary, favouring the Mother of God with another of his furtive winks. No point causing offence, when all was said and done.

* * *

''S like a care home in here.'

'*Keep your voice down*,' Kate Burton hissed. '*She'll hear you.*'

But Noakes's observation was undoubtedly true, Markham reflected. Nerys Wynne's house was as far removed as possible from the sleek lines of Michael Dominguez's property next door. Indeed, it looked as though the décor hadn't changed in decades, with fussy doilies and antimacassars very much in the ascendant. Modern fixtures and fittings, however, were conspicuous by their absence.

'Top spread though,' Noakes conceded generously with his mouth full of savoury. 'I were right about ole Nerys being Welsh. Them Caerphilly tarts are champion.'

Behold the Christian Carnivora.

Somehow, the DI suspected that the deceased would have enjoyed his sergeant's unabashed focus on the rations. Dominguez was the kind of man to have relished the sight of so many well-heeled vultures crowding round the funeral baked meats.

Kate Burton, however, looked embarrassed by the entire proceedings, eyeing her fellow DS with a basilisk glare.

Poor Kate. She'd far rather be at Worthington's PM than dancing attendance here.

'Inspector, I need to speak with you.'

Rosemary Kernan had come up alongside him like an alligator sizing up its prey.

The MP looked ill, he thought, her doughy complexion rough and uneven beneath a thick layer of foundation. Her eyes were red-rimmed and bloodshot.

'I'm at your disposal, Mrs Kernan,' he replied courteously.

'Later this afternoon then.' She spoke with the arrogance of one accustomed to instant compliance from the hoi polloi. 'I'll come to the station.'

Bernard Gallagher and Judith Lockyer stood close together by a tired-looking display of dried flowers on the living-room sideboard. The DI had a feeling the drab pair were watching his exchange with Kernan closely. But as soon as he turned his eyes towards them, theirs were instantly withdrawn.

On the other side of the room, Susan Caldicott and Andrew Boughton were locked in earnest conversation. Boughton looked distinctly put out. Markham wondered whether the presence of Chris Mayne had rattled him. Whatever it was, the organist's florid face was high-coloured and sweaty, his booming voice dialled down to half its usual megawatt volume.

'Can I offer you another vol-au-vent . . . or perhaps some quiche, Inspector?' Simon Wynne was doing the honours manfully.

'We don't have anything stronger than tea or coffee, I'm afraid. Mum's teetotal, you see, and . . . well, I'm happy to go along with that.'

'Your mother's laid on a marvellous buffet, Mr Wynne.'

Her son looked pleased.

'Time for us to get back to the station, though.'

Once I've prised my sergeant away from those flapjacks.

'I'll just pass on my thanks,' he murmured, moving across to their hostess who appeared tired but delighted by Noakes's enthusiasm for the edibles.

'Step away from the cake, Sergeant,' he muttered sotto voce, drawing his wingman away from the buffet.

'I'll jus' . . .'

A paper package disappeared into Noakes's jacket pocket.

'Nerys said I could have a doggy bag,' he pointed out with a touch of defiance.

With a supreme effort, Kate Burton managed to refrain from raising her eyes to heaven.

The DI took pity on her.

'You can get off to Mr Worthington's PM, Kate,' he said. Then, as it appeared Doyle was trying to make himself invisible, 'And take the constable with you.'

The DC looked as though he now regretted having consumed three sausage rolls. But there was no help for it with Burton making her way towards the front door.

Noakes smirked at the youngster's discomfiture.

An eloquent eye roll directed at Noakes and Doyle was gone.

'Right, Sergeant, duty calls.'

Back in the DI's car, Noakes was uncharacteristically silent.

After a time, Markham found this unnerving.

'Something's bothering you, Noakesy. Come on, spit it out.'

'C'n I have a word with you back at the station? In confidence, like . . .'

'Of course you can, Sergeant.' The DI paused delicately. 'Can you give me an idea of what it's about?'

'It's Nat, guv.' The DS cleared his throat noisily. 'My Natalie,' he added for the avoidance of doubt. A tide of crimson was creeping up his beefy neck. 'I wanna report a rape.'

9. BOMBSHELL

The DI had a brainwave.

'We can sit outside St Chad's. It's turning into a lovely afternoon and no one will disturb us.'

In minutes, they were sitting on a bench next to the cenotaph, enjoying the warm grass-scented air of the terraced graveyard, which seemed to quiver with its own green life.

Noakes divested himself of the straitjacket, bundling it into a ball with a carelessness which would have brought down the wrath of his 'missus' on him had she been there to witness it.

His striped tie got the same treatment. Then Noakes loosened his belt a couple of notches, eyeing his gut ruefully as he did so.

'*Thass better*,' he sighed.

'Striptease over, Noakesy?' the DI enquired.

'It were murder in church in them tight trousers.'

Not the most felicitous choice of words in the circumstances, but Markham merely smiled.

Now that they were settled, the DS didn't seem to know how to begin.

But his boss merely sat back, stretching his long legs in front of him, letting the silence cast its tranquilizing spell.

Truth to tell, for all that the DI had on his plate — and with the vicar's murder, there was no chance of avoiding a press conference — he felt a lazy reluctance to move. Never had the prospect of CID's stale fug seemed less appealing.

Noakes belched loudly then coughed apologetically for this breach of cemetery etiquette, looking round as though he expected one of the stone angels to swoop down from its monument and chastise him.

'Stuffed my face a bit back there,' he admitted.

A bit!

'But ole Nerys did 'em proud. It were all home-made . . . none of your Mister Kipling or owt like that.'

Markham smiled. 'Olivia says funerals always make her hungry,' he observed mildly.

'Me an' all. Summat to do with the caterwauling an' having to be all po-faced an' polite . . . It's stressful, that's what it is.'

'Well, you certainly did justice to Mrs Wynne's hospitality, Noakes. She looked pleased as punch to see you tucking in.'

'Nice ole biddy. Mind, she looked a bit tottery bringing the bread an' wine up . . . I thought she were going to drop the lot.'

'So did her son by the looks of him.'

'Yeah.' Noakes chuckled. 'Sweating cobs in case she didn't make it.'

It felt companionable mulling things over together.

Quite like old times.

Don't rush him.

'Did you . . . like, *feel anything* back there, boss . . . ? Y'know . . . get any *vibes* in church to say the murderer were hanging out with us?'

His faith in Markham's ESP was touching. Especially since DCI Sidney was wont to dismiss it as 'feyness' and an over-reliance on 'hunches'.

'That was just it, Noakesy. I didn't really pick up anything from the congregation today.'

'Folk allus merge into one. Everyone looks the same at a funeral . . . kinda washed-out an' insignificant,' the DS said comfortingly.

'There *was* just one moment . . .'

'Oh aye?'

'Just before the offertory procession . . . quite strange, as though all the air was sucked out of the building . . . like some sort of drop in atmospheric pressure . . . It lasted a moment or two and then everything was back to normal.'

Noakes preserved a respectful silence.

Then, 'Your intuition *could've* been trying to tell you summat, guv.' He rumpled his untidy hair. 'Or mebbe you were coming over faint an' needed to put your head between your knees.'

From the sublime to the ridiculous, thought Markham wryly.

'You could be right about the faintness,' he agreed. 'Too much coffee and nothing to eat this morning. Olivia warned me I'd regret it.'

Noakes looked pleased at this confirmation of his diagnosis.

'Your Olivia' — his ears turned slightly pink — 'allus gets to the heart of things.'

She's certainly burrowed her way into your *heart*, Markham thought with amusement.

As though Olivia's name was some kind of talisman, the DS screwed his courage to the sticking point.

'My Nat — *Natalie*,' he corrected himself as though this formality was a bulwark to stop his feelings from breaking through. 'She tole me she were . . . raped.'

The big meaty fists clenched and unclenched.

How far did you go to stop Natalie learning she wasn't your biological daughter?

Markham forced the question back to the inner recesses of his mind.

That was for another time. What he needed to focus on now was supporting a devastated father — the only father Natalie had ever known.

'When did this happen to Natalie?' he asked gently.

The fact that Markham took the sexual assault as a given — never doubted Natalie's veracity — made the little graveyard suddenly swim before Noakes's eyes.

The DI feigned intense interest in the activities of two magpies on a nearby tomb until his sergeant had recovered himself.

'Three weeks ago. She'd been out with her mates at the Krazyhouse,' Noakes said. 'First proper night out since . . . well, since what happened at the Bluebell . . .'

Natalie Noakes had once been the undisputed doyenne of Bromgrove's least salubrious nightclubs. There was a time Markham would have rejoiced to hear she had rediscovered her mojo, but not like this . . . God, not like this.

'She were supposed to call me for a lift, but she fancied a walk . . . clear her head an' that.' He paused for a moment, looking perplexed. 'Happen I come on too strong sometimes . . . after what happened, y'see . . . too protective.'

'Totally understandable. Any father would be the same.'

The DS swallowed painfully.

'The bastard grabbed her in Quarry Street . . . the bit where there ain't any streetlamps. Bloke in a balaclava.' He mopped his forehead. 'Next thing she knew, he'd dragged her into Cuckoo Lane . . . an' then she were on her back trying to fight him off . . . but she weren't strong enough, see.'

'Take your time, Noakesy. Take your time.'

Theirs had never been a touchy-feely partnership, but now he put a reassuring hand on his friend's shoulder.

'No need for details. Natalie's assailant raped her.'

'She didn't tell her mum or me till after she missed two CBT appointments. Turned out she weren't even able to tell the therapist . . . after all the chuffing poking round in her subconscious an' all that empowerment bollocks or whatever the fuck they call it, she couldn't say a word.'

Which explained the explosion of anger when Kate Burton had mentioned therapy — the rant about it being all 'emperor's new clothes'.

'An' now it's too late to get forensics or any of that.' Angrily, the DS kicked at the gravel on the path in front of them. Startled, the magpies flew up into the overhanging elms with a burst of indignant chatter.

More scuffing of gravel.

'She didn't have any experience in that direction.' He cleared his throat, unable to meet Markham's eyes. 'Didn't let lads take liberties . . . a good girl, our Nat . . .'

The DI felt a spasm of pity so sharp he had to look away so that his features didn't betray him.

Natalie Noakes was no virgin if the local grapevine was anything to go by. But as far as her father was concerned, she was pure as the driven snow.

Very gently, he said, 'Sounds like she just blocked it out, Noakesy. Shock does that . . . makes the brain shut down . . . a sort of survival mechanism.'

The DI had thought he knew every inch of Noakes's mind. But that was until the Bluebell investigation and its shocking conclusion.

Now he felt his way carefully, tentatively around the perimeter, testing words before he uttered them. Weighing their capacity to reassure and comfort.

'Also, I'm sure she didn't want to worry you and Muriel,' he went on quietly. 'After . . . everything that had happened . . . especially since she was making progress and gradually getting back to normal.'

'She won't never get back to normal now.'

Noakes's mastiff features were working convulsively while his shock of rumpled hair was standing more on end than ever.

'She'll pull through, Noakesy. You and Muriel will bring her through.' Markham's face was suddenly as implacable as any of the stone effigies tucked out of sight inside the little church. 'And in the meantime, we need to liaise with the rape enquiry.'

'You reckon the piece of shit who attacked Nat is the same one who assaulted them other poor lasses?'

'Yes, I do. There's the balaclava for one thing.' Markham examined the Celtic knotwork on a nearby gravestone as though it might hold the answer to the riddle.

'Obviously, we'll need to talk to Natalie.' Aware of the DS stiffening, he added, 'Don't worry. I'll put Lindsay Hollis on it. She's the best, *and* she's got experience with PTSD.' Almost casually, he continued, 'Did Natalie notice anything about her attacker — pick up on anything unusual?' He smiled at his wingman. 'She's her father's daughter, after all, and I seem to remember her keeping a cool head in an emergency.'

There was a shy look of pride as the other said, 'She clocked the expensive smell of him. An' he kept muttering summat . . .'

The DI waited.

'Yeah . . . About wanting pleasure in dark places.'

Pleasure in dark places.

Woods, dark alleys, badly lit back streets . . .

'Jus' lemme have five minutes in a dark place with him.'

They would need to keep Noakes well away from the rape investigation, Markham reflected. At any cost.

But the DS's next words blew that plan clean out of the water.

'An' he said he wanted to make a bonfire of all the books. *Yeah, thassright* . . . cos demons fly out of the pages.'

The day was mild, but Markham felt a succession of little chills chase down his spine at these words — icy fingers running over the vertebrae like they were keys on a piano.

Noakes scowled. 'Bloody gibberish . . . like some nutty professor . . .'

A reader.

Or a member of a book club.

The DI knew he needed to tread carefully. 'It could point to an academic background. On the other hand, if he's mentally deranged then maybe they were just random utterances.'

'Yeah, nutters allus talk about satanic stuff an' all that.'

'Was Natalie able to say if her attacker was young or old?'

Noakes shook his head.

'Like you said, guv, she must've froze an' blotted it out . . . It were jus' the weirdy words an' that smell . . . Mind' — Noakes suddenly remembered something — 'Nat said it weren't aftershave or owt like that . . . Yeah, *thassright* . . . It were lily of the valley or summat old-fashioned . . . like my missus wears.'

The DS looked momentarily embarrassed to have described his wife as 'old-fashioned'.

Affecting not to have noticed, Markham said, 'So the rapist was wearing *women's perfume*?'

'That's a clue — right, guv?' His wingman's voice was eager.

'Well, it's an interesting kink, Noakes.'

Kate Burton would have a field day checking out all the variables in her *Diagnostic and Statistical Manual of Mental Disorders*.

Were they looking for someone with a mother fixation? Or was this a man who had enjoyed a relationship with an older woman then later come to regret it, associating sex with shame and the dark side of his nature?

Dark places and demons.

Cautiously, Markham said, 'I think we can't rule out the possibility of a link with the book-club murders, Noakes.'

The DS stared at him.

'*Fuck me sideways.*'

'I do hope not.' The DI kept his tone deliberately light.

'I shoulda seen it, guv. I thought he were some kind of religious screwball . . . Like the Yorkshire Ripper an' pervy types who bang on about God an' bibles an' voices from heaven . . . when deep down they're jus' sex maniacs.'

'Totally understandable that you didn't make the connection, Noakes. I'm not even sure about it myself.'

But the other's curranty eyes were gleaming with enthusiasm.

'So the same bloke who did the murders might be the Bromgrove Rapist . . . *Jesus*. That means it's gotta be a man, guv.'

'Not necessarily.'

'How come?'

'There's another possibility — a connection between our book-club killer and the rapist. Don't forget, when were in the sacristy at St Barnabas's, Dimples wouldn't rule out the possibility of *two* people working together.'

'So there could be a woman covering for the rapist, bumping off anyone who gets near the truth . . .'

'Hmmm. Somehow that explanation feels too contrived and "oven-ready", Noakes. And I could be reading way too much into the rapist's words — what he said about wanting to burn books and demons flying out of the pages.'

There was also the chance that a traumatized Natalie Noakes had misremembered the details of her ordeal, this being far from uncommon with victims of sexual assault.

However, Markham's gut told him there *was* a connection, although its precise nature remained in the shadows.

'If there's a woman helping the rapist, mebbe she's in a relationship with him.' Noakes's imagination had gone into overdrive.

'Or perhaps he's been damaged by a previous relationship and that's what's triggering the assaults?'

'It could be one of them women from the book club.' His DS was clearly reviewing the contenders. 'Older an' bossy . . . a ball-breaker . . .'

While pleased to see animation replace dull-eyed despair, Markham felt obliged to call a halt to the sergeant's gallop.

'This is all just speculation, Noakesy.'

'Yeah, but you've got a hunch, guv. *I can tell*.'

'And you know what the DCI thinks about "hunches".'

Especially mine.

'Let's get an interview set up for Natalie with Lindsay Hollis. No pressure on her to say or do anything she isn't happy with.'

'I c'n live with that.'

Noakes's words were gruff, but the grateful look that accompanied them was balm to the DI's soul.

We're getting back on track, he thought exultantly.

'D'you think we'll catch him, boss?'

'We'll do our damnedest, Noakesy.'

'Do the others need to know about Nat — Burton an' Doyle? Are you gonna tell 'em?'

'That's your call, Sergeant. Yours and Natalie's. For now, we'll keep it between ourselves and DS Hollis. However, I'm going to ask Kate to review all the paperwork from the rapes on the basis that the DCI wants us to check out all contemporaneous offences of violent assault.'

In the hope of pinning the Grasmere Park killings on some random psychopath as opposed to a well-heeled member of the community.

'Right up Burton's street,' the DS conceded. 'An' she's good at sweating the small stuff,' he added generously.

'Indeed she is.'

The DI was loath to leave the little graveyard. With its soft rustlings and the drowsy hum of fat bumblebees, it made Bromgrove CID seem a million miles away.

But duty called.

'We've got Rosemary Kernan coming in,' he said glancing at his watch. 'And knowing that lady, I would imagine she doesn't care to be kept waiting.'

'Watcha think she wants to talk about?'

'I suspect she's going to tell us that Michael Dominguez knew what went down at Everglades.'

'The abuse an' her husband being mixed up in it?'

Until Sidney offered an escape route.

'Something along those lines, yes.'

'*Hey*.' A thought struck Noakes. 'Mebbe the rapist was abused at Everglades when he were a kid an' never got over it.' His doggy features creased in thought. 'An' mebbe Manuel said summat dead tactless so me laddo ended up turning round and battering him. Sheila said Domingo didn't have a filter . . . bit of a big mouth, like.' More cogitation, then, '*Hey*

— mebbe *Kernan*'s the one the rapist is having a relationship with.' The DS shuddered. 'Talk about being squashed in the sack . . . *That*'d give you a frigging hang-up alright.'

Registering the DI's expression, he muttered, 'I know, I know . . . mustn't jump to conclusions cos we gotta join up all the dots.'

Markham smiled at him, mustering a confidence that he was far from feeling.

'I know it feels like it's anyone's game at the minute, Noakesy, but I swear we're getting closer.'

'Copper's nose,' the other said happily. 'You can't beat it.'

Noakes lurched to his feet, watching as the magpies flew back down to the neighbouring tomb.

'Someone should take an air rifle to them little pests.'

And on that uplifting note, they headed away from the peaceful little nook towards the station.

* * *

Back in CID, they found Kate Burton sitting at her desk, raking the gravel in her miniature Zen garden.

The DI knew a displacement activity when he saw one.

'How was Mr Worthington's PM, Kate?' he asked gently.

'Well, at least Dimples played Classic FM and didn't inflict any choral stuff on me.' A savage jab of the little bamboo rake. 'I just couldn't have faced *Aida* or *Madama Butterfly* today.'

Noakes grunted sympathetically, having endured ordeal by opera at the pathologist's hands more times than he cared to remember.

'Turns out Mr Worthington was riddled with cancer, guv,' Burton went on. 'Secondaries in the liver. Didn't look like he'd gone for treatment either.'

Markham thought of Michael Dominguez, his corpse in the earth . . . soon to be joined by Timothy Appleyard in his shroud.

And now Derek Worthington had joined that dismal procession to extinction.

The vicar might have been terminally ill, but the poor wretch deserved to enjoy the time he had left.

God, sometimes he hated this job.

Aloud, he commented quietly, 'No surprises other than that, Kate?'

'No, guv. He was strangled with his own stole and then hoisted up using that lift mechanism in the turn.'

'What's one of them?' Noakes enquired. 'A *turn*?'

'It means a revolving cupboard in church, sarge.' She smiled weakly. 'You know how I like quaint old terms.'

And, wonder of wonders, her fellow DS smiled back.

Peace in our time, Markham thought with an inward chuckle.

'I suppose it's too much to hope the SOCOs came up with anything,' he said.

'The killer's forensically aware, sir. Everything wiped down.' With a sigh, she laid down the little rake and straightened the tray containing her bonsai tree. It was now perfectly aligned with her psychology library. 'Mr Worthington would have been in contact with everyone from Grasmere at some time or another, so nothing to get excited about in terms of trace evidence. And' — she shivered — 'it was a clean kill in terms of there being no blood spatter or anything like that.'

'Dominguez and Appleyard sure as hell weren't clean kills,' Noakes growled. 'Sonny boy must've been *covered* in blood.'

Burton groaned.

'I've already had Brian Rafferty bore me rigid about blood transfer patterns and drip stains.'

'Don' tell me,' Noakes put in sarcastically, 'cos of cross-contamination there's zilch chance of pinning it on any of 'em in Grasmere.'

'Well, once we've got someone in the frame, they can zero in on him and look for specific incriminating evidence.'

'Flaming boffins . . . Waste of frigging space if you ask me.'

Noakes's scowl was a powerful inducement to change the subject.

'Judith Lockyer called earlier, sir,' Burton said. 'Wondered if we fancied coming to a meeting of the book club at her house tomorrow morning.'

'More like they wanna find out what's going on,' Noakes muttered.

'You're probably right, sarge,' his colleague said pacifically. 'I got the impression she was fishing for info.'

Doyle appeared in time to hear this last exchange.

'Bit insensitive, isn't it?' he said. 'Starting up the book club again when three of the group have snuffed it—'

'And most likely one of them's the killer,' Noakes finished.

'Lockyer said it's "what the deceased would have wanted".' Burton air-quoted with a grimace. 'I think she was trying to say it was kind of a *memorial*.'

Before Noakes could say where Judith Lockyer could stick her 'memorial', Markham observed, 'It might be useful. We'd get to see them all together—'

'In their natural habitat,' Doyle grinned.

'Precisely, Constable.'

The DI turned to Burton.

'Get back to Ms Lockyer please, Kate, and tell her we'll be there.'

'Will do, guv. She said the meeting usually starts around half past ten.'

'Just in time for elevenses, sarge,' Doyle said mischievously.

'Huh. With that one we'll be lucky to get owt decent . . . You can tell jus' by looking at her it's cottage cheese and crappy rice cakes all the way.'

Burton frowned and Doyle bit his lip to stop himself laughing.

'*Sir.*'

Markham looked across the office to see DS Giggs signalling to him.

'What is it, Sergeant?'

'A visitor's on her way up, sir. Mrs Rosemary Kernan. The desk sergeant said she's got an appointment.'

He felt his heart sink.

'D'you want me to get rid of her, sir?'

'No, that's alright, Giggs. Best get it over with.'

The other flashed a sympathetic thumbs up.

'I'll tell 'em to send her up.'

'Fuck. I'd forgotten about her,' Noakes groused. 'Mind you' — he looked meaningfully at Markham tapping the side of his nose — 'she *might* be useful.'

Burton watched this dumbshow in some bafflement but didn't pass comment.

Once we're finished with Kernan, I need to get Kate looking at the rapes, the DI thought. *Should be able to sell it to her as a pre-emptive strike in case Sidney wants a trawl of all local deviants.*

In the meantime . . .

'Let's see what Mrs Kernan has to say,' he said wearily, ushering the team towards his office.

* * *

An hour later, the four detectives huddled around Markham's desk.

'*Phew!*'

'*Phew* indeed, Kate.'

'So Kernan *did* have a barney with Domingo!' Noakes exclaimed.

'*Dominguez*,' Burton corrected automatically, but there was no energy in the rebuke.

'Sounds like he really got on his soapbox with her,' Doyle observed.

Markham's face was closed, shuttered, as though he had retreated somewhere deep inside himself.

'*So*,' he exhaled heavily as the team regarded him expectantly. 'Mr Dominguez challenged Mrs Kernan about the cover-up of her husband's . . . impropriety.'

'He felt strongly about child abuse,' Burton said, watching her boss closely.

Noakes caught the look.

Time to deflect attention away from the guv'nor.

'Kernan were pretty keen to dob Gallagher in,' he said. 'Who'd a thought the likes of *him* would turn out to be a perv?'

'"Perv" is putting it a bit strong, Sergeant.' The DI was back with them. 'Bernard Gallagher faced an investigation, yes — into allegations of overfamiliarity with certain male students. But he was eventually cleared of all complaints.'

'Only cos they all closed ranks an' shut the thing down.' Noakes's tone was derisive.

'Could Gallagher have killed Dominguez and the other two?' Doyle asked bluntly.

'Yes, given that the element of surprise was on the killer's side.' Markham's voice was bleak.

He locked eyes with Noakes.

But what about the rapes?

Kate Burton saw them exchange glances and her insides constricted.

What is it? What are they sharing that I don't know about?

The DI got up from his desk and walked across to the window.

Late afternoon.

Normally he loved this time of day, when the boundary between earth and sky dissolved, when the colours gently leached out of the landscape with the fading of the light . . . leaving a sepia montage.

But not today.

Not when time was running out and they were up against one, maybe two, killers on the loose.

'I'll see you here tomorrow morning — nine a.m. sharp,' he told the team. 'We'll discuss strategy' — including a strategy to keep Sidney at bay — 'and then go to Judith Lockyer's for this book-club meeting.'

'Will we be doing a press conference, sir?'

‘Looks like it, Kate. But that’ll be Monday, so let’s see what the weekend brings.’

* * *

After the team had gone, Markham sat staring at paperwork until it seemed the letters were dancing diabolically on the page.

Time to go home.

Time to walk out into the darkening air, wondering fearfully what the next day would bring.

10. HAMMER BLOW

Saturday, 28 March dawned fine and clear, and Markham felt his spirits lift.

Contemplating the pale, perfect morning from the bay window of his study, he looked out across the neighbouring cemetery.

Sometimes he felt as though he was destined to drag murdered corpses behind him until the end of his days. At other times, he had a sense of things being more hopeful — that he might perhaps lay down his pain and sadness in the safe, consecrated space of the cemetery and then walk on, trusting to a better future and the prospect of stopping a murderer in his tracks.

Perhaps this morning would be the turning point. When they saw the suspects in — what had Doyle called it? — their natural habitat?

Sipping hot, unsweetened black coffee, his thoughts moved to Natalie Noakes.

An interview with Lindsay Hollis had been provisionally arranged for Monday afternoon when Mrs Noakes would accompany her daughter to the station's rape suite.

'Muriel's feeling pretty paranoid about it all,' Markham had told Olivia, who was shocked to learn of Natalie's ordeal. 'Worrying whether anyone will see them and "draw conclusions".'

'Poor woman.' Olivia's compassion was genuine. 'I'd say she has a shrewder idea than Noakes about Natalie's love life . . . but she clings to that fiction of her being innocent and inexperienced.'

'Most likely because she's always been terrified of Natalie repeating her own mistakes — having a child with completely the wrong man.'

'If Muriel's lurking in the background, won't that put Natalie off?'

'DS Hollis knows the score. She's arranging for a regression therapist to come in. It'll only work if Natalie's defences are totally down, so no relatives allowed.'

'Muriel won't like it.'

He sighed. 'Lashings of tact should help . . . and Hollis is good at that. She'll find a way of distracting her.'

'Poor Muriel,' Olivia repeated. 'There's no genteel gloss you can put on rape . . . It's definitely not The Done Thing. But underneath all that provincial snobbery and her obsession with twitching lace curtains, she's tough as old boots.'

'Talking about twitching lace curtains, Judith Lockyer's invited us to a meeting of Grasmere Park's book club this morning.'

Olivia stared at him.

'Isn't that a bit soon?' Her response was an echo of Doyle's. 'I mean, right after Mr Worthington being found like that.' Her face spasmed. 'Do they know he was murdered?'

'Oh, the *Gazette*'s intrepid hacks and CID's "deep throat" took care of that.' His voice dripped with chilly disdain. 'Everyone knows alright, though thankfully no one had the bad taste to accost me about it at Michael Dominguez's requiem. It'll be the same old story on alibis,' he continued wearily. 'The vicar died early in the morning, so everyone was no doubt virtuously employed having breakfast or pottering about, setting off for work or whatever.'

'They probably want to pick your brains.'

'More than likely. Kate said Lockyer was clearly on a fishing expedition, though she tried to dress it up as something more noble — a commemoration of Dominguez.'

Olivia laughed. 'If it's some kind of twee poetry recital, how will you keep George muzzled? You know what he's like about all things "arty farty".'

'Don't I just!' He grinned. 'On the other hand, it might be useful to have him cut through all the posturing — shock them into some kind of honesty.' His expression turned suddenly sober. 'One or more of them's a killer, Liv, so we've got to get through their defences.'

'Well, good luck detonating the H-bomb. If anyone can get under their skin, it's George!'

* * *

'Must be doing alright with them bodice-rippers,' Noakes observed an hour later as he and Markham stood outside Judith Lockyer's detached period lodge. 'Much better'n the poor old padre's gaff.'

It certainly was, the DI thought, taking in the one-storey, compact but beautifully maintained property.

With its pediment and pilastered porch, the white-rendered frontage gave the residence a classical air that was somehow perfectly in keeping with the properties on either side: a former coach house and a Queen Anne cottage.

Yes, Grasmere Park might be an architectural hotchpotch, but there was no denying its picturesque charm. And he had no doubt that the interior of the lodge would be every bit as high spec as that of Michael Dominguez's house.

'I seem to recall Ms Lockyer mentioning that she inherited this place from her parents,' Markham murmured, keen eyes raking the leafy side road that led down to the river.

'She landed on her feet alright,' Noakes grunted but with less rancour than might have been expected.

Telling me about Natalie lanced a boil, Markham thought, his heart lifting as he took in his colleague's appearance, which was far more chipper than on the previous day. Noakes had even made some sort of attempt at colour-coordination. Today, his fawn sweater and dark cords seemed infinitely less jarring than the usual bilious combinations that he inflicted on the general public. His tie, sober and respectable, was neatly knotted, and his haystack hair brushed into submission. Altogether, the omens were promising.

Kate Burton's Corsa drew up, closely followed by Doyle's Skoda.

'Nice place,' the DC said in an appraising tone. 'No need to worry about noisy neighbours out here.' There was a wistful inflection in his voice as he thought of his own housing association flat in Medway; a canny first step on the property ladder but a long way from his dream home.

Noakes winked at him. 'You jus' wait, ginger. With that law degree, you'll be a chief super in no time with a luxury pad an' all the trappings.'

'Cheers, sarge.' The youngster looked pleased at Noakesy's vote of confidence. With a becoming show of modesty, he gestured to Burton. 'I reckon someone else might beat me to it.'

Markham smiled at these courtesies.

'C'mon,' he laughed. 'Let's agree I've got a crack team and turn our attention to the suspects in there.'

'What're they meant to be doing anyway?' Suspicion crept into Noakes's voice as though he very much feared an outbreak of joss sticks and other bohemian paraphernalia.

'Relax, sarge,' Burton reassured him. 'It'll just be some speechifying about the late lamented. One of them'll read a poem or some such . . . talk about Dominguez's contribution to the community, that kind of thing. Only someone in there won't mean a word of it,' she finished trenchantly.

Although it was a mild day, she shivered. Grasmere Park was infected with an insidious virus in the form of someone posing as a good citizen . . . Or maybe, if Dimples was right, they were up against a malign tag team that would always be two steps ahead of them.

Burton wondered what lay behind the DI's request for her to review the rape files. He had looked oddly intense when he handed her the assignment, asking her to be discreet about it. There was something he wasn't telling her . . . and she was pretty certain Noakes knew what it was.

Another secret shared between the DI and his wingman — from which she'd been excluded. Her sense of injustice flared up along with a hard, bitter feeling . . .

But then she saw the DI's absorbed expression and reproached herself.

They were a *team* and it was for Markham to allocate their roles. She knew he trusted her and in the final analysis *that* was what mattered, not who got the lion's share of his attention.

'We just watch and listen.' The DI's instructions snapped her back to reality. 'Check their body language . . . Who seems unusually tense . . . ? Who looks ill at ease . . . ? Who—'

'Looks like they spent yesterday morning finishing off the vicar,' put in Noakes.

'Would that it were so simple, Sergeant.' Markham shot him the kind of look Burton hoped never to receive from him, but her colleague was unabashed.

'This one's a cunning bastard,' Noakes declared. *In more ways than one if they turned out to be a sex attacker*. 'They'll be ready for us.'

'If Dimples is right and we're looking for a partnership, maybe the relationship between them has come under strain,' Burton said uncertainly. 'I mean, *three murders* . . .'

'Yeah.' Doyle liked the idea. 'Or maybe one of 'em's gone rogue . . . doing their own thing with the other panicking cos they've lost control of the script.'

The DI could see they were thinking outside the box. And he approved.

'We've got to be open to all possibilities.'

'Kernan looked pretty stressed yesterday,' Noakes pointed out. 'And she was defo keen to put us onto Gallagher.'

'Hmmm.' Markham's eyes followed the line of the low wall that enclosed the secluded gardens of Judith Lockyer's house. He was willing to bet their little conclave was being observed from somewhere inside. 'I'm certain our killer belongs to this book club,' he said gravely. Turning to Burton, he enquired, 'Did you manage to trace the whereabouts of Derek Worthington's accusers from that abortive court case, Kate?'

'Yes, sir. They're in the clear for yesterday . . . Nowhere near here and witnesses to vouch for them.'

'And nothing significant from the railway volunteers?'

'Nothing, sir,' Doyle told him. 'Actually, they're a really nice crowd . . . mostly OAPs with a sprinkling of young ones. Not much in common 'cept for being star-struck about steam engines.'

'Whereas with the book-club crowd there's an *edge*,' Markham said. 'Fenella Staunton resented Mr Dominguez's rejection—'

'Plus, there was the plagiarism — pinching her ideas,' Burton explained for the benefit of Noakes.

'Same with Gallagher — some sort of rivalry or touchiness.' This was Doyle.

'An' mebbe Gallagher an' Boughton were cruising the gay scene like Domingo, if what the ex-boyfriend says is right.' Trust Noakes to zero in on the homosexual angle. 'Could've been either of them who was the stalker — the Queen of Mean or whatever he was called.'

'Queen of the Night,' Markham amended, thinking of Olivia's suggestion that Michael Dominguez might, in fact, have been referring to a woman.

'Then we've got Susan Caldicott saying Dominguez had no business dishing out relationship advice,' Doyle ruminated. 'Something a bit off there . . . and she was jealous of his money.'

'Boughton resented him too . . . blamed Domingo for spoiling his chances of being a JP.' Noakes's mind was running on Muriel's thwarted ambitions in that direction.

'Judith Lockyer hated Dominguez putting her down,' Burton said. 'Hated the way he made her seem like a second-rater with her romantic fiction, whereas he was the real thing: a bona fide *author*.'

Markham's temples were beginning to throb, his earlier optimism evaporating fast.

But once started, Kate Burton was remorseless.

'The Wynnes were fed up of him too,' she said. 'Not the easiest neighbour in the world and always expecting them to sort out his domestic stuff — even though Nerys has a bunch of health issues.'

'Yes, he wasn't a particularly considerate individual,' the DI agreed. 'And he had a mischievous streak. That quicksilver wit of his could be cruel.'

But where did the rapes fit in? Had Michael Dominguez discovered the identity of the perpetrator and been silenced for that knowledge? Or was this all just pure coincidence — two predators each with their own hideous agenda?

Suddenly his earlier conviction that there was a connection between these murders and the sexual assaults seemed insubstantial and flimsy, dissolving into thin air. Just like when he tried to read late at night and the words grew dim, skating and sliding across the page into a river of ink . . . until at last he felt as though he had slipped the limits of himself . . .

Books, books, always books. It all came back to this infernal book club.

He became aware that Doyle was looking at him curiously.

'Better get in there,' he announced, attempting to speak lightly, though the splitting headache he'd been dreading had already begun.

'Lockyer's prob'ly hiding behind the curtains trying to lip-read,' Noakes said sardonically. 'Can't wait to grill us like as not.'

* * *

But when Judith Lockyer opened the door to them, the expression on her face immediately alerted Markham to the fact that something was wrong.

'What is it, Ms Lockyer?' he asked as they stood in her elegant hallway with its primrose-coloured walls, thin-legged chairs and tables, and deep-pile cream carpet. *Not very practical for hoovering,* Burton found herself thinking before giving herself a mental shake for such shallowness.

'Fenella's late,' Lockyer replied.

''S only quarter to eleven, luv.' Noakes put out a steadying hand. 'Or d'you go by the book?'

He was rather pleased with himself for this pun.

'No, you don't understand. She's never ever late. Has a real thing about it being bad manners. If anything, she turns up half an hour early for everything.' The inflection of these words suggested she regarded her neighbour's hyper-punctuality as something of a mixed blessing.

'Have you tried her mobile?' Burton snapped into efficient mode.

'It's switched off.'

'Mebbe she jus' wanted time out or summat,' Noakes suggested.

As in, a bleeding break from you lot.

Hearing a murmur of voices from the neighbouring room, Markham beckoned the woman outside.

Standing in the forecourt, he smelled the sharp scent of a rosemary bush.

Rosemary, that's for remembrance.

'Where might Mrs Staunton go if she wanted to be on her own? Does she have a favourite place? A walk perhaps?'

'Bromgrove Rise is her usual haunt,' Judith Lockyer replied promptly. 'She likes tramping around the woods early in the morning . . . Says it helps her get things in perspective.'

Imperceptibly, the DI gestured to Burton who moved away down the drive, reaching for her mobile.

'Ms Lockyer, I want you to leave this with us now. Go on with your meeting while we try to locate Mrs Staunton.'

His voice sounded rusty and grating even to his own ears, as though he was trying to turn the key on a fearful truth.

She backed away from him towards the house, chewing the end of her grey plait in a way that had Noakes casting his eyes to heaven.

Once the front door was closed on them, the team regrouped at the bottom of the drive.

Burton put away her phone, grim-faced.

'They've found Fenella Staunton, guv.'

'Where?'

'The woods. Lockyer was spot on.'

'What condition was she in?'

'Strung up from a tree.' Burton swallowed hard. 'Dog walkers called it in. Looks like she's been sexually assaulted.'

This confirmation of his fears knocked Markham backwards. Later, he would remember that the sound of birdsong in Grasmere Park seemed suddenly to stop with his sergeant's announcement.

* * *

There was something surreal about the afternoon's proceedings.

As the DI watched Fenella Staunton's body being cut down by the paramedics, his mind wandered to St Barnabas's church where he'd glimpsed images of another twisted figure tied to a tree, bleeding from his head, hands and heart . . .

'She wasn't battered or tortured. Death due to cerebral hypoxia.'

Dimples Davidson was there with his bag, coordinating preparations for removal of the body.

'But there was an assault, yes?'

'Unconsummated by the looks of it. Her clothing was disturbed.' The pathologist's eyes travelled over the surrounding foliage, speckled with bluebells and dog violets. 'Wasn't this where—'

'Yeah.' Noakes too was looking about him with an expression of superstitious apprehension. 'It's the place the Newman Hospital murders kicked off. Right here.'

Davidson regarded the two men narrowly as if debating with himself whether to produce his hip flask. But the uptight female sergeant and gangling constable were hovering in the background, so he decided against it.

'When did it happen, doc?' Noakes asked, his wistful look suggesting a nip of something wouldn't have gone amiss.

'Sometime early this morning.'

The doctor snapped his fingers at the two paramedics who promptly zipped the dead woman into a waiting body bag, giving Markham no chance to linger on the contorted purple features, unnaturally elongated neck and lolling tongue. Another signal from Davidson and they carried the stretcher towards the gravel path that bordered the woods.

Again, that unnatural silence — as though all the birds had been shot out of the sky.

Above them clouds flapped like monstrous winding sheets.

The air had turned damp and cottony, as though the banks of catkins had conspired to bring down a perfect storm of pollen on the intruders. Kate Burton's eyes and nose were now streaming uncontrollably.

'Let's get outa here.' Noakes regarded his colleague sympathetically, reflecting that she looked all of twelve years old as she mopped away desperately at her runny nose and bleary eyes.

'C'mon, sarge.' Doyle took her arm. 'Let me give you a hand . . . easy to twist an ankle if you can't see where you're going.'

Noakes moved up on her other side ever so casually, as if hardly aware of what he was doing. Even so, Markham could see him watching carefully to ensure his colleague didn't come a cropper on any protruding tree roots.

The DI and Davidson watched them wend their way up the overgrown slope.

'The age of chivalry is not dead,' Dimples observed with an indulgent chuckle. Then he asked more seriously, 'Everything alright with Noakes? He was looking a bit green about the gills back there.'

'Double whammy what with it coming so soon after the vicar.'

The DI was glad his wingman was safely out of earshot.

'Can you get me the specifics asap, Dimples?' he said urgently. 'I want to know if this was an abortive rape.'

'Whatever this was, it was done with considerable rage,' the medic replied. 'The victim was a well-built woman. And it seems like at some point she fought back . . . defensive bruising on her forearms.' He looked round and shivered. 'I've always thought this was a desolate spot. Not like on the hilltop where there's all that wavy heather and sand. Up there's grand for clearing the head. But these rank little thickets and copses . . .' He shook his head. 'Just the place for someone to jump out at you.' A glance at the tree where Fenella Staunton had been found swinging. 'She was wearing walking shoes, so it looks like she was planning on a ramble and then . . . someone caught up with her . . .'

'One person or two?'

A shrewd glance from under Dimples' beetling eyebrows.

'Could've been just the one. Force the woman's head through the noose . . . loop the end of the rope over that branch and then pull hard on the running knot or what have you . . . all over in minutes.'

Minutes.

'So a single person could have done this?'

'Yes. If your vic was stunned or threatened with a weapon — maybe a knife — to ensure her compliance, that'd make it easier. We found a bump on the back of her head, so I figure she took quite a knock. By the time she recovered her balance, it would have been too late to fight him off.'

'*Him* . . . so you're ruling out a female killer this time?'

Davidson thought for a moment. 'Not impossible, but I'd be more inclined to say a male — or possibly two assailants working as a team.'

Markham's eyes fixed on the dark undergrowth.

The pathologist followed his gaze. 'You're off the beaten track here.' His tone darkened. 'Nice and private. If this was her usual walk, then someone who knew her movements could have followed and "accidentally" bumped into her.'

'Accidentally on purpose.'

'Yes. And then once the trap was baited and she was lulled into a false sense of security—'

'The other one joined the party.' Markham's face was grim as he visualized the ambush.

The DI was clearly taking this death hard.

'Who was she?' Davidson asked gently.

'Fenella Staunton. Retired academic from the university.' Markham took a deep breath. 'Michael Dominguez's neighbour and a member of his book club to boot.'

The other whistled.

'Any connection between the Bromgrove Rapist and your Grasmere killer then, Markham?'

The DI looked up at the darkening sky.

'I have reason to think there could be, yes.'

'Reckon Sidney'll buy it?'

'I think you can guess the answer to that one, Doug!'

The other gave a mirthless chuckle.

'Grasmere Park's very own serial killer with a sideline in sexual assault — good luck with that!'

'Well, there's a press conference on Monday to look forward to. You're welcome to attend if you like blood sports.'

Davidson slapped him on the back.

'Think I'll pass, Inspector,' he said as fat drops of rain began to fall. 'I'll get back to you about the assault before then.'

White-suited SOCOs with arc lights and crime-scene tape had begun to descend on the scene like giant ghostly moths.

Side by side, the two men made their way back towards their cars.

* * *

Two paracetamol and two cups of coffee later, Markham was beginning to feel marginally more human.

Kate Burton had provided the medication. 'Like a mobile pharmacy that one,' Noakes commented, but it was clear Burton herself needed dosing with something.

'I've taken some Piriton for the hay fever,' she said somewhat defensively, clearly embarrassed by her swollen face and inflamed eyes.

'Have a swig of tea?' Noakes offered, proffering a manky-looking plastic cup.

Somehow she managed not to shudder.

''S alright, sarge.' She smiled weakly. 'I'll only be peeing all afternoon.'

It was all downhill after a certain age, her grizzled colleague reflected gloomily.

'Right,' said the DI. 'If we're finished comparing ailments, how about we apply ourselves to the murder of Fenella Staunton?'

It was a hammer blow and no mistake. The *fourth* murder in the investigation and not a single suspect to bless themselves with.

'Just as you thought, they all had their explanations off pat, boss,' said Doyle who had been deputed to return to Grasmere Park and check the residents' alibis for that morning. 'Taking a lie-in; having a late breakfast; organ practice — that's Boughton. Pottering in the garden and DIY — the Wynnes. Messing about on Google . . . Take your pick.' He sounded thoroughly exasperated. 'And all of 'em doing the shock-horror routine when I broke the news about Mrs Staunton.'

'I'd pegged Staunton for the other murders, y'know,' Noakes said. 'That snooty Cruella de Vil look of hers . . . You could tell she were a good hater. An' *now* . . .'

Back to bleeding square one.

Outside, there was the faint roll of thunder and the station gutters began to gurgle and drip.

Swollen clouds scudded relentlessly above the town centre, shafts of light criss-crossing between them in the eerie eye of the storm.

Markham's mobile trilled.

Three faces watched attentively as he took the call.

'That was Mr McLeod,' he said. 'An unexpected development in one of the cold cases.'

'*Don' tell me*,' Noakes guffawed. 'Timothy Appleyard's missus has turned up at last.'

Then, watching Markham's face, '*Jesus*,' he whispered. 'She *has* . . .'

'Some bones have been found at the heritage railway station.'

Burton was the first to find her voice.

'Whereabouts, guv?'

'Tangled among some cabling under the main signal box.'

Doyle looked poleaxed. 'What put them onto it?'

'Apparently there was an anonymous tip-off.'

'After all these years.' Noakes looked round at them. 'She ended up stuck down some pipe . . . That's *sick*.'

'Dominguez must have known about it, sir.' Burton's hay fever was forgotten now. 'It had to have been him who helped Appleyard.'

'I think that's the most likely scenario, yes.' The DI was impassive.

'But how'd she end up . . . well, in *bits*?' Doyle was very pale. 'Did Appleyard *dismember* her? Or did he stash her somewhere and wait till she was a skeleton before getting Dominguez to do a Burke and Hare number with him?'

'Grave robbers,' Burton murmured to Noakes by way of explanation.

Her fellow DS looked as though he regretted having returned to CID by way of Greggs.

'And why would Dominguez agree to cover for him?' Doyle was utterly bewildered.

'After so many years, I'm not sure we'll ever know, Constable.' Markham smiled wearily. 'But *there's* the secret that Dominguez was holding over Timothy Appleyard — the one we thought might have made Appleyard finally snap and batter Dominguez to death.'

‘Only it weren’t him.’ Something about Noakes’s tone suggested regret at having to pass up such a neat solution — one they could have gift-wrapped for that bastard Sidney with a ruddy great bow plonked on top.

‘There must be someone else out there who knows what happened,’ Doyle said.

‘Yes, whoever called in with the tip-off,’ Burton concurred.

The DI regarded them steadily.

‘We can’t allow ourselves to be distracted by this,’ he said. ‘I’m going to see Mr McLeod tomorrow, but we’ve the press conference on Monday to get through.’

‘Will there be an announcement about the . . . bones, sir?’ Doyle sounded hopeful. ‘It’d give the *Gazette* lot *something* at any rate.’

‘Have a word with Barry Lynch, Kate.’ The DI knew she regarded the oleaginous press officer with about as much enthusiasm as root-canal work, but it couldn’t be helped. ‘See if he can drum something up: “several promising lines of enquiry including a tragic cold case . . . no details released at this stage out of respect for relatives, blah blah.”’ He sighed. ‘Lots of flimflam about the history of Grasmere Park and the eminence of its residents down the years. And you can bung in the usual about random violence being the price of a divided society — alienation, lack of respect for authority, drugs . . .’

The DI felt slightly sickened by his own glibness.

‘Class warfare, sir?’

‘Yes, with the emphasis firmly on the *righteousness* of the deceased —contributors to society, givers rather than takers, supporters of the cultural edifice . . .’

‘And defo nowt about queers an’ stalkers or randy Revs going off the rails.’

Burton looked pained at Noakes’s interjection while Doyle merely grinned.

‘Think you can do it, Kate?’

‘Absolutely, sir. Distraction tactics.’ *Along with fending off octopus-mitts Lynch.*

‘Talking of randy Revs, there’s some sort of memorial service for Worthington on Monday afternoon in St Barnabas’s.’

Noakes scowled at the young DC.

‘*Chuffing Nora, not another one*.’

‘Not a funeral, sarge.’ Doyle was soothing. ‘Nothing fancy. Just a few prayers from the vicar at St Austin’s. The two parishes are doubling up, so he probably thinks it’d look bad not to say *something*.’

‘Right, that’s enough for now,’ Markham said decisively as the rain began to lash down. ‘Let’s review everything we’ve got first thing on Monday before the press conference. Witness statements, notes about all of Grasmere’s residents — everything.’

* * *

After his colleagues had trooped off to enjoy the rest of their weekend, the DI sat in his darkening office for a long time with the lights switched off. As he listened to the downpour, the rain seemed to hiss, *You’re running out of time*.

11. A GLIMMER OF LIGHT

Sunday was uneventful, though Markham spent several hours in his study reviewing paperwork from the case.

Dimples Davidson telephoned as requested to discuss Fenella Staunton.

'There was some kind of attempted sex act, Markham.'

'Attempted?'

'As in the type which doesn't yield biological evidence.' The pathologist was not his usual calm and collected self. 'It's likely a foreign object was involved. A log or branch, something like that . . . SOCOs didn't turn it up when they searched the woodland.'

'Was this pre- or post-mortem, doc?'

'Pre-, I'm sorry to say.'

So she *had* been tortured after all. It was just that her wounds were invisible.

'I've emailed you a report, Markham. It's all in there.' Davidson cleared his throat. 'I didn't want any of your lot with me for this one. Figured they needed a break from the grisly stuff.'

He meant Kate Burton, Markham thought with a sudden rush of affection for the curmudgeonly medic who operated according to his own idiosyncratic code of chivalry.

After the call, he sat thinking for a long time.

Unnatural sex with a foreign object.

Hinky sex.

Did this point to a woman being involved?

Did it mean their book-club killer was also the Bromgrove Rapist?

He said a swift prayer for Fenella Staunton, falling back on the familiar cadences of his Catholic boyhood.

How gut-wrenching to recall her declamation from Lamentations at Michael Dominguez's requiem on Friday. She had been unaware then that she was reading the last rites for herself as well.

My soul is shut out from peace; I have forgotten happiness.

Despite religious orthodoxy, thoughts of a more pagan complexion invaded his thoughts . . . Charon the ferryman — that sordid god — taking Fenella Staunton across the Styx to the land of the dead.

Would she be greeted there by Michael Dominguez, Timothy Appleyard and Derek Worthington? Would she hail them with grateful recognition or ignore them with characteristic regal disdain? Would she curse Dominguez for setting in motion the chain of events that had condemned her to torture and a gruesome untimely death?

Olivia crept into the room as he sat there contemplating the pillowy banks of cloud which raced above the cemetery as though they would outpace death itself.

'Tea and Hobnobs,' she pronounced, setting down a tray at his elbow.

Then, she curled up in a neighbouring swivel chair, which her boyfriend had imported for her comfort. 'Don't torment yourself, Gil,' she said softly. 'No way you could have seen this coming.'

'Mrs Staunton had taken over the hot spot as Noakesy's favourite suspect,' he said sadly.

'I can't imagine George taking a shine to her. Not with her condescending manner.'

'He called her Cruella de Vil.'

'Ah.' A smile tugged the corners of Olivia's mouth. 'He has a gift for summing folk up.'

No way was Markham going to share the full details of Fenella Staunton's death with Olivia. *No way.*

Her smile faltered, grew uncertain. 'Gil . . .'

'It's alright, sweetheart. The best I can do for that poor woman now is to nail the unspeakable bastard who left her like that.'

'D'you have any leads?'

He sighed. 'All the alibis seem watertight. Superficially, anyway. No sign of anyone slipping out of the Park to waylay Mrs Staunton in those woods.'

'How about that MP woman?'

'Her PA's been calling in her whereabouts. She clocked in with Kate on Saturday morning to say Mrs Kernan was at home tucking into a full English.'

'And was she?'

'God knows.' His tone was flat. 'For all I know, she was up there in the woods waiting for Fenella Staunton.'

'C'mon, Gil. Have a biscuit . . . Otherwise I'll end up scoffing the lot.' She groaned theatrically. 'Another diet bites the dust!'

Markham regarded his girlfriend affectionately. Fresh from a brisk windswept walk on Bromgrove Rise, copper hair whipped into a wild tangle, she was flushed with exhilaration and energy. He had considered asking her not to go up there but, on reflection, decided against it . . . as though her presence might somehow cancel out — *exorcize* — that other walk which had ended in torture and death.

'You've earned a pig-out after that hike,' he laughed. 'I'm just sorry I couldn't come with you, my love.'

'That's alright, Gil. I know how it is.'

Living with the ghosts of all those he couldn't save.

What was it Princess Di had said? 'There were three of us in the marriage, so it was a bit crowded.' How about a shadowy host forever lurking on the margins of your life . . . eternally present rivals you could never shake off?

Where are you? she asked him in silent colloquy.

Half in love with easeful death, came the answer.

Aloud, she said, 'Maybe the press conference tomorrow will turn up something.'

'I'm not counting on it, Liv. Our best bet is distracting the *Gazette*'s slavering newshounds with that find at the railway.'

'Did you get an ID on . . . the bones?'

'It's Appleyard's wife alright. In the circumstances, we put a rush on the DNA testing, and it came back positive.'

'How horrible.' Olivia spun round on the swivel chair a few times before coming to rest, in a childlike reflex that made Markham smile.

'Are you going to tell them you've found Mrs Appleyard, Gil?'

'Not in so many words. Sidney'll go into orbit if we let Grasmere Park become a scandal-fest, so it's more a case of a nod and a wink . . . While Gavin Conors and Co go haring off to research "bygone tragedies", it should give us a chance to regroup.'

Her forehead puckered.

'D'you think whoever killed Mrs Staunton attacked Natalie?'

Keep it light, he told himself, *keep it light.* He couldn't even bear to contemplate explaining to Liv about 'attempted sex' and 'foreign objects'.

'They're bound to ask about that — if the Grasmere Park murders are related to the rapes,' he said.

A voice inside told him there was a link . . . a voice that spoke the truth, whatever Sidney said to the contrary.

'Kate's aiming for vague,' he added.

'Ah, I see. *Operation Throw Sand in Their Eyes*.'

He grinned. 'Well, Kate's a virtuoso at that.'

'What else have you got lined up?'

'There's a memorial prayer service or something along those lines for Derek Worthington tomorrow afternoon.'

'Sorry I can't come with you, sweetheart. Double lower sixth on the beauties of John Donne.'

Death, be not proud, though some have called thee
Mighty and dreadful, for thou art not so . . .

Fenella Staunton was proud if ever a woman was. But death had triumphed over her.

With an effort, Markham recalled himself to the present.

'No worries, Liv. It's only a prayer service anyway. The funeral's some way off.'

'Anglicans not so good at pulling strings as Monseigneur Slimy?'

'More likely the diocese doesn't want those allegations of impropriety against Worthington being raked over,' he said drily.

'From what you say, Mr Worthington was a good man, Gil. How awful that he should be judged by something that happened way back in the past.'

Privately, Markham vowed that, although Derek Worthington's tomb might remain unacknowledged by the world at large, it would not be unvisited by *him*. An answering flash from Olivia's eyes told him that she shared his feelings.

The clouds had ceased their restless pursuit and a vitreous half-light bathed the cemetery's graves and monuments.

'C'mon, darling,' Olivia coaxed. 'Time to take a break.' She smiled winningly. 'As you said, there's nobody so good as Kate when it comes to the gentle art of bluff. You can count on her to buy you some time.' She glided to Markham's side, a gentle hand on his arm. 'And who knows, perhaps tomorrow will give you the break you need.'

'Right, Liv. What'll it be then? *Line of Duty* or *Unforgotten*?'

'Neither,' she riposted firmly. 'Tonight, it's *The Chase*.'

Markham raised his eyebrows at this reference to the fiendishly competitive game show.

'Just in case you're ever tempted to forget you hitched your star to a right smart cookie.'

The exchange terminated in a burst of laughter.

Meanwhile, the cemetery's ghostly cohorts watched and waited in their mounds for Judgement Day.

* * *

'You played a blinder back there, luv. Proper devious,' Noakes told Kate Burton admiringly after the press conference on Monday. 'An' all that twaddle 'bout Grasmere being a conservation area an' full of historic buildings were brilliant — got their minds running on slebs rather than pervs. You could tell Sidney liked it.'

His fellow DS told herself helplessly that there was a compliment in there somewhere.

'Well, I thought if we could distract them with human-interest stuff and unsolved crimes from the past, then maybe they'd stop asking questions about a connection between the book-club murders and these rapes.'

'Seems you pulled it off, Kate. Or, as Barry Lynch would say, "it looks like we got away with it."' Markham's dark eyes gleamed with amusement as he cited Call Me Bazza's catchphrase, the station press officer having a reputation for getting unnecessarily up close and personal with female officers.

'Where'd you dig up that stuff about there being a railway ghost, sarge?' Doyle asked curiously.

'Oh, there are always tales about railway stations being haunted,' she grinned. 'Especially the old-fashioned narrow-gauge ones.'

Noakes leaned in. 'You mean you made it up? Even the bit about the dog?'

'Oh, I cobbled stuff together from the internet. All these places have Beast of Bodmin or *Hound of the Baskervilles*-type stories. Pulls in the tourists, see?'

'Like I said, *devious*.' Noakes's approval was unfeigned. 'Gavin Conors is prob'ly hoping for a story about some sicko feeding body parts to Rover.' He guffawed. 'Puts a whole new spin on Pedigree Chum.'

'God, d'you think so?' his colleague said weakly. 'I only meant to put them off the scent.'

'Don' worry, luv.' Noakes gestured expansively. 'You know what Conors is like. He'll jus' make it up anyway.'

'Never lets the truth get in the way of a good story,' Doyle agreed grimly.

'The thing is, as a diversionary tactic, it did the trick.' The DI's relief was plain. 'The DCI wants us to keep a lid on those remains being Mrs Appleyard's.'

'Good luck with that,' Noakes muttered. 'Sidney knows this place leaks like a freaking sieve.'

'He also wants us to leave Rosemary Kernan well alone.'

The DI's face darkened as he recalled the 'free and frank exchange of views' between himself and the DCI on that subject.

'She's a bleeding suspect like the rest of 'em.' Noakes looked thunderous. 'An' Sidney more'n likely covered for her perv of a husband.'

'There's no doubt her tentacles reach well beyond that constituency office,' Markham said flatly. 'For the moment we keep unofficial tabs via her PA.'

'Kernan's at the town hall this morning,' Burton said. 'I checked.'

'Good. And they should all be going along to St Barnabas's for the prayer service this afternoon.' Markham steepled his fingers in characteristic meditative pose. 'All of them in one place.'

'Un-get-at-able,' Doyle said with quiet satisfaction.

'All of them bar one,' Burton pointed out.

The DI frowned. 'Oh, who's that?'

'I had a call from Susan Caldicott this morning,' she said. 'Apparently Nerys Wynne had a fall on Sunday—'

'You could tell she weren't steady on her pins. Thass why the son kept having heart attacks,' Noakes observed sagely. Then, struck by a happy thought, '*Hey* — why don' I granny-sit while you lot do the praying bit?'

Kate Burton's pained expression at this made it look, DC Doyle said afterwards, as if she had piles.

'Your suggestion wouldn't have anything to do with Mrs Wynne's excellent hospitality, would it, Sergeant?'

'Nah, boss.' The thing about Noakes was he was absolutely brazen. 'She took a bit of a shine to me, that's all.' He endeavoured to look modest without success. 'An' you lot don' mind the caterwauling an' carrying on' — a crafty look came over his face — 'plus the damp in that place ain't good for arthritis.'

'Our hearts bleed, Noakesy,' the DI laughed as Doyle mimed playing a violin. 'Nice try but no dice.'

He'd just eat the poor woman out of house and home while outraging her genteel sensibilities with his own scabrous commentary on all her neighbours.

'I think Kate might be a better bet on this occasion,' Markham continued.

Better bedside manner and no risk of her sounding off about all and sundry.

'In the circumstances Mrs Wynne might prefer a woman,' he said emolliently. 'In case she needs help with the *personal* side of things.'

'Yeah, I s'pose she wouldn't want me going to the bog with her.'

Too right.

'Mrs Caldicott volunteered to stay with Nerys,' Burton said. 'The son's girlfriend offered too. But Nerys wouldn't hear of it. Insisted she'll be fine. I had an aunt like that,' she said reminiscently. 'All stiff upper lip and putting your best foot forward.'

Markham was thoughtful. 'In the circumstances I want eyes on *all* the Grasmere residents,' he said. 'Plus, you might be able to get her to open up, Kate. She struck me as a shrewd judge of character.'

Doyle pursed his lips. 'Not the type you could have a good goss with,' he said. 'Too stiff and starchy for that.'

'Worth a shot,' the DI countered swiftly. 'Because as things stand—'

'We've got sweet FA.'

'You took the words right out of my mouth, Sergeant.'

The DS looked resigned to his fate.

'Cheer up, Noakesy. Kate may get your share of Nerys's barmbrack, but we'll have a chance to observe the rest of the residents at close quarters.'

'Oh aye.' His wingman was clearly underwhelmed by the prospect.

Doyle grinned. 'Maybe Mrs Wynne'll send something home-made over for you, sarge.'

'Don't put ideas into his head,' Burton snapped. 'We can't treat the poor woman like flaming Deliveroo.'

'Wanna bet?' the young DC challenged.

'Enough, Constable. Stop teasing,' Markham admonished. He cast a despairing look at his number two. 'I want you to find something suitable for Noakes to wear.'

'Whass wrong with what I've got on?' came the indignant rumble.

Where to start?

'I don't think an orange jumper and green cords strike quite the right note. And you could do with a decent blazer.' *As opposed to the donkey jacket affair he was sporting*. 'To say nothing of a quieter tie.'

'It's meant to be impressionist wotsit . . . like them ones we saw in the art gallery.'

'Looks more like someone's sneezed on you, sarge.'

Noakes glared at the youngster. 'Cost me a pretty penny that did.'

The DC's expression said *You woz robbed*!

'Sort it out between you,' Markham said in a tone that brooked no argument. 'I'll expect to see you suited and booted at the church, Sergeant.'

'Sidney an' Bretherton ain't gonna be there,' Noakes said mutinously.

'But I want to show Derek Worthington appropriate respect,' the DI said quietly. 'So I won't have you turning up looking like a colour-blind binman.'

Doyle smirked. Just wait till he told the lads what Markham said. They'd serenade Noakes with a chorus of 'My Old Man's a Dustman'. The silly old sod would never live it down!

He became aware of the DI's cool gaze on him.

'Care to share the joke, Constable?'

'Just remembering some of my own style disasters, sir,' he improvised wildly.

'Indeed.'

Time to beat a hasty retreat.

'Okay if sarge and I shoot off now, boss?'

'Certainly. I'd like you to swing by Mr Lynch's office en route please. See where we're up to with the press release.'

That wiped the smile off his face, Burton thought with savage satisfaction as she took in Doyle's crestfallen expression. *Your turn for a dose of Call Me Bazza!*

* * *

The vicar of St Austin's was a barrel-chested little man of around fifty with lively brown eyes.

Markham liked the dignity with which he conducted the short service, personalizing it by including some tributes from parishioners whom Derek Worthington had helped. Even Noakes, clad in a sober grey lounge suit which Doyle had magicked up from somewhere (most likely with help from Chris Carstairs), was impressed.

'I thought it'd be some old fart chuntering on about it being Worthington's time to go an' tears being wiped away.' Clearly the DS rated the Book of Revelation no more highly than Lamentations. 'But fair play to this bloke, he made you feel Worthington weren't bad . . . for a sky pilot.'

'Yeah,' Doyle agreed. 'He was tactful too. Almost made it sound like Worthington was a roaring success as a vicar.'

'In the only sense that really matters, I think he was,' Markham said quietly.

'None of 'em from Grasmere really stood out, though,' Doyle mused. 'Looked a bit zonked, if you ask me.'

'They'll be coming to terms with Fenella Staunton's death,' the DI pointed out. 'And, let's face it, they're not all spring chickens.'

'Nice of Simon Wynne to drag the girlfriend along. I'd say Wynne's punching above his weight,' Doyle sniffed, with a man-of-the-world air which made Markham suppress a smile.

‘She looked a decent lass.’ Noakes too had liked what he saw. ‘Stopped the Lockyer woman keeling over halfway through.’

‘Boughton had to lend Bernard Gallagher an arm,’ Doyle pointed out. ‘Made sure we noticed him doing it.’

The retired principal had looked distinctly papery, Markham reflected. But was it genuine frailty, or was there something overdone in his reliance on Andrew Boughton’s trusty right arm?

‘What happened to Kernan?’ Noakes asked. ‘Seemed like she took a hike halfway through.’

‘Her mobile went off,’ the DI replied. ‘Urgent call from a constituent. I checked with her PA.’

‘An’ then the teacher woman got ants in her pants and buggered off. What was that about?’

‘She had to get back to school, Sergeant. It was kosher.’

‘Lockyer said there were eats at her gaff,’ Noakes said accusingly.

‘I felt we were better off out of it, Noakesy.’

The DI was hard-pressed to say why he had made the team’s excuses and bowed out of the buffet at Judith Lockyer’s.

‘I wanted to get back to the station,’ he said.

Noakes’s piggy eyes regarded him intently.

‘Whatcha waiting for, guv?’

‘Hard to say.’ Markham raked the thick dark locks which somehow never looked as though he had a hair out of place. *Like a freaking tailor’s dummy*, Noakes reflected, entirely without irritation. The guv’nor was no more aware of his effortless style than the sharpest-suited scrote that ran the county lines.

The DI smiled at the two men.

‘I just have this feeling something’s going to break,’ he said simply. ‘That our killer’s luck is about to run out.’

Restlessly, he paced across to his office window and yanked it open a few more centimetres.

A slight breeze stirred the papers on his desk.

It felt almost like a sign.

A tingling electric current started at his feet and seemed to rise to his very fingertips.

This is it, he thought. *This is it.*

A gentle tap at the office door and Kate Burton joined them.

* * *

As soon as he saw her face, Markham knew he had his break.

'Sit down, Kate,' he said.

'Lemme get you a drink,' Noakes offered awkwardly.

'Ta, sarge. Coffee or whatever they've got. Don't mind, so long as it's hot.'

Gratefully, she sank into a chair on the other side of Markham's desk.

Doyle got to his feet.

'I've got some digestives in my desk,' he said shyly.

Clearly the big reveal required appropriate sustenance.

A few minutes later, the team had reassembled.

'Give us what you've got, Kate,' the DI said once she was settled with drink and biscuits to hand.

'It's Nerys,' she said.

'As in Nerys *Whack-a-Mole*?' Noakes guffawed. Then, observing his colleague's expression, '*Hell*, you don' mean . . . ?'

'I don't know what to think, sarge,' she said shakily, gulping down the noxious brew that passed for coffee in CID.

'Why not take it from the top, Kate,' Markham said watching her closely. 'What happened with Nerys?'

'I was worried about her when I turned up there, guv. She looked really sick . . . And I could tell she wasn't happy to be left with the police babysitting her.'

'Go on.' Markham never rushed anyone, and his calm demeanour seemed to give her strength.

'I thought Nerys seemed twitchy . . . uncomfortable . . . Like she had something to hide.'

Burton sipped her revolting over-sugared coffee, trying not to grimace at Noakes's offering from the CID machine.

'I asked if she'd mind putting on a brew,' she told them, 'and could I use the loo.'

'Nice one,' Noakes put in, as though to underline, *devious*.

'No, I really fancied a drink, sarge. I was parched.'

'You took the opportunity for a quick snoop, yeah?' Doyle winked at her.

'Well, yes . . . I dunno . . . I got the feeling she was desperate to stop me looking around . . .'

'An' you fancied a quick look-see, right?' Her fellow DS saw no problem.

'That's right.' Burton smoothed her hands along neatly suited trouser legs in a gesture long familiar to Markham.

The three men watched her expectantly.

'Whatcha find then?' Noakes rumbled. 'Body parts in the spare room or what?'

'It was a kind of shrine.'

'*You what?*' Noakes boggled. 'A religious thingummy . . . a shrine to what, for God's sake?'

'Michael Dominguez.'

'*Eh?*'

'There was this back room next to the loo upstairs.' Burton's face registered confusion. 'It was practically *papered* with pictures of Mr Dominguez . . . press cuttings, the lot . . .'

'Did Nerys realize you'd seen it, Kate?'

'No, I don't think so, sir.' Again, that smoothing of the trouser crease. 'I moved like the clappers, got downstairs pronto. Complained of bladder problems . . . what it's like being a woman in CID when you can't get to the loo — made her think it was cystitis.'

'*Nice one*,' Noakes said again, with unfeigned admiration. Miss Fussy Knickers was showing signs of real promise. A credit to his training.

'Tell us your thinking, Kate.' Markham was very calm, very gentle.

'Well, I'm wondering, sir . . . Nerys clearly had some kind of fixation with Michael Dominguez . . .'

'You think *she's* the book-club killer?' Doyle burst out. 'An old biddy like that?'

'There's something wrong there somewhere, guv,' Burton went on, gulping down Noakes's horrible brew as though her life depended on it. 'You should've seen it. She obviously had a thing about Dominguez.'

'*Christ*. Poor Simon,' Noakes shook his head. 'Dead embarrassing when your ole mum goes doolally.'

'Nerys couldn't have killed Dominguez and the others,' Doyle said. 'I mean, she's obviously got Parkinson's or something like that. Can barely stand upright, the poor cow.'

'Well, she's friendly with Andrew Boughton,' Burton said. 'Plenty of pics of *him* on the photomontage.'

'You mean *conspirators*?' Noakes's voice was sharp.

'I don't know what to think, sarge.' Burton raised her hands, palms upwards. 'The whole thing's so peculiar. I mean, *Nerys Wynne* . . .'

'*'Course it is, luv.*'

Where fallibility was once conceded, Noakes was prepared to be magnanimous.

'A sweet ole housewife type . . . 'S like thinking the Queen Mum could do it!'

'We ruled Nerys out of the equation early on,' Markham said slowly. 'The nice, dependable next-door neighbour. But she could have had her own issues with Michael Dominguez—'

'Maybe she wanted to be more than jus' Mrs Sensible who'd allus help him out whenever the utility room or wotsit flooded.'

'There was no sign of anything like that, Noakes.' The DI's hands were steady on his desk, but his mind was in turmoil.

There's no art to find the mind's construction in the face.

'Nerys couldn't have killed Michael Dominguez and the rest of 'em on her own.' DC Doyle thought of his own grandma and was adamant. 'Not a chance, boss,' he went on. 'And anyway, she's the most normal of the lot. Nice lady.'

The DI thought so too. In fact, Nerys Wynne reminded him of Miss Maudie in *To Kill a Mockingbird*, the wonderful novel he was enjoying from Olivia's library of audio books.

Level-headed. Compassionate. Magnificently sane.

There's no art to find the mind's construction in the face.

He could not get the refrain out of his mind.

Time and again, he had been disappointed by humanity. Why should this case be any different?

'What about the son, then?' Doyle demanded.

'*You what*?'

'The son. Simon Wynne.' The DC managed to face down his glowering mentor.

'*Come off it.*' Noakes plucked off his tie, a sure sign of agitation. 'He's pukka . . . a stand-up guy.' The DS swiped one of Doyle's digestives and put it down again, a sure sign of unusual perturbation.

'Wynne's young . . . well, *young-ish*.' Doyle pressed on, undaunted. And then, in a desperate rush, 'He could be our rapist too.'

'How d'you make that out, then?' Noakes growled.

'The age fits, sarge.' You had to hand it to Doyle, he never backed down from a quarrel.

'The guy's got a *girlfriend* for Chrissakes.'

'I know, sarge. But that doesn't mean he couldn't have had some kind of . . . *thing* for Dominguez.'

'What kind of a *thing*?' Noakes wanted clarity. 'You mean like a *woofter*?'

The DI intervened before Burton found her voice.

'Sergeant, let's try and find less pejorative terminology, shall we?'

Fat chance of that.

'You're having a laugh, aintcha?'

Noakes's dander was well and truly up.

'Alright, so he's not love's young dream. But you're not seriously telling me Simon Wynne could be Domingo's stalker — the Queen of the Night or Queen of Mean or whatever it is . . . I mean, the guy's a *surveyor*, for crying out loud.'

'Murder isn't job-specific, Sergeant.' The DI was inscrutable.

'Yeah, but I mean . . . *a surveyor*!' The DS just couldn't get his head round it.

'Look, sarge.' Burton was suddenly intent. 'He's the only one really young enough to be our rapist. *Think about it*.'

In that instant, Markham knew his wingman was visualizing Simon Wynne crouched over his beloved daughter.

'*Not him . . . it couldn't be*.' The DS's voice was hoarse.

'*It could*, sarge.' Burton wouldn't back down. 'On the surface, him and his mum are all-round good eggs. But what if each of them had expectations of Dominguez?'

'Whatcha mean *expectations*?'

'They may both have been intimately involved with him, sarge. Nerys as his go-to troubleshooter and number-one fan, and Simon as his—'

'*Lover?*'

'*Yes*.' Burton faced her colleague down. 'Simon Wynne could've been involved with Michael Dominguez back in the day . . . while mum fancied herself indispensable to him.'

'*Jesus*.'

'A prayer, I trust, Sergeant.' Markham's voce was brittle.

'You mean he could be the rapist? *Bloody Simon Wynne*?'

The DI locked eyes with Noakes.

Easy, easy, Noakesy.

'We're a long way off anything like that,' he said levelly.

Both men knew Natalie was scheduled to do her interview with DS Hollis and the rape team later that afternoon.

'I want everything you've got on Nerys and Simon Wynne,' the DI told Burton. '*Everything*.'

'You're not serious 'bout Nerys an' her lad, guv?' Noakes was incredulous.

'Yes, I am, Noakes.' Markham was firm. 'At last I think we may have a glimmer of light.' His gaze steady and unwavering, he added, 'The press conference on those rapes is first thing tomorrow. Which means I want every last piece of information on the Wynnes on my desk before then.'

He locked eyes with Noakes.

Natalie's evidence too, Sergeant.

'I'm on it, guv.'

He had no doubt that Kate Burton meant every word.

With interest.

* * *

At last, at last!

Markham's finger reached for Lindsay Hollis's number.

Keep the line open with Natalie Noakes, he prayed. *Give us something, Linds. Anything.*

Outside, the rain lashed down noisily in great fat drops.

Like someone's knell, he thought. *Unless I can get there first.*

12. THE CHASE IS ON

When the team reassembled on the morning of Tuesday, 31 March, it struck the DI that his colleagues looked distinctly ropey — like they were in want of a good night's sleep.

They cheered up, however, at the sight of the bag of treats he had ordered in from the neighbouring Tesco Express together with a tray of hot drinks.

'Cheers, guv,' said Noakes, reaching for a double chocolate-chip muffin while Doyle snaffled a cinnamon pastry and Burton opted for a granola cookie.

'What's the plan, sir?' As ever, Burton was keen to get down to it.

'There's a press conference on the rapes at half past ten,' Markham said evenly. 'I'd like you and Doyle to attend that please, Kate. Strictly speaking that investigation belongs to Chris Carstairs, so yours is just a "watching brief". Chris'll keep Gavin Conors in his place.' A brittle smile. 'Plus, I understand the DCI's away attending that firearms conference in Leeds.'

'*Every little helps*,' Doyle grinned.

'Meanwhile, Noakes and I are going to go through all the paperwork again with a fine-tooth comb.' *And discuss what transpired at Natalie's session with DS Hollis.*

'Are the Wynnes our prime suspects, sir?'

'Yes they are, Kate.'

The light of battle was in the DI's eyes. He knew he faced an uphill struggle to convince Noakes in particular that they could be looking at an unholy alliance between mother and son.

Calmly, he got up and walked over to the window. Outside it was a breezy, blustery day, with the banks of leylandii (which screened the station from the hoi polloi) writhing and twisting as though possessed.

Possessed.

He turned back to the team.

'If Simon and Nerys were somehow in thrall to Michael Dominguez, then it would have been easy for things to spiral out of control,' he said.

He had their full attention now.

'Dominguez was a compelling and charismatic character, whereas the Wynnes are staid and lacklustre by comparison. Would it be so surprising if they wanted some of his stardust to rub off on them . . . ? Bring some glamour and excitement into their lives?' A sad smile. 'Let's face it, life was never dull when Dominguez was around. They were neighbours but riding on his coat-tails. It could have fostered an unhealthy dependence.'

'*Stardust*,' Burton repeated thoughtfully. Then, 'Didn't you say Nerys mentioned something about the BBC being interested in Dominguez, sir?'

'That's right, Kate, she did.'

'I get the feeling Dominguez thought of the Wynnes almost like medieval serfs or something,' Doyle observed.

'Yeah,' Noakes conceded through a mouthful of muffin. 'Sheila Birtle said she an' Nerys managed him between them. Like Nerys thought it were a privilege.'

'There's something else now I come to think about it.' Fastidiously, Burton brushed crumbs from her immaculate charcoal trousers. 'Only I didn't see it as being important when she mentioned it.'

'When who mentioned what?' Noakes mumbled.

'Susan Caldicott. It was when I asked her whether folk in Grasmere ever fell out . . . You know, tiffs, people being sent to Coventry, stuff like that.' Burton rummaged in the shiny executive briefcase and flipped through a notebook while her male colleagues exchanged meaningful looks. 'Hold on, here it is. She said Dominguez could be' — a faint blush — 'a right arsehole at times.'

'Go on, Kate.' Back at his desk, the DI leaned forward intently. 'Was Mrs Caldicott referring to a specific incident?'

'She said Dominguez put Nerys down . . . said something cutting to her after the book-club gang went round to his place for drinks and snacks. Apparently Simon went back afterwards and called him out on it. She thought they might've had a bit of a barney.'

'Yeah, but he's a bit of a mummy's boy, ain't he? If someone had a go at ole Nerys' — Noakes shrugged — 'well, no surprise he waded in.'

'How healthy is that relationship?' Markham wondered.

Oh God, Noakes thought, Burton was getting *The Look*. The one that meant she was gagging to whip out her psychology textbooks and bore everyone witless about childhood complexes and whatnot.

Doyle too looked apprehensive, as though he feared his colleague's portable library was about to make an appearance.

The DI knew exactly what they were thinking.

'It's alright. We're not going to start on Oedipus.'

Whoever he *is*, said Noakes's expression.

Burton was disappointed but swiftly recovered.

'If the relationship with Nerys is dysfunctional — perhaps because she's domineering and trying to run his life — it might explain what happened with Fenella Staunton . . . the, er, unusual injuries . . . the ones in Dimples's report.'

Doyle looked as if he had suddenly lost his appetite, abruptly removing his hand from the remaining yum yums in the Tesco bag.

Noakes too felt queasy.

'You mean, deep down Wynne is angry at older women?' he asked, his eyes sliding away from Burton's. Like the pathologist, he was never comfortable discussing sexual matters around females, even hard-boiled cops. It made the DI wonder how frank he had been with Muriel. Whether he had ever brought up the fling which had produced Natalie.

Perhaps he'd been content to bury the past . . . especially if dredging it up meant facing up to what had happened at the end of the Bluebell case and confronting those inner demons.

How far were you prepared to go, Noakesy? How far?

Burton's voice jolted the DI out of his own thoughts.

'The foreign object could have represented a sort of substitute penis, supposing the killer's childhood issues with his mother had left him impotent with women.'

Doyle gulped but was anxious to demonstrate the appropriate sangfroid.

'Wynne's got a girlfriend,' he croaked.

'Doesn't mean he mightn't also have some serious hang-ups,' she retorted.

'Sheila Birtle said she thought Wynne might be a bit AC/DC till she saw 'em snogging in the town centre,' Noakes cut in.

'I believe she said "shopping" not "snogging", Sergeant,' his boss pointed out austerely.

'Yeah, well, the point is mebbe Wynne's got his secrets like everyone else.'

Secrets.

'I ran Simon Wynne's name past Chris Mayne,' the DI said quietly. 'Mayne didn't show any recognition, but it doesn't mean Wynne's never been involved with Dominguez. Maybe it's a secret that no one knows about.'

'You don' think he's Domingo's stalker though — do you, boss?' Noakes helped himself to a yum yum. Seemed rude not to when the guv'nor had gone to all that trouble. 'I mean, they were jus' neighbours, right? An' none of the rest of 'em in Grasmere picked up on any vibes.' He licked jam off his fingers with leisurely thoroughness, undeterred by Burton's shudder of distaste. 'They'd be bound to notice if owt was going on.'

'Not if the affair was long over and Wynne was happy to stay in Dominguez's life on any terms — as the ever-helpful, reliable neighbour and unpaid factotum.'

'But thass the thing, guv. He *weren't* happy if he's the one Domingo called the Queen of Mean.'

Markham didn't correct his subordinate. Once Noakes got a name into his head, nothing would shift it.

'Maybe Wynne was hoping Dominguez would take him back,' Doyle put in. 'And then he found out about the Spanish guy.'

'Antonio Escobar.'

'Right, sir.' The young DC was animated. 'Maybe that's when things turned ugly and Wynne started getting nasty . . . making threats.'

'Could've been the tipping point,' Burton commented sagely, with a wistful glance towards her psychology bible in the outer office.

'Dominguez was scared,' the DI mused. 'But he thought he could handle it.'

It was a miscalculation that had cost him his life.

'D'you think Nerys knows what her blue-eyed boy has been getting up to with' — Noakes caught Burton's eye — 'other fellas?'

His fellow DS ruffled her bangs, giving her the air of a head prefect straight out of Enid Blyton.

'I don't see it.' She shook her head. 'But if Simon lost the plot with Dominguez and then made up a story for Mum about being provoked — told her he'd been taunted or goaded into doing it, maybe cos he was defending her, something like that — then I reckon she'd be prepared to cover for him.'

'He could've told her it was self-defence.' Noakes's speculative tone told the DI his wingman was slowly coming round to the idea of the Wynnes as potential collaborators in murder.

He rumpled his haystack hair in an amusing mirror-image of Burton's gesture. 'But how'd it work with Appleyard an' Worthington? I mean, Nerys is into the church big time. Can you honestly see her being up for murdering a padre?'

'I think she might if there was a threat to her son,' Markham pointed out.

'So . . . what? You reckon Appleyard an' the sky pilot sussed Wynne — saw him doing summat iffy or wondered about him an' Domingo — an' were gonna dob him in?'

'Maybe they worked out Wynne could be a rapist?' Doyle suggested tentatively.

Noakes's corned-beef complexion turned purple.

The DI watched his wingman closely, conscious that they were on dangerous ground.

'I'll buy him doing summat dodgy to Staunton on account of this childhood shit or having a screw loose . . . An' his mum might have covered for him over Domingo. But frigging rape . . . prowling round Bromgrove an' doing that to young lasses? *No Way, Jose*. Nerys is old-school — the type with principles. It'd be a step too far.'

'I'm not so sure,' Markham said as the DS stared at him. 'If she was in on the murders, who's to say how flexible her conscience might prove to be.' He held Noakes's accusing gaze. 'And, remember, a parent will do *anything* to protect her child.' Noakes's eyes dropped at that, but he continued to mutter under his breath, '*You gotta be kidding me*.'

'The thing is, boss,' Doyle piped up, 'Nerys is in her seventies, right? She's never strong enough to have done any actual killing.'

'Correct.'

'But she could've lured 'em somehow.'

'Agreed.'

'She'd never go along with owt pervy.' Noakes's reputation for stubbornness was well deserved. 'If Wynne *is* a sex offender, she wouldn't go along with any cover-up.'

'She might if she thought boyo was falsely accused,' Doyle continued bravely.

'How d'you make that out?' Noakes asked belligerently.

'Well, the guy's got a nice girlfriend — you said so yourself, sarge. Nerys might think any stuff about rape was bullshit . . . got blinkers on . . . not prepared to admit the truth.'

'This is all hypothetical,' Markham said firmly. 'As yet we haven't got nearly enough to back it up.'

'You're liking 'em for it though, boss,' Doyle observed shrewdly.

'Yes, I am, Constable. There's the fact of that shrine to Dominguez — it tells me Nerys could be unhinged enough to form part of a double act. And let's face facts' — he looked at each of them in turn — 'it wouldn't be the first time.'

'God, no.' Doyle shuddered as he recalled some of their previous investigations.

'So, you reckon Nerys had the hots for Domingo, guv?' Noakes got down to brass tacks.

'I think it's possible she may have developed some form of erotomania . . . It's sometimes called de Clérambault's syndrome—'

'What did this French Wossname do, then?' Noakes asked suspiciously.

Burton was visibly chafing at the bit to enlighten him.

'Why don't you do the honours, Kate?' the DI urged.

'It's a delusional belief that someone's madly in love with you, sarge. Someone unattainable or of higher status. *De Clérambault* was the doctor who identified the condition.' Burton looked longingly towards her desk with its copy of *Diagnostic and Statistical Manual of Mental Disorders* but somehow managed to resist sprinting over to fetch her beloved textbook. 'Most often it's sexually inexperienced or socially naive women who have it. Sometimes they have a persecution complex or other types of paranoia too, so it's difficult to treat. One famous patient was convinced King George the Fifth was crazy about her — stood outside Buck House for hours on end cos she thought he was sending her secret signals by moving the curtains.'

‘*Chuffing Nora.*’

Burton appeared highly gratified at the effect of her explanation.

‘So even though Manuel never fancied her back, she reckoned she were in with a chance?’ Noakes was intrigued despite himself.

‘Dominguez was pretty obtuse when it came to Nerys,’ Burton pointed out. ‘Happy to exploit her interest when it suited him.’

‘You could say he *used* her.’ Doyle too was drawn in by the theory.

‘That’s right.’ Burton’s brows furrowed with concentration. ‘He did the same thing with Timothy Appleyard.’ She turned to the DI. ‘You said he liked having a coterie of faithful retainers, sir.’

‘Indeed. And Doyle said earlier that the Wynnes put him in mind of medieval serfs — an apt comparison.’

Now it was the youngster’s turn to look gratified.

‘Nerys is widowed, unworldly and socially insecure,’ the DI continued. ‘Her fixation with Michael Dominguez was probably slow burn but intense.’

‘*Creepy*,’ Noakes said with feeling. ‘An’ her son stalking him as well. Like a shared hobby or summat . . . *Hey*,’ he exclaimed, ‘does Wynne have this French thingy too . . . ? Is he one of them erotic mentalists or whatever you call it?’

Burton permitted herself a small smile.

‘I don’t think so, sarge. But he must’ve known his mum had this obsession and used it for his own ends.’

‘But if Wynne went an’ killed Domingo, how could she have gone an’ covered for him? I mean, wouldn’t she have *hated* him for offing her pin-up?’ The DS was confused and no wonder.

‘Perhaps there was some joint explosion of resentment,’ Markham suggested. ‘Maybe they discovered he was leaving all his money to his new boyfriend’s arts foundation.’

‘Yeah,’ Doyle said eagerly. ‘They could have felt Dominguez *owed* them after the way they’d danced attendance all those years . . . and then he betrayed them in favour of some dodgy continental.' *His grizzled mentor's xenophobia must be catching*, Markham reflected with wry amusement.

'Perhaps it was an accumulation of stuff.' Burton's earnestness would have been comical were the stakes not so high. 'What Mrs Caldicott said about Dominguez humiliating Nerys, slapping her down in front of the other residents . . . That could have sparked something.'

'The persecution complex.' This, surprisingly, was Noakes. The DI suspected that when it came to psychology, he might prove an apt pupil, particularly given his addiction to *True Crime* on Sky.

Taken aback, Burton blinked.

'Yeah, sarge. She might well have seen herself as an injured woman — nursed a grievance.'

'Especially if there'd been other put-downs.' Doyle was not to be left out.

'Happen them two meant us to go after Appleyard,' Noakes hazarded.

'I'd say that was the plan alright.' The DI's face was like a chiselled bas-relief on an ancient marble monument, so cold did it suddenly appear. 'No doubt the Wynnes imagined we'd be keen to get him for Dominguez if we couldn't get him for his wife,' he observed with an icy tone to match.

'An' if Plod were too slow arresting Appleyard, they'd have thrown out a few "clues",' Noakes said disgustedly.

A disturbing thought occurred to Doyle. 'You don't think they knew anything about Appleyard murdering his missus, do you?'

'*Nah.*' Noakes shook his head. 'But they might have guessed the truth. I mean, Caldicott heard Appleyard talking 'bout Domingo turning the screw and making him suffer, so mebbe *they* heard summat like that as well an' put two and two together.'

'Maybe when the red mist descended, they justified it on the basis that Dominguez got his just deserts, because he had connived at murder,' the DI theorized.

'If Nerys wasn't in on the bashing an' throttling an' . . . thingy' — Noakes still shied away from the specifics of the assault on Fenella Staunton — 'what 'xactly *did* she do?'

'Pass info along to Simon, presumably.' Markham's tone was sombre. 'We can hypothesize that the murder of Michael Dominguez was some sort of *crime passionnel* for which Nerys gave Simon an alibi — said he was at home with her. But with the other victims, something must have happened to make Wynne believe they were a liability. He could have acted on information received . . .'

'You mean tip-offs from his ole mum?'

'Precisely, Noakes.'

'D'you think any of the vics tried blackmail on Norman Bates?'

Doyle grinned. The old warhorse had come up with the perfect tag. If they were on the right lines, the Wynnes were certainly shaping up like something out of *Psycho*.

'Everything's conjecture at this stage, Noakesy.' The DI rubbed his tired eyes. 'But I believe this pair may be our killers.'

'It's not as though the rest of 'em didn't have their reasons for wanting to stick it to Domingo, though.'

'That shrine's the thing.' Burton sounded chipper about the way things were shaping up. 'It means Nerys isn't just some cosy Old Mother Hubbard type. She could actually be seriously disturbed. Simon too, if he was in on it . . .'

'Or it could be just a senile crush.' Being so close to collecting his law degree, Doyle felt it was incumbent on him to take an objective approach and argue things from both sides. 'For all we know it might be Andrew Boughton working with one of 'em.' He turned to Burton. 'Didn't you say his picture was up there too?'

'Yes it was,' she conceded, 'and Nerys gets on quite well with him even though most other people think—'

'He's a grade-A prick,' Noakes concluded the sentence for her.

'You took the words right out of my mouth, sarge,' came the stoic reply.

After this, silence fell over the team, interrupted only by the buzz of the strip lighting.

Outside, the leylandii jerked and twisted in their interminable St Vitus's dance.

Markham contemplated his desk for a long minute then said, 'I'd like you to interview Susan Caldicott again, Kate. See if you can lean on her for more about the Wynnes.' Remembering what Olivia had said about the woman and her barbed comment about Dominguez having no business dishing out relationship advice, he added, 'I'd be surprised if she doesn't know more than she's telling.'

At that moment, the DI's email inbox pinged.

A message from DS Lindsay Hollis.

Marked urgent.

He clicked on it.

The email read:

Not sure if this is a breakthrough on the rapes, but Natalie Noakes's EMDR regression turned up something interesting. She said the man who attacked her used the word 'cariad'. That's 'darling' or 'sweetheart' in Welsh. Got any Celts on the list of suspects?!
Cheers
Linds

He gave no sign of interest in the email's contents other than a flexing of his long, elegant fingers, but suddenly the atmosphere in Markham's stuffy little office was charged with a peculiar electricity.

They all felt it, especially Kate Burton, who instinctively deduced this was something to do with George Noakes. Something the DI didn't intend on sharing with the rest of his team.

So, was it connected with the Bluebell case or something else? She was almost certain she'd clocked Natalie Noakes being whisked through reception the previous afternoon . . .

Were the higher-ups digging deeper into what happened at the Bluebell Dance Studio?

Or was it something completely unrelated? Was Markham calling in favours to get Noakes's daughter out of some sort of trouble? After all, those friends of hers from the Krazyhouse were certainly no strangers to the station's custody suite.

Or was Natalie a *victim* . . . ?

In a sudden blinding flash of intuition, she knew.

The rapes. Natalie Noakes must be the latest . . . the girl attacked in Cuckoo Lane.

Her eyes locked with Markham's and she knew the boss had registered her reaction.

Then the DS looked away and made a great show of consulting her watch.

'We'd better get off to see DI Carstairs before this press conference,' she said, turning to Doyle. 'We can go along to Hope after that and interview Mrs Caldicott.'

'Reckon she'll be glad of a break from the little scrotes she teaches,' Noakes grunted. He nudged Doyle. 'Mind you, don't get distracted by them lasses with their big hair and spray tans.'

'Ta, sarge,' the other replied amicably with a mock leer. 'Makes me sound like Benny Hill that does.'

Kate Burton wore the expression of one who has swallowed a wasp before suddenly remembering that Noakes was quite possibly a grievously wronged father. With an effort, she arranged her features into a caring expression.

'You okay, luv?' Her fellow DS was all solicitude.

'Perfectly thanks,' came the tight response.

''S jus' that your face . . . well, looked like you got toothache or summat.'

That's what came of trying to be the bigger person, Burton reflected grimly, her smile congealing, as she left the office trailed by a sheepish Doyle.

Noakes smirked as he watched his colleagues depart. Idly, he pulled the magnetic pendulum on the DI's desk towards him and set the balance balls in motion, something he had been itching to do for the last hour. Wouldn't do to mess with it in front of Burton. Didn't want Miss Goody Two Shoes thinking he was immature . . .

The DI watched with tolerant amusement underlaid by concern.

How was his number two going to take this?

Best give it to him straight.

Without preamble, he told the DS what he had learned from DS Hollis.

For several minutes, the clacking of the executive gadget was the only sound to be heard.

Then Noakes spoke, his big hands twitching violently as though, in his imagination, they were already wrapped round the prime suspect's throat.

'*The bastard. The frigging Welsh bastard.*'

'Here, I'm just going to get you some water, Sergeant.'

A trip to the water cooler would give the man space. Though, by the look of Noakes, a whisky and soda was called for rather than H_2O.

'He's a *surveyor*,' the DS growled as Markham set the plastic cup in front of him. 'They don' do stuff like that.'

Noakes's non sequiturs being as legendary as his stubbornness, the DI simply nodded.

'A nerdy office type . . . like John Major . . . the sort who tucks his shirt into his Y-fronts.'

Markham swallowed his laughter. To think of Noakes setting up as an arbiter of fashion . . .

'It was good camouflage,' he said gently. 'I read him all wrong too . . . figured he was a nice guy who found Dominguez a bit tiresome but put up with him for his mother's sake.' Now it was Markham who set the balance balls in motion as though something in their rhythmic motion could cancel the turmoil in his mind.

The two men watched the balls gradually click to a halt.

The DI prayed Noakes could feel his profound sympathy. Theirs was not a relationship founded on confidential exchanges, but they had a special connection nonetheless. Sometimes, indeed, it felt almost as though Noakes, with his forest pygmy primitivism, was the only colleague to understand him. 'Markham's hand puppet' the DCI's clique was wont to sneer, but to him George Noakes represented *humanity*.

There was a knock and an exhibits officer appeared in the doorway.

Inwardly, he cursed the interruption. *Not now.*

''S alright, guv. Could be important.'

The DS was about to lumber away to the outer office.

'No, hang on, Sergeant. I want you with me.'

The slumped shoulders lifted and Noakes returned to his seat.

'Margaret Ford, sir. Sorry to disturb you but there's something you might want to see.'

'Oh?'

'They found it on Bromgrove Rise . . . property of the lady whose body turned up in the woods — Mrs Fenella Staunton. Looks like she dropped it.'

She held out a plastic evidence bag containing what looked like a slim pocket diary.

Somewhat disconcerted by the stunned silence that greeted her announcement, Margaret Ford advanced uncertainly. She set down the package on Markham's desk with as much care as warranted by an unexploded bomb before making good her escape.

'Wynne wanted us to think it was the Bromgrove Rapist who did for Staunton,' Noakes said hoarsely. 'That's why he . . . messed with the body. But cos he were a perv with a thing about his mum' — his face twisted — 'a head case jus' like Burton said . . . he had to make it extra specially nasty.'

'Mrs Staunton may have left us a clue, Noakes.'

A voice speaking to them from beyond the grave, from wherever the dead existed after they left this life.

Slowly, deliberately, the DI took a pair of latex gloves from his desk drawer and began to unseal the bag.

13. BAITING THE TRAP

'My God, Gil. It's like that poor woman had a *premonition* something terrible was going to happen to her . . . like she left that diary deliberately for you to find.'

Olivia and Markham were sitting at the kitchen table in their apartment on Tuesday evening mulling over the latest developments. Suddenly ravenously hungry, having main-lined black coffee all day without pausing for food, Markham did full justice to the spread of crispy spring rolls, sweet-and-sour pork, vegetable chow mein and prawn dim sum that Olivia had ordered in from their favourite local restaurant, Chung Ku. Slowly, some of the strain left his face and he felt a resurgence of energy.

'Well, we haven't got enough to justify an immediate arrest, Liv.'

'But at least it puts the Wynnes in the frame, right?'

'To the extent that those jottings show Fenella Staunton may have had her suspicions about the two of them, yes.' He reached for his beer. 'Problem being, it's pretty cryptic. Just a scrap of paper stuffed in the back pocket . . .'

'Quite incriminating, though — saying she'd "caught N out about MD!" Next to a reminder to "see where it goes with the Wynnes" with a row of pound signs.' Olivia scooped up some water chestnuts and pak choi. 'This is seriously good,' she sighed ecstatically. 'Just what I needed after that toxic department meeting.'

Markham grinned. His girlfriend invariably claimed to have lost the will to live after a day at the chalkface, but a decent takeaway never failed to recharge her batteries.

'She doesn't mention any other Grasmere residents in the diary?' she pressed him.

'No — just reminders about dates of book-club meetings.'

'So it's got to be more than just coincidence that she scribbles down something about Nerys and Simon — something that links back to "MD", which has to be Michael Dominguez — then turns up dead.'

And horribly violated.

'We don't know when she wrote the note, Liv,' Markham said. 'Or even why.' He sighed. 'Any half-decent lawyer would laugh us out of court . . . interpret it as meaning any number of things.'

'What about that funny little doodle? The word "NO" in capitals in a circle with a line through it . . .'

'Again, it could mean anything, sweetheart.'

'But it's a *MeToo*-type logo, Gil. Anti-rape and sexual assault. Why would she have drawn something like that next to the other stuff?'

'Mrs Staunton was a retired feminist academic. It could have been a reminder of some activist meeting, or maybe it was just what you said — a casual doodle and she wasn't thinking of anything in particular.'

Olivia concentrated on her crispy noodles for a few moments then returned to the fray.

'What if she suspected Simon Wynne might be the Bromgrove Rapist? What if those pound signs mean she planned to blackmail the Wynnes?'

'I think she'd have come to the police if she had any firm suspicions about Simon Wynne,' Markham replied. 'But maybe he triggered something in her subconscious mind, and it surfaced in that doodle.' A faraway look came into his eyes. 'It was graffiti that cracked the art gallery case, remember . . . ?'

Olivia was keen to bring him back from those gloomy labyrinthine byways where his mind was all too prone to linger.

'How did George react?' she enquired swiftly.

'Well, at first he just couldn't get his head around the idea that a John Major lookalike could be the Bromgrove Rapist. Y'know, the whole shirt-inside-underpants thing.'

Her lips quirked. The heroic and the sublimely ridiculous were somehow inextricably blended in Noakes's personality. And yet she trusted him as she did few others.

'Is Simon Wynne really Mister Weetabix then?'

'He's not *that* unattractive actually — probably a bit of a catch before getting the middle-aged, stuck-in-a-rut look.' He shivered. 'Difficult to imagine him leading some sort of double life—'

'A gay past . . . and then going on to attack those women.'

'Somehow, when we worked through the whole scenario, the Wynnes seemed to fit.'

'Was it the creepy room Kate came across in their house that clinched it for you, Gil?'

'Well, hearing about that made things suddenly slot into place. The idea of Nerys being unhealthily fixated with Dominguez . . . and then I got to thinking Simon might have shared his mother's obsession. There was definitely something odd about the way he seemed to want to stay in Dominguez's orbit. I remembered Sheila Birtle saying he was a bit AC/DC — it made me wonder about his sexual orientation.'

'You don't think he ended up killing Dominguez to avenge his mother's honour or something — if he felt she'd been wronged by him, belittled somehow . . . ?' Olivia speared a pork ball as though recreating that violent encounter in her mind's eye. 'Maybe he just lost it when Dominguez was taunting him or said something tactless. And then after that it was all about self-preservation and Nerys covering for him.'

'I'm sure there was an element of revenge, Liv.' Markham helped himself to some dim sum from the carton she pushed towards him. 'Payback for the way Dominguez had made fools of him and his mother, using them while laughing up his sleeve. But I think sex was in the mix as well and Wynne was the gay stalker Dominguez was afraid of.'

'The Queen of the Night.'

'Yes. But it's a leap in the dark, really. I just had the feeling it had to be someone close at hand . . . someone Dominguez felt unable to report to the police because it wasn't straightforward. That got me thinking about a neighbour. Then, when I found out about Nerys's idol worship—'

'You had the idea of it being a family affair,' she concluded. Suddenly, she laughed. 'I take it you haven't run your "hunch" past Slimy Sid?' She narrowed her eyes and squinted balefully at him in a perfect take-off of the DCI.

'God, no.' Markham rolled his eyes. 'He's away till Thursday, so it's all hands to the pump to see if we can break this case wide open before then.'

'That Celtic word Natalie came up with under hypnosis or whatever it was they tried on her—'

'*Cariad*. It means "darling" or "sweetheart".'

Olivia leaned forward eagerly. 'Well, that definitely points to a Welsh connection of some sort. And the Wynnes *are* Welsh, right?'

'Yes. The family hail from Caerphilly originally and Nerys definitely has a lilt, though Simon seems to have lost it.'

She began to tidy up the foil trays.

'I know you probably shouldn't have any more caffeine,' she said, 'but what the hell? We could both do with it.'

'You read my mind, love.'

As she prepared the cafetière, Olivia continued to turn things over.

'What happened with Kate and Susan Caldicott?' She inhaled the aroma of the ground coffee appreciatively before pouring on hot water. 'I saw Susan skulking round the staff room, but never got a chance to suss the vibes.'

Markham contemplated her flushed, happy face. With her slender delicacy, she reminded him of the irises in St Chad's graveyard.

'I don't want you anywhere near this case, Inspector Clouseau,' he teased her. Then, more gravely, 'Seriously, Liv. There's something uniquely horrible about the level of violence.'

To say nothing of the details he had kept from her.

A mock pout.

'At least you can tell me if our resident snoop came good.'

'She *did* say she'd noticed Fenella Staunton acting jittery round Nerys and Simon. This was at the wake after Dominguez's requiem.'

Olivia was struck by a thought. 'Hey, maybe Fenella got a peek at Nerys's shrine.'

'I imagine it was safely under lock and key that day. Pure chance really that Kate ever got inside.'

'Hmm. But *something* must've spooked her.'

'Agreed. And then, for some reason, she wrote herself that note.'

'Weird that she went and jotted it down, Gil. I mean, she wasn't likely to *forget*.'

'According to Mrs Caldicott, Fenella was eccentric that way. Always writing herself little messages, even pinning them to her clothes. Susan wonders if it wasn't the beginning of Alzheimer's or something like that.'

Olivia set two steaming mugs in front of them, helping herself to lashings of cream and sugar while Markham stuck to black.

'Or maybe it was just some inner instinct that made Fenella want to get it down on paper,' he said. 'Some inexplicable whim.'

'A *premonition*.' Olivia shuddered. 'D'you think she could have chucked the diary into the undergrowth when she saw Simon Wynne coming for her?'

'Her shoulder bag was missing. The diary might just have dropped out . . . or, as you say, when she realized this was the end maybe she tried to leave us a message.'

Olivia's hands tightened involuntarily on her mug as she visualized Fenella Staunton's last desperate minutes.

'D'you know,' Markham said inconsequentially, 'at Dominguez's requiem I remember having the oddest sensation . . . as if all the oxygen were being sucked out of the church. It was during the offertory when the Wynnes moved to the back to bring up the gifts . . . the feeling of there being this vortex.'

'As if there was an evil force field round them,' she said, enrapt by the possibility. 'Sounds like a paranormal phenomenon — as in cold spots and ESP.'

'Something like that.' He smiled at her, trying to suppress memories of those cold spots in the Bluebell investigation. 'Or maybe *Domingo* was trying to tell us something.'

'*Domingo*?'

'Noakesy persists in calling him that . . . I think on account of him being Spanish like Plácido Domingo.'

Olivia chuckled.

'Typical George.' Then she asked sympathetically, 'How's it going with Natalie?' She had always found Noakes's brash and blowsy daughter hard to like, but her heart ached for the whole family.

'Lindsay Hollis said the EMDR went well — that's eye movement desensitizing and reprocessing. How it works is you relive a traumatic experience while watching either lights or the therapist's fingers moving backwards and forwards.'

'Blimey.' Olivia's face was sombre. 'How long does it take to have some effect?'

'Well, you keep reliving and reliving the experience — over and over — until you get to the point that you can remember what happened without having a meltdown.'

'So, it wipes the mind clean,' Olivia said thoughtfully, 'till it's blank like a fresh sheet of paper. And then presumably the victim can write a new script and take back control.'

'Exactly like that.'

'Was it the first time Natalie did this eye-movement thingy?'

‘They first suggested it when she was having CBT after the Bluebell case.’ He saw Olivia wince at the recollection of how that investigation had ended. ‘But she said no to it, and Muriel backed her up.’

‘That figures.’ She grimaced. ‘Definitely not The Done Thing to have a doolally daughter.’

‘To be fair to Muriel, I think she just wanted them to be able to draw a line under what happened.’

And seal up those painful family secrets.

‘At any rate,’ he continued, ‘nobody was going to force EMDR on Natalie. But after the rape things were different . . . She realized she needed help and’ — a rueful smile — ‘the fighter in her wants the man who did this caught and punished.’

‘She’s a fighter all right,’ Olivia said. ‘Good for her!’

‘To be honest, they’d normally want to carry out a detailed assessment before starting with eye processing. But time isn’t on our side, and with Natalie willing to go ahead . . .’

She heard the undertone of guilt.

‘Don’t feel bad, Gil. You’re up against it and, believe me, no one forces Natalie Noakes into anything she doesn’t want to do.’

For a few minutes, they savoured their coffee. Then Olivia asked, ‘Did anything else come out of the session? Or just the fact that the attacker called her *cariad*?’

‘Natalie identified the scent of the perfume she remembered smelling. She’s positive it was Lily of the Valley by Coty — happens to be one of Muriel’s favourites, so she recognized it.’

‘God, Muriel ain’t going to like that — her and the Bromgrove Rapist having the same taste in beauty products.’

He laughed. ‘I imagine she’ll switch brands pronto.’

‘Is it any use to you, Gil . . . this about the perfume?’

‘Kate Burton got quite excited when I told her. Obviously, I didn’t mention Natalie’s name, just said we had a potential lead. Anyway, Kate is almost certain it’s the same fragrance Nerys Wynne uses. She had a quick look in the bathroom cabinet when she went to the house and remembers seeing a box of the stuff still in its wrapper. She really liked the vintage packaging, that's why it stuck in her mind.'

'Wow.'

'Also, she said Nerys reminded her of her aunt. She thought it was just because of them both being quite old-fashioned, but now she realizes they have the same scent.'

'Lily of the Valley by Coty.'

'Yes.'

Olivia excitedly twirled strands of long red hair around her fingers, as was her inveterate habit in emotionally charged moments like this.

'So, if Simon Wynne's your rapist, then he goes out wearing his mum's perfume,' she said.

'Correct. Under EMDR, Natalie remembered her attacker had been *drenched* in the stuff — her words.'

'He must have some kind of psychosis connected to his childhood.' A grim chuckle. '*Oedipus Schmoedipus, just so long as he loves his mother*.'

Now Markham was laughing too.

'Don't try that joke out on Noakes. You should have seen his face when we started on the psychoanalysis . . . clearly terrified we were going to drag Freud into it.'

She bit her lip. 'Poor George.' Then, with elation in her voice, 'But it all fits, doesn't it, Gil? *It all fits*.'

'Won't be enough for the DCI, sweetheart. Not by a long way. I mean, can you imagine Sidney's face when I tell him I plan to arrest a respected local surveyor and his mother cos she wears Lily of the Valley!'

'But there's all the other stuff too.'

'All circumstantial, Liv. The CPS wouldn't wear it for a minute.' His lips quirked. 'And *I'd* probably end up back in uniform directing traffic for the foreseeable.'

'But there was all the stuff Natalie's attacker said about demons flying out of books, wasn't there?' Clearly Olivia was not going down without a fight. '*That's* another link between the rapist and the book club.'

'Again, purely circumstantial.'

Markham got up and came round to her side of the table. He began gently massaging her shoulders.

'I know, I know,' he murmured into her hair. 'You and me and the team, *we* think it's the Wynnes, but as things stand it's not enough to get a conviction.'

'Sorry, Gil. I understand. It's just . . . the idea that they might get away with this.'

Unseen by her, a muscle leaped in his jaw. That was his biggest fear too. And then a new procession of nightmares would join the old familiar ones.

'What're you going to do?' she asked.

'We have to bait the trap.'

'How?'

'Susan Caldicott.'

Olivia whirled round.

'You said it yourself, Liv. She's mega nosy, the kind of woman who listens at doors.'

Gently, he resumed his rhythmic kneading of her shoulders.

'The book-club folk will certainly know she's like that,' he continued, 'so it'll be more convincing when she approaches Simon Wynne with her "concerns".'

'*Concerns*?'

'I haven't thought through all the details yet, sweetheart. But let's say she goes to him with something she's overheard, something that's got her wondering if Wynne and Michael Dominguez were once more than just neighbours. She feels it's her duty to go to the police but gives the impression she could be . . . dissuaded.'

'*Blackmail*?' Olivia thought intently. 'Surely he won't buy it, Gil. I mean, there's four people dead.'

'Mrs Caldicott's hard up and it's well known the husband's a bully. She could easily be desperate enough to want to start over somewhere a long way from Bromgrove.'

'But she's a respectable teacher. I don't much like the woman, but the idea of her turning a blind eye to serial murder provided the price is right . . .' Her tone was incredulous.

'Susan Caldicott was hostile to Michael Dominguez, Liv,' he countered. 'Oh, she was happy enough to go to his little soirées and bathe in reflected glory, but she was spiky about him too. I'm hoping there was enough simmering animosity between them for Wynne to credit the idea that she wasn't exactly heartbroken when he died.'

'But what about Timothy Appleyard and the vicar and Mrs Staunton? Those were brutal killings.'

'She can assuage her conscience by insisting Wynne gets treatment: psychiatric help. Then there's her regard for his mother . . . It would kill Nerys if Susan went to the police and turned him in, so out of compassion for Mum, etcetera, etcetera . . .'

'That sounds more plausible,' Olivia conceded.

'The "mother love" card's worth playing because Caldicott gets on well with Nerys. She didn't like it when Dominguez put her down. So it stands to reason she wouldn't want her good friend's life ruined.'

'Nerys is in it up to her neck.'

'Yes, *we* know that, Liv. But as far as Simon Wynne is concerned, Mrs Caldicott has no idea his mother is involved.'

'Have you told Susan you think Nerys is implicated in the murders?'

'Not in so many words, no.' He leaned down and buried his face in her abundant hair.

'Even so, she may have an inkling.'

Markham straightened up, drawing her with him.

'We haven't told her about the shrine to Michael Dominguez. The less she knows, the better. The idea is she'll be helping us get a dangerous killer and serial rapist off the streets. If we give her the full picture, she might inadvertently alert Nerys.'

Olivia leaned into him. 'To appropriate your delightful press officer's catchphrase, you just might get away with it.'

'It's high-risk,' he said, 'but we've got to try something — and fast.' Now he rubbed his own shoulders as though to dislodge an impossible weight.

'Are you going to let the top brass in on your plan?'

'*No way.* Sidney and Bretherton would only start squealing about oppression and entrapment — the whole damned caboodle.' He sighed. 'Then Caldicott would get cold feet and the whole thing would be off.'

'When are you going to have Susan go and see Simon?'

'Hopefully tomorrow afternoon, Liv.'

'Then what?'

'I reckon he'll ask for time to think it over. He won't say anything explicit just in case she's wearing a wire.'

Something in his face alerted her.

'You're expecting him to go after her,' she whispered.

'Yes.' He reached for her hand. 'We'll tell her to say they can't meet at her house.'

'Thank God for that. She's got four kids, you know.'

'That's why, Liv. I promise, there's no risk to her family. The house will be under round-the-clock surveillance.'

'Where are they going to meet, then?'

'Bromgrove Rise.' He held Olivia's gaze. 'Less risk for her because it's outdoors and we can flood the area with undercovers. Plus, there'll be the memories of Fenella Staunton to unsettle him.'

'I bloody well hope so,' she said with some vehemence. 'I want the ghosts of all of them to haunt him for the rest of his days.'

'We'll prepare the ground with Mrs Caldicott tomorrow morning. When she goes to him, it's got to be convincing — no improvisation or doing her own thing.'

Olivia was struck by his look of exhaustion.

'It's knocked you sideways, hasn't it, this case?' she said. 'The Wynnes came totally out of left field.'

'True. With the other Grasmere residents, there was a kind of subterranean strain of jealousy — resentment of Dominguez's charm and success — or, in Rosemary Kernan's case, fear for her reputation. Plus, there was the fact that they all had issues with him — something to cast a shadow over the relationship. I warmed to the Wynnes just because they seemed so straightforward by comparison—'

'Boring but salt of the earth.'

'That's it. The dull but dutiful middle-aged surveyor and his quaint, old-fashioned mother.'

'Maybe it's not so surprising that he should turn out to be the Bromgrove Rapist,' Olivia observed as they started on the washing-up.

'Oh yes?'

'His domestic set-up is weird for a man of that age. Just him and Nerys . . . that one mother-child relationship has dominated his life. I mean, even though he looks after her, by the sound of it he is still the child.' She plunged her hands into the suds. 'It could've made him aggressive beneath all that surface meekness, Gil. Could've given him a fear of adult women as being somehow dangerous and threatening . . .'

'Kate Burton would enjoy this,' he said wryly, reaching for a tea towel. 'She was checking out autistic aggression, psychosis in Asperger's syndrome and any number of interesting diagnoses when I saw her last.'

'Oh dear. I suppose George was none too happy about it.'

'Well, Natalie's EMDR means he's more receptive than usual when Kate starts sounding off about psychology.'

'What do the team reckon to your plans for Susan Caldicott?'

'This is our Cresta Run and they know it, Liv.'

Without brakes.

* * *

The morning of Wednesday, 1 April saw the team in conclave with Susan Caldicott.

The woman looked even more washed-out than normal. She wore her lank, unwashed hair scraped back to the nape of her neck and speared with a plastic slide. The hem of her skirt was trailing and there was a food stain on her blouse. This dispiriting ensemble had the overall effect of making Noakes look positively dapper.

The pale blue eyes regarded them with suspicion.

'*I can't do it*,' she hissed.

'You can and you must, Mrs Caldicott.'

The DI's voice was quiet and controlled, but there was no doubting his intensity of purpose.

Her voice rose almost to a shriek.

'If you're right about this, then you're expecting me to put my life on the line.'

She promptly burst into noisy weeping.

Markham looked on unmoved, waiting until she subsided into hiccoughing sobs.

'What if he attacks me when I go to see him?' she demanded.

'You're going to phone him at work asking if you can meet at lunchtime "for a confidential word" back at his house,' the DI instructed calmly. 'He won't try anything then — too risky given that his office will have a record of your call to him. Plus, he'll want to plan his next move and draw attention away from Grasmere Park.'

God, she looks a real bag of washing, thought Noakes, eyeing the strand of saliva which streaked the woman's chin.

'After the confab, you jus' go home, luv, an' wait for him to suggest a meet,' he said reassuringly. 'Then when he asks where, you say Bromgrove Rise.'

'Won't he wonder why?' She shuddered. 'With it being where Fenella Staunton ended up.'

'It don' have to be down by the woods.' Noakes was the soul of wheedling patience. 'You jus' say you fancy being out in the fresh air after them stuffy classrooms . . . cos they give you a migraine . . . Jus' lay it on thick. You wanna stretch your legs an' go to the top of the hill. It's one of your favourite places an' you feel safe cos there's joggers an' people out walking their dogs an' whatnot.' He smiled at her insinuatingly. 'Only this time there won't be. We'll have the place sealed off, so he thinks he's got it all to hisself.'

'And then you wait for him to grab me. Is that it?'

'Pretty much, yeah.' Another disarmingly beatific smile from Noakes.

To Markham's astonishment, Susan Caldicott smiled faintly back. Despite her damp nose and smudged lipstick, she pulled herself together in the face of Noakes's unique brand of honesty.

'At least you're not sugar-coating it,' she said.

''Course not.' The DS beamed. 'You're a professional woman . . . intelligent. You c'n do this. 'Sides,' he added almost casually, 'you'll be a local hero: the teacher who stopped a serial killer an' rapist in his tracks.'

She blew her nose so vigorously that Doyle winced.

'We'll have eyes on you at all times, Mrs Caldicott, never fear,' Burton put in earnestly.

'We need someone with the balls to lure Wynne into the open.' As Noakes said this, he showed no sign of unusual agitation beyond a puffing of the cheeks, but Markham felt his determination.

This is for Natalie. For my daughter.

Susan Caldicott looked steadily at Noakes. Perhaps she sensed something beneath what he had said — some plea of a personal nature. Or perhaps she was simply responding to the upfront way he put CID's cards on the table. Whichever it was, she simply said, 'Okay, I'll do it then.'

'Thank you, Mrs Caldicott. You will be doing the public a very considerable service.'

The sense of relief was so great that, as he said this, Markham's leg went into an involuntary spasm which almost made him leap out of his seat. But he controlled the tremor.

'DS Burton and DC Doyle will take you to an interview room and go through your script,' he said to her. 'DS Noakes and I will be along shortly.'

When they had left the room, he turned to his wingman.

Drawing a deep breath, he said, 'Well done, Sergeant.'

‘We’re gonna get the bastard, guv,’ the other replied gruffly, with a reflex constriction of the hangdog features almost equal to the violence of Markham’s spasming leg.

Either that or we go down in flames, his boss thought.

‘What if Wynne won’t give us Nerys?’ Noakes asked. He tugged at the bulging grey suit he had chosen to reflect the importance of the day’s enterprise. ‘She’s dangerous too . . . In fact . . .’

‘Go on, Noakes?’

‘D’you remember the anonymous tip-off ’bout Timothy Appleyard’s missing wife — the one that said where to find her bones?’

‘What about it?’

‘Nerys coulda been the one who rang it in,’ he said. ‘Coulda been mixed up in the woman’s death somehow. Who’s to say the wickedness didn’t start long before what happened with Domingo.’

Oh, God. A potentially new Pandora’s box of secrets.

‘We can’t afford to be distracted by that now, Noakesy,’ he said firmly. ‘But if you’re right, it’s even more vital that we end this.’

His wingman nodded gravely.

Time to lay the snare.

14. INTO THE LIGHT

The day had turned darker while the DI took Susan Caldicott through the essentials of their plan to trap Simon Wynne. Now he and Noakes watched as the rain began to fall, its steady patter oddly soothing to their jangled nerves.

Murky abysses had opened in Markham's mind at Noakes's suggestion that Nerys Wynne might be the elusive killer of Timothy Appleyard's wife, his brain teeming with possibilities and scenarios.

Was it conceivable that *Nerys* murdered the woman who had gone missing so long ago? Had Timothy Appleyard merely come upon his wife's body and panicked, asking Michael Dominguez to help dispose of her remains through fear of being wrongly accused? Did Nerys suspect that Dominguez knew what she had done . . . ? Would they ever know the truth of it all?

'See, the thing is, she don' have a troll face,' Noakes interrupted his thoughts.

'A troll face?'

''S right.' The DS felt he had come up with the *mot juste*. 'Nerys looks like someone's nan. Kindly, *safe* . . . No one's gonna figure *her* for a grade-A whack job.' Then he frowned. 'Don' see sonny boy giving her up.'

'If we can get Wynne, we'll build a watertight case against them both, Noakes.' The DI knew that tunnel vision was what they required — for now. 'Let's focus on *him* for now.' An image of Derek Worthington's throttled corpse swam before him. *It takes three and a half minutes to strangle someone to death* . . .

This plan *had* to work.

The rain was coming down heavier now, the sodden leylandii bowing before its onslaught.

'If this thing goes tits up, we'll most likely end up in Traffic.'

'Oddly enough, the thought had occurred to me, Sergeant.'

'Sidney an' Bretherton c'n jus' jog on,' Noakes said amiably. 'You gotta try summat before Wynne does for another poor lass. Them two numbnuts would only—'

'Spoil the party?'

''Xactly, boss.'

The DS was pleased they were in perfect accord as regards their assessment of the top brass.

'D'you think Wynne'll take the bait, Noakesy?'

'Bound to,' the other said comfortably. 'If Caldicott comes up to snuff.'

'But will she? That's the question.'

'By the time Burton's finished rehearsing the poor cow, she'll be desperate to get it over with.'

Noakes clearly considered Kate Burton to be CID's secret weapon when it came to boring members of the public into submission.

'He might smell a rat.'

'Nah. There's summat desperate about Caldicott . . . like she wants to run and keep on running.' The DS sniffed. 'Mind, if I had to teach at Shitty High, I'd feel the same.' He suddenly became aware of what he had said. 'No offence to your Olivia, guv,' he added, wriggling in his seat as the tips of his ears turned pink. 'Obviously she's different . . . idealistic . . . got a *whatchamacallit* . . . vocation.' He shook his head decisively. 'But you c'n tell Caldicott's had a bellyful of all that school bullshit an' the bullying husband. Prob'ly needs a break from her bratty kids an' all.' A hitch of the grey suit, which unfortunately screamed gone-to-seed bookie rather than ace CID detective. 'We've gotta nail the bastard an' she's the one who's gonna help us do it.'

Something about the DS's scowling implacability made goose pimples break out on Markham's arms.

How far would you be prepared to go for your daughter, Noakesy? How far have you already gone?

The DS jerked him back to reality.

'So Caldicott puts in the call to Wynne's office from her mobile making out she wants a word with him at lunchtime. Then, after she's done the blackmail script thingy, she goes back home an' waits for him to ring her back.'

'Correct.'

'How long d'you reckon he'll take to call her?'

'I think he'll move quickly, Noakes. Very quickly, so we need to be ready.'

'Where are we gonna park the undercovers? It's jus' dog crap an' weeds on the top of Bromgrove Rise.'

Noakes never had much time for the picturesque.

'You may recall the Folly, Sergeant.'

'Oh aye, yeah. That funny little crumbling jobby. Some sort of tower, right?'

'It's a defensive lookout dating back to World War Two. If Mrs Caldicott suggests meeting there, then it means we can monitor the situation from inside.'

'Won't he check it out, guv? I mean, he might wonder if Caldicott's gonna do the dirty on him or summat. He's a sneaky bastard hisself, so no surprise if he thinks she's the same.'

'I've had a word with Peter Geraghty in the Territorials.'

'Oh aye.' Noakes took great satisfaction in never, ever appearing to be taken by surprise.

'Pete's agreed to rig up some temporary notices and barriers plus a bit of barbed wire — enough to suggest the Folly's temporarily out of bounds due to MOD exercises.'

Notwithstanding his assumed nonchalance, Noakes's shaggy eyebrows went up as far as they could go.

'Sidney'll frigging crucify you, guv.'

'Sidney doesn't need to know, Sergeant.' Markham allowed himself his first proper smile of the day. 'Let's face it, he'd only ruin everything.'

There was no arguing with this logic.

'Thing is, boss . . . Can we count on Wynne trying to kill Caldicott given his office will have a record of her calling him? That makes him the last person to have contact with her — bumps him right up the leader board.'

'He can always come up with some plausible reason to explain their meeting. She was having marriage problems and wanted to sound him out as a friend . . . cry on his shoulder . . . Or she was having problems with someone in Grasmere . . . Or she was unhappy at work . . . Or she had the hots for him—'

'She ain't that desperate, guv!'

Markham went on inexorably. 'Or she was frightened and wanted to talk about the murders . . . wondered who would be next to die.'

'So, he tops her an' sends us haring after the husband or one of the others in that sodding book club.'

'Precisely. And if all else fails, he can fall back on Sidney's old favourite — the Bushy-Haired Stranger.'

The ferocious expression that settled over Noakes's features was such that a casual observer might have mistaken him for the homicidal maniac in question. However, he contented himself with grunting, 'You mean, pin it on a local nutter — some loony on day release from the Newman or a Trot from the uni.' In Noakes's estimation, patients from the local mental hospital and tree-hugging lefties were pretty much interchangeable.

'Well, I don't see the DCI embracing the idea of the Wynnes as Grasmere's answer to Norman and Norma Bates. Do you?'

'He never wants poshos mixed up in owt dodgy,' the DS agreed. Then, returning to this theme with lugubrious relish, 'So you reckon Wynne'll go for the jugular?'

'Yes, if he thinks he can get away with it.'

'Same way as he did Staunton?'

'Strangulation seems indicated.' Markham's eyes wandered to the leylandii, doubled over in the drenching tempest like some sort of diabolic Greek chorus preparing for the final act in the drama.

'It don' matter how dirty the bugger fights, he ain't gonna win.'

The DI regarded his number two levelly.

'Of course, we won't be fighting dirty, Noakesy,' he said very deliberately. 'No matter what the provocation.'

It was the nearest he had ever come to saying that he knew the DS had temporarily lost his moral compass at the end of the Bluebell investigation.

That he knew and understood.

A pulse was beating near Noakes's right temple. At that moment it looked as thick as corded rope.

But he looked Markham straight in the eye and didn't turn away.

'You can count on me, guv,' he said simply. 'I won't screw this up.'

And the DI, who so rarely made physical contact with anyone, reached across his desk and patted Noakes's arm as the latter sat there in his horrible bookie's suit.

'Of course you won't,' he smiled. 'Otherwise we'll be the station's very own Keystone Kops, destined to see out our days with Superintendent Nicely-Nicely Craig in RPU.'

'Christ, his head's further up his own backside than Sidney's.'

'Well, there you go then.' The DI spoke lightly. 'Failure isn't an option if you want to avoid a fate worse than death.'

In the strange half-light of the late-spring afternoon, Markham's face had a haggard cast.

Noakes knew some of the popular designations for his boss that were current in CID.

Big girl's blouse.

Wimp.

So wet you could wring him out.

But the big uncouth DS had never thought any the less of Markham for the tormented sensitivity that ran through him like a mineral deposit.

He knew the guv'nor was like a Pied Piper of the dead, dogged by a shadowy host that included a lost sibling whose life had been ravaged by drink and drugs. Then there was the mother with whom he had never been able to make his peace.

The big words and arty-fartiness took some getting used to, granted, but when all was said and done he knew he could never work so easily in harness with anyone else.

'Fancy a cuppa in the canteen before we check in with Caldicott an' Burton, guv?' he enquired craftily, tugging self-consciously at the grey suit as though aware it had somehow missed the mark. 'It'll be a while before she's word-perfect an' you know Burton. She'll have her going over an' over it like a freaking election lesson.'

Eliza Doolittle, eat your heart out, thought Markham, his lips twitching despite himself.

'Excellent idea, Sergeant. Egg and chips should set us up nicely for a spot of attempted strangulation.'

The DS wisely chose to ignore the undercurrent of sarcasm.

'Champion,' he said.

* * *

Two and a half hours later, the team were out on Bromgrove Rise, crouching within the derelict tower known locally as the Folly.

'Where the bleeding hell is she?'

'Take it easy, Noakesy.'

Mercifully the rain had finally stopped, but the arched recess felt uncomfortably dank against Markham's back. An MOD mesh aluminium screen provided by the Territorials enabled them to see out without being detected by anyone coming up the hill, and they had taken it in turns to act as lookout.

Inside the ground-floor circular enclosure, strange stone slabs and benches put the DI uncomfortably in mind of sarcophagi. The wind seemed to have picked up too, whistling through the monument like a one-stringed harp.

'We're well placed to hear what they say,' the DI pointed out, 'and Mrs Caldicott knows to lead him as close as she can get to the wall.'

'Where're the undercovers?'

'Down in the heather and woods, sarge,' Burton piped up. 'No chance he'll spot them . . . Me and Doyle never clocked them.'

'Here comes Caldicott,' Noakes hissed suddenly. 'An' I c'n see Wynne coming up the other path.' An intake of breath. 'Oh, fuck.'

A cold wave flushed through Markham's body, but he forced himself to speak calmly.

'What is it, Sergeant?'

'I thought it were a dot . . . but it's freaking Nerys . . .'

'Has she come with him or by herself?'

'Looks like she's followed him up here, boss,' the DS muttered. 'Somehow I don' think this is part of his game plan.'

The DI turned to his other sergeant. 'Wasn't their house supposed to be under surveillance, Kate?'

'Yes, boss.' She raked a hand through her pageboy. 'I don't know how they missed her. Maybe once they saw Wynne set off, they dropped their guard.'

'Joint enterprise, boss,' Doyle said eagerly. 'We can get them both.'

Markham felt a deep uneasiness spread through him like the oozing damp that blotched the cement walls of the folly.

He signalled his team.

'Radio silence from here on in,' he said quietly, and they nodded, checking that all devices were switched off for fear of any betraying crackle.

* * *

As Simon Wynne and Susan Caldicott made their way steadily up towards the folly, Markham felt as though time was somehow suspended, and they were just dream figures moving through a dim and clogging medium.

The sensation was heightened by the almost primeval eeriness of the strange little fort, which seemed full of timeless whispers and murmurs inaudible to everyone except himself.

He thought of the guns that had once stood in this place, roaring their readiness to avenge.

Now there was only the wind, keening and skirling round the tower's arches like some unearthly banshee. Even so, to Markham's overwrought senses the noise was as shrill and insistent as the voice of the recording angel calling Simon Wynne to judgement.

Susan Caldicott sounded loud and surprisingly confident, though Markham could detect the thread of fear running through her words.

'Have you thought about what I said back at your house, Simon?'

'Yes, and it's no-go I'm afraid.'

The pleasant, light baritone might as well have been discussing the weather.

'I just want enough to get away and start over,' Susan said, her tone now ragged enough to be perfectly convincing. 'Once I'm clear of Bromgrove, you'll never hear from me again. Just the money plus your promise to get treatment, that's all I'm asking.'

'Your price is too high, my dear.'

Again, it could have been the most inconsequential chit-chat rather than a matter of life and death.

'Do you honestly think I'm fool enough to let you walk away from here alive?' he asked pleasantly.

The woman's next words came so hoarsely that they were almost a croak. She knew Markham and the team were close by, but in that instant her peril felt very real.

‘What about your mother, Simon? You can kill me, but the net’s closing in and they’ll catch you in the end. Think what it’ll do to her.’

‘Why should they catch me?’ It was a sneer. ‘I’ve got away with it so far’ — he almost spat the words — ‘and none of you ever guessed a thing. Fools.’

‘They’ll know you were the last person to speak to me.’

‘So what? A sad, neurotic woman wanting attention, but I wasn’t interested. Susy no-mates . . . Came up here looking for casual sex with a stranger. Very sad . . . bound to end badly.’

Noakes nudged the DI hard and his boss returned the pressure with interest.

‘Tell me why you did it, Simon. At least give me that.’

‘Playing for time, are you? Hoping someone’ll come galloping to the rescue . . . ? The handsome sleuth and his dull-witted sidekicks?’ Burton jerked at this, Doyle later put it, as though someone had shoved a poker up her backside. ‘Oh, what the hell. Why not?’ The killer sounded bored, speaking in an oddly monotonous tone that was almost totally without emotion.

‘Michael Dominguez was a total shit. We were lovers back in the day and then he dumped me — just like that. If I wanted to stay in his life, then it had to be on his terms.’ Wynne stuttered over the last words and the pace of his speech quickened noticeably. ‘He treated Mum and me like lackeys — there to run his errands and do all the menial stuff he couldn’t be bothered with . . . And he put Mum down all the time, though she’d have done anything for him.’

In that instant, Markham decided Simon Wynne almost certainly knew of his mother’s idolatry and her creepy shrine to their neighbour.

‘He always said we’d be looked after . . . and then it turned out he’d changed his will. Left everything to some fucking Spanish bumboy.’

This sudden coarseness was shocking, coming as it did from the mouth of the mild-mannered surveyor.

'But why did they all have to die, Simon? Why did you kill them?'

Well done. Burton nodded grimly. *Get him to spell out how he did it*, she had told Susan Caldicott. And the woman, aware of her hidden audience, was sticking to the brief.

'Michael sniped at mum once too often. And I just couldn't take it any more. I asked him if we couldn't start over, but he wouldn't even hear me out.' Now his voice was almost a snarl. 'He'd closed that chapter, was how he put it . . . Like I was something that needed to be tidied away so he could fucking move on.'

Perhaps conscious he was losing control, the killer drew a deep breath and paused before resuming in the same colourless tone as before.

'It was easy to lure him out to that steam railway place. He loved anything like that . . . intrigue . . . play-acting.'

Only there was nothing remotely playful about what had been done to Michel Dominguez out there in the sidings, Markham recollected with a shudder.

'He taunted me . . . said things . . .'

Unlikely they would ever know the precise trigger, but meeting Kate Burton's eyes Markham was willing to bet the answer was located somewhere in her psychology manuals.

'I know Michael could be a complete bastard,' the woman agreed softly.

'He certainly had your number,' was the brutally cold response.

Stay calm, Susan. Keep him talking.

'What about Tim, Derek and Fenella. What had they ever done to you, Simon? They were your friends for God's sake.'

'Tim saw me letting myself in to Michael's house that night. It was just my bad luck he was doing one of his damned late-night walkabouts. Mum had keys . . . I needed to get rid of any evidence of me and Michael.'

The missing computer with its cache of incriminating emails.

'Look, Tim was only half-alive . . . a functioning alcoholic ever since his wife died. In the end it was a kindness to put him out of his misery.'

The DI felt sick. *A kindness.* Like Appleyard was a dog needing to be put down.

'Tim wasn't sure what to think. He wanted to hear my side of it, but I couldn't risk letting him live. He'd only have gone on wondering and turned me in eventually . . . especially if it looked like the police had decided to go after him.'

'But crushing him to death . . .'

'It wasn't meant to happen like that, but he fought me. In the end I had no choice.'

There's always a choice, Markham thought grimly.

'It was meant to be neat . . . peaceful. I knew all about the library set-up. My firm was contracted for the renovations. Nicking a visitor's pass was child's play. And if Tim hadn't struggled . . . If he had only accepted it . . .'

It was chilling hearing Simon Wynne blame his victims for the brutality with which had dispatched them into eternity. *How very dare you!* Burton felt a wave of hysterical laughter welling up but fought it down.

'Fenella Staunton was an interfering bitch who didn't know when to leave well alone.'

'How was that?' They could hear Susan Caldicott force the whispered question past a golf-ball-sized lump in her throat.

'Mum slipped up.' Simon Wynne was oblivious of his mother's proximity. 'We weren't supposed to know what was in Michael's will, then Mum let slip to Fenella that he'd left everything to the Spaniard. Poor Mum . . . She's on antidepressants and all sorts . . . all over the place really . . . said more than she meant to . . .'

'So your mum knows it was you who killed Michael?'

'Yeah. I told her I just couldn't take any more of the mind games . . . told her I'd totally lost it. She understood.'

'Does she know you and he were—'

'Lovers?' An impatient laugh, jarringly discordant. 'I'm sure on some level she does, but we've never talked about it.'

'Did Fenella tackle you?'

'She started looking sideways at us. It was obvious at Michael's wake, so I knew what had to be done. Mum just left it to me to take care of her.'

So clinical, so detached. Doyle shivered from causes that had nothing to do with the wind or the damp.

'And Derek?' The teacher could barely get her words out at this point. Hearing how traumatized she was, Burton was glad they'd made the decision to withhold details of Fenella Staunton's violation from Susan Caldicott. It might well have tipped her over the edge.

And now came a high-pitched giggle, so unexpected that the hairs on the back of Markham's neck stood up.

'Worthington had nothing to do with Michael at all.' Another snigger. 'He wanted to ask if I was the Bromgrove Rapist.'

'And are you?'

'Yep, guilty as charged.' There was a lazy smile in his voice. 'Some slag — a parishioner — came to him and said something. I dunno what, but our holy man asked to see me, wanted to "talk things out" and "give me a chance to explain".'

Of course he would, Markham thought sadly. After what he himself had been through, Derek Worthington was the last man on earth to condemn someone out of hand.

Another unearthly whinnying sound.

'He talked about hearing my confession — can you imagine! Even put on his stole, the daft old queen.' A hard edge crept into his voice. 'At least I sent him on his way in the correct rig-out . . . full canonicals. No doubt the handsome sleuth appreciated it.'

The DI raised a hand to his mouth as though to bite down on the knuckles.

But no sound came from him.

The cries that echoed round the hilltop came from someone else.

Unseen by anyone, Nerys Wynne, white-faced and trembling from head to toe, had risen beside her son like a wraith.

She must have covered the ground between them with preternatural speed.

The DI signalled to the team.

Wait!

'You raped those women?'

'There's a part of me that people don't know . . . that you don't know, Mum.'

A small boy's voice was now issuing from the full-grown man by some species of grotesque ventriloquism that would haunt Markham for a long time afterwards. No trace of his earlier smart-alec disdain remained.

'I'm sorry to give you all this grief. I've kept this part of me hidden all this time.' The stutter was back. 'But the son you know also exists.'

'He never existed!'

'Listen to me, Mum. It was like something took me over. I never understood. It would just consume me . . . I've fought it for the longest time, but it's just too strong.' His voice faded for a moment. 'I knew it wasn't normal . . . all the time this force building in me, taking over my whole life.'

'You're evil . . . subhuman. You did *that* to those young girls . . . And then' — she was shaking with the force of her emotion — 'you killed that good, decent man for trying to help you.'

Wynne's tone turned sickeningly wheedling. 'C'mon, Mum. You thought his past had caught up with him.'

'I'd have done anything to protect you over Michael Dominguez — even if it meant turning a blind eye to murder. But *the vicar* . . . *that's* different. I should never have believed you . . . manipulative lies, all of it.'

The cold hatred in her voice hit Simon like a smack in the face. From his vantage point, Markham saw him stagger back as though she had indeed struck him.

And then the DI felt his blood run cold.

Wynne produced a cigarette lighter and, from his inside jacket pocket, a small jerrycan.

Tearing back the mesh screen, Markham practically vaulted through the archway, closely followed by the other three.

'Don't come near me.' With a flick of the wrist, the top was off the can and Wynne had doused himself in petrol.

The pupils of the killer's eyes had become tiny, like pin-pricks. A deathly rattle came from the back of his throat.

'*Do it*,' commanded his mother and the next minute he was engulfed in flames, a white column of fire.

Noakes moved to grab Nerys, but she was too quick for him. As though moving into the embrace of a dance partner, she stepped into the heart of the inferno, arms outstretched.

The detectives were forced to fall back, watching in stunned horror as the two figures became one, subsumed in the blaze that whirled and danced and soared many feet overhead.

In an instant, the tower on the hill became a funeral pyre.

Like Valhalla, was Markham's last dazed thought as they retreated before the conflagration and watched as choking smoke spiralled into the sky.

* * *

'So Nerys never connected Simon with the rapes at all,' Olivia said wonderingly.

It was two weeks after the conclusion of the book-club case and Markham's gang were ensconced in the back room of their favourite pub, the Grapes.

Denise, the bosomy landlady, being highly susceptible to Markham's reserved charm, had shooed other drinkers away from this inner sanctum, ensuring they were able to enjoy their drinks away from curious glances.

And the conclusion of the Grasmere Park murders had sparked unprecedented local interest, not least when Simon Wynne was unmasked as the Bromgrove Rapist.

‘God knows what was going on in that poor woman’s mind,’ Markham said as he sipped his gin and tonic.

‘A textbook case of denial,’ Burton announced solemnly as Noakes and Doyle exchanged grins.

‘Apart from that, it was all pretty much as we thought,’ Markham observed.

‘Antonio whatshisface made the right call staying put on the Costa del Sol,’ Noakes grunted. ‘Otherwise he’d have copped it too.’

Markham and Olivia smiled at each other.

They had reclaimed Bromgrove Rise for themselves earlier that day, wandering along the trails until they no longer saw a killer behind every bend in the path.

But Markham knew it would be many years before the pillar of fire ceased to brand his dreams along with the sight of those charred corpses locked in their claw-like embrace.

‘What about Timothy Appleyard’s wife?’ Doyle asked. ‘Could that have been Nerys?’

‘Jim McLeod’s reopening the investigation,’ his boss replied, ‘but I’m not sure we’ll ever find out what really happened. Not after all this time.’

‘Thank God the two of ’em went together in that freaking bonfire,’ Noakes said. ‘Can you imagine the circus if it’d gone to trial?’

‘I’m sure Sidney wouldn’t have objected.’ Olivia’s delicate features were flushed with indignation. ‘The press conference on the news round-up was nauseating. All that guff about always knowing the answer lay in Grasmere Park . . . I wanted to punch him.’

Noakes’s troubadour’s soul swelled with admiration at this outburst.

‘Too right. He didn’t even mention you in them pukey photospreads he did for Gavin Conors, boss.’

‘I’m not worried about Sidney grabbing the glory. And besides’ — with a sidelong smile — ‘a little bird tells me the IOPC may be going to take another look at Everglades and the Kernans.’

'Nice one.' The DS was delighted. 'Should keep ole baldy boots busy for a while.'

Afterwards, walking home to The Sweepstakes in the sweet-scented evening, Olivia asked, 'How's it going with Natalie?'

'Like you said, Liv. She's a survivor . . . I think she'll be damned before she lets a pervert like Simon Wynne ruin the rest of her life.'

'And George?'

'Somehow it came alright between us without the need to say anything.'

At that moment, two sparrows swooped down out of the summer sky in a barrel roll before soaring joyfully upwards.

Arms intertwined, Markham and his girlfriend watched till the little visitors were out of sight and then continued on their way, leaving the book-club case behind them.

THE END

ALSO BY CATHERINE MOLONEY

THE DI GILBERT MARKHAM SERIES

Book 1: CRIME IN THE CHOIR
Book 2: CRIME IN THE SCHOOL
Book 3: CRIME IN THE CONVENT
Book 4: CRIME IN THE HOSPITAL
Book 5: CRIME IN THE BALLET
Book 6: CRIME IN THE GALLERY
Book 7: CRIME IN THE HEAT
Book 8: CRIME AT HOME
Book 9: CRIME IN THE BALLROOM
Book 10: CRIME IN THE BOOK CLUB

FREE KINDLE BOOKS

Thank you for reading this book. If you enjoyed it please leave feedback on Amazon or Goodreads, and if there is anything we missed or you have a question about, then please get in touch. The author and publishing team appreciate your feedback and time reading this book.

We're very grateful to eagle-eyed readers who take the time to contact us. Please send any errors you find to corrections@joffebooks.com. We'll get them fixed ASAP.

Printed in Great Britain
by Amazon

61199460R00135